THE JILTER

A Series of Worthy Young Ladies
Book Five

Kate Archer

Dragonblade Publishing, Inc. is an imprint of Kathryn Le Veque Novels, Inc.
P.O. Box 23
Moreno Valley, CA 92556
ceo@dragonbladepublishing.com

Produced in the United States of America

First Edition September 2022
Trade Paperback Edition

ARE YOU SIGNED UP FOR DRAGONBLADE'S BLOG?

You'll get the latest news and information on exclusive giveaways, exclusive excerpts, coming releases, sales, free books, cover reveals and more.

Check out our complete list of authors, too!

No spam, no junk. That's a promise!

Sign Up Here

www.dragonbladepublishing.com

Dearest Reader;

Thank you for your support of a small press. At Dragonblade Publishing, we strive to bring you the highest quality Historical Romance from some of the best authors in the business. Without your support, there is no 'us', so we sincerely hope you adore these stories and find some new favorite authors along the way.

Happy Reading!

CEO, Dragonblade Publishing

Additional Dragonblade books by Author Kate Archer

A Series of Worthy Young Ladies
The Meddler (Book 1)
The Sprinter (Book 2)
The Undaunted (Book 3)
The Champion (Book 4)
The Jilter (Book 5)

The Dukes' Pact Series
The Viscount's Sinful Bargain (Book 1)
The Marquess' Daring Wager (Book 2)
The Lord's Desperate Pledge (Book 3)
The Baron's Dangerous Contract (Book 4)
The Peer's Roguish Word (Book 5)
The Earl's Iron Warrant (Book 6)

PROLOGUE

Number 7, Russell Square, 1813

ANNE BUXTON, VISCOUNTESS Featherstone, readied herself to descend to her drawing room and receive her friends.

It was a momentous occasion. She felt herself a veritable actress poised to tread the boards, launching the theatrical sensation of the season. The ladies' carriages had arrived and now the air in her bedchamber crackled with anticipation.

This was her moment. It was the moment she would announce that she had found her girl. Other of her friends had already walked that starry path of maternal happiness. Now, it was *her* turn.

Meggy carefully lifted her emerald brooch from its silk-lined case and pinned it on her dress. It was not just any emerald, it had been owned by Catherine the Great. Lady Featherstone had won it by decisively prevailing at one of Lord Ryland's mystery suppers. There was some power to the gem, she was certain, as if the tsarina's spirit traveled with it.

Lady Featherstone stretched one hand out to receive her walking stick. It was the very walking stick once in the hands of the famed Monsieur Vidocq, founder of the Sûreté in Paris. That accoutrement had also been won from Lord Ryland and she did not go anywhere without it.

Those two items were testaments to her perseverance in

learning to understand the criminal mind and unravel mysteries of all sorts. It had taken years of work, but she had sharpened her mind to a razor's edge.

She suspected her incisive thinking would be crucial to managing a young lady through a London season. Especially this young lady, who came with a mystery.

Finally, the last item she required was handed to her before she would descend the stairs.

Tulip.

As she gazed into the soulful eyes of her spaniel, her maid somewhat ruined the moment by muttering, "That dog needs a good scrubbing in the tub."

Ignoring Meggy's rather pedestrian observation, Lady Featherstone threw her shoulders back. "I am ready," she said.

CHAPTER ONE

THE WOMEN OF *The Society of Sponsoring Ladies* had been gathered in Lady Featherstone's drawing room for above a quarter hour. They had been called, and now they waited.

"This is all very mysterious," Lady Redfield said.

"Well, it would be," Lady Easton said. "Her note claimed she was on the verge of the mystery of her investigative career."

"*Is* it a career, though?" Lady Heathway said.

"I really do not see why we are to be dragged into one of Anne's endless criminal mysteries. What can it possibly have to do with our society?" the duchess asked.

"She calls me *Bwandbaba*," Lady Mendleton said to nobody in particular.

This statement might have confounded any group of ladies gathered in a drawing room, as they might be led to believe that Lady Featherstone had, for unfathomable reasons, begun calling Lady Mendleton by the name of *Bwandbaba*.

However, this particular group were all perfectly aware that the *she* in question was not Lady Featherstone, but rather Lady Mendleton's granddaughter. That baby had been deemed exceedingly advanced since the moment of her birth, despite what seemed to be her less than perfect pronunciation now.

"She hasn't learned to ride a horse or dance the quadrille yet?" Lady Easton said with no little aspersion. "Well, I am surprised."

Lady Mendleton looked condescendingly at Lady Easton. The arrival of a granddaughter fourteen months ago had seemed to arm her in iron. Nobody could discompose her. She was the grandmother of the very advanced baby, or the VAB, as the duchess called her.

"You shall not be the only one with a granddaughter in tow," Lady Heathway said. "Grace is due for her confinement in a month."

"That is excellent news!" Lady Redfield said. "But Penelope, how can you know the baby will be a girl?"

Lady Heathway sipped her tea and said, "I know it because the fates would not cross me on this matter."

As the ladies considered the notion of Lady Heathway directing the fates at their work, Lady Easton said, "Theodosia, is it true that your son's butler has become suddenly rich?"

"Oh yes, Peregrine says Mr. Sindu is a proper gentleman now and looking for a house in Town. Though, I imagine it was not a terribly big leap, as he always did seem to live as a gentleman, despite being a butler. My son was terribly indulgent of the fellow as they'd known each other since they were boys."

"Arabella says they will look for a butler to take his place, but there shall never be another Mr. Sindu," Lady Redfield said.

Lady Featherstone swept into the room with the full regalia of an emerald brooch, a storied walking stick, and a rather musty-smelling spaniel.

"My friends," she said, her manner that of a queen welcoming her favored ladies-in-waiting.

"What's this mystery you wrote us about, Anne?" the duchess asked. "You do not attempt to drag us into one of Lord Ryland's investigations? None of us has the least interest in his criminal society you dabble in."

The ladies round the table nodded in agreement. They were all happy to attend Lord Ryland's ball each season, and the mystery supper that accompanied it, but they would hardly find themselves at his society meetings. Only Anne was at all interested in attending those gatherings, where the facts of some horrible crime were examined and theories developed on who the perpetrator might be.

"This," she said, whipping out a letter that had been tucked into her bosom, "is not a mystery for Lord Ryland. This particular question is more suited to *us*. This letter was received by me yesterday, sent by my cousin the Earl of Copeland."

Lady Featherstone applied her lorgnette and read out the letter.

My dear Lady Featherstone,

I fear it has been too long a time since we have corresponded and the awkwardness of applying to you now is not lost on me. However, I am driven to seek your help as I have recently found myself hardly knowing where to turn.

My daughter Prudence and I have, for all intents and purposes, barricaded ourselves inside Copeland Hall. We go nowhere for fear of what, or I should say who, we might encounter.

A month ago, a certain Lord Luckstone who has recently located to our neighborhood began to claim that he was affianced to Prudence. This was never true, but somehow he insists that I did not oppose the match and that he asked Prudence, and she also did not refuse.

We do not quite understand how he comes to this conclusion, nor how any gentleman considers himself accepted on the basis of claiming he was not rejected. Prudence does not have the slightest interest in Luckstone and neither do I—I find him rather distasteful.

He seeks admittance every day and is stopped at the doors. We dare go nowhere as he always seems to be about and we think he watches the drive. We have become prisoners in our own house.

The only answer to this thorny situation is to remove Prudence from the neighborhood, though I am not fit to do this. As you know, I married rather late in life. My dear wife has long passed on and now I am a frail old man who suffers greatly from the gout.

Aside from Lord Luckstone, I have been long fretting over how to give Prudence a season so that she may have a future befitting her, though she claims she is happiest by my side. Now, my fretting has increased to fear. Prudence must be got away from here.

Dare I impose upon you to such a degree, cousin? I have of course heard that you and your friends have been instrumental in launching several young ladies—might not my dear Prudence take a place among their ranks?

I wish for nothing more than to see my darling girl settled with a gentleman I can respect and admire. In her current circumstances, she will meet nobody of that description. Most of all, I must get her out of the reach of Lord Luckstone. If, one day soon, I am not here, who will protect her?

All my best,
Jonathan Hastings

"The Earl of Copeland," Lady Heathway said thoughtfully, "I remember the gentleman, very congenial. His estate is just south of Maidstone in Kent."

"You do all see?" Lady Featherstone asked. "She must be rescued from the clutches of this Lord Luckstone."

"But who is Luckstone?" Lady Easton asked. "I am sure I've never heard of him."

"Nor I," Lady Featherstone said, "though I have contacted Lord Ryland and asked him to make inquiries. This mystery of how the man thinks himself engaged when there is no engagement must be unraveled. After all, what's to stop him from coming to Town after her?"

"*Bwandbaba.* Is that not darling?" Lady Mendleton said softly and apropos of absolutely nothing.

"First things first," Lady Easton said. "Bring the girl here, and then we will see what to do if this Luckstone person comes calling round."

Lady Featherstone nodded. "Yes, as to retrieving her, though…I do believe I will require reinforcements."

"Oh Anne, you were so good to come with me to collect Arabella last season…" Lady Redfield trailed off.

Naturally, the ladies all took this to mean Lady Redfield thought she ought to volunteer her services, though she also thought she'd like to be refused. The lady had grown bolder over the course of her adventures with Lady Arabella, her own young protégé, but she remained less than a tower of strength. Rescuing might well be beyond her abilities.

"Nonsense, Cecilia," Lady Heathway said to Lady Redfield. "Overpowering people is not exactly your strong suit and it may be required as this Luckstone person seems to haunt the earl's neighborhood. *I will go.*"

To Lady Featherstone, Lady Heathway said, "Once we have retrieved Lady Prudence, you may take me to Swanley to join Grace and my nephew at Barlow Hall as we prepare to welcome my granddaughter, who on no account will ever be permitted to call me *Bwandbaba.*"

All the party was approving of Lady Heathway acting as second-in-command to Lady Featherstone's general. Why would they not be? If there were a person standing about who needed to be overpowered, then certainly Lady Heathway was the one to overpower them.

They were also likely approving of the idea that there would be no second baby floating about who called a person *Bwandbaba.*

LADY PRUDENCE LANDRY, only child of the Earl of Copeland, regarded her poor father as he slept in his favored chair. She was grateful that he'd not woken from the distant sound of the door knocker.

It was Luckstone attempting to gain entrance again. He came

as he did every day, insisting that they were engaged.

She did not understand why he went on with it. He would never be admitted. The butler, Mr. Jonas, was a steadfast sort who would never falter in the face of this intruder. The four footmen were rather galvanized by the situation. Prudence got the distinct feeling that they enjoyed the confrontations at the front doors, as she had overheard them gleefully rehashing various encounters.

The stress of these daily incursions was not doing her father any good at all. She knew that in his heart he wished to go out to the courtyard and thrash Luckstone to within an inch of his life.

He could not, though. He was far too frail. Though he could still walk with the use of a cane, she knew the gout pained him with every step.

What was to be the end of it?

As she heard the footmen's far-off voices discussing another successful sortie on the drive, she could not foresee how it would end.

Rather, her mind drifted back to the beginning of it.

Lady Reston had hosted a dinner and the new inhabitant of the neighborhood, Lord Luckstone, had been invited. Until then, he had been the subject of intense curiosity. Where had he come from? Why had he taken the lease on Morris House? Was there a Lady Luckstone?

Information spread in dribs and drabs—he was unmarried and the house on his own estate, said to be in Lancashire, had experienced a terrible fire some months ago. He'd rented the Morris estate for at least a year while his house was rebuilt.

Though Prudence had been interested to see him, she hadn't liked him much when she had. He was perhaps in his late thirties, tall and thin, with rather greasy hair. He proved himself a very voluble and glib talker—he asked her no end of questions. At first, she found him exhausting, and then she'd found him irritating.

He'd called on the house the following day and spent a deal of time with her father. As he was taking his leave, he thanked

Lord Copeland for inviting him to dine the following Tuesday. After he'd gone, her father said he recalled no such invitation.

They viewed it as very odd, but supposed there was nothing to be done about it.

They should have done something about it. It was the dinner that started it all.

After a tedious hour at the table, Prudence had left the men to their port. She'd finally gone to bed after they did not come into the drawing room.

Then, the following morning, Lord Luckstone was somehow there again, and found her in the garden.

He'd said a rush of things Prudence could hardly keep track of and then declared that they were to marry.

She was speechless and only stared at him. He'd bowed and taken himself off.

Later, she would discover from her father that he'd done just the same over port—talked and talked and talked and then thanked him for his daughter's hand. As her father sputtered at the effrontery of it, Lord Luckstone had leapt up and taken his leave.

The lord had since told all and sundry in the neighborhood that they would wed, while her father wrote letters to those same individuals explaining that they would not.

Prudence felt a chill run down her back, as it did whenever she considered Lord Luckstone. He was like a runaway horse that could not be stopped.

She did not like that sort of forcefulness in men. No, she did not like it at all. She knew well enough a woman's place in the world and what power they did and did not have. But it was another thing entirely to be treated as if one had not expressed any opinion at all.

Prudence heard the door knocker again and prayed Lord Luckstone had not come a second time in one day. Listening, she thought not, as she did not hear any muffled voices coming from the hall.

Jonas entered the room, carrying a letter on a silver salver. "Lady Prudence," he said quietly, "I believe Lord Copeland will wish to be woken for this letter. It has come by fast messenger from the house of Lady Featherstone."

"Lady Featherstone?" Prudence asked. Who was Lady Featherstone?

AMBROSE THORPE, MARQUESS of Ryland, had been made the marquess at far too young an age. When he'd been just fifteen and away at school, he'd been pulled out of a lesson to hear the dire news—his father was dead.

It had not been at the moment that he'd been apprised of the full circumstances. Then, he'd only been told that his father had met with an accident on the road.

Later though, his mother had told him all. She had been with his father in the carriage and they'd been set upon by highwaymen. His father had fought back and been murdered for his trouble. The coachman had been shot too, but had survived. One groom came away with a broken leg, another had been knocked unconscious and had never been quite right since.

The attack was thought to have been planned, though very much mistaken. All through it, as the three highwaymen tore through the carriage's contents, their leader demanded the diamond from Lisbon.

Neither Ambrose's mother nor his father knew what the Lisbon Diamond was. Lady Ryland had diamonds in her case and the men had taken them, but they'd made it clear those were not the particular one they looked for.

Since then, Ambrose had become acquainted with the story of the Lisbon Diamond—mined in Brazil and gone missing in Portugal. It was said to be six carats which was large but not what made it sought after. It was the one and only diamond shaped by the famed mathematician Gregoro Silva. By way of geometry and a steady hand, its fifty-eight facets were cut so precisely as to make it sparkle like no diamond ever had.

It was a beautiful item, and yet a dangerous one too. Its allure and brilliancy might easily spark envy and so it had been rarely seen even before it disappeared.

It had belonged to the Távora dukedom of Portugal, until it did not.

In 1759, the entire Távora family and their close relatives were executed in the aftermath of an attempt on the life of King Joseph I. Only some of the women and children were spared, and then only because of the intervention of the Queen of Portugal and her daughter. The Távora riches were taken by the crown, their houses burnt to the ground, and the soil where their houses stood was salted so that nothing would grow there again.

Somehow, though, the Lisbon Diamond never made it into the king's coffers.

Ambrose was of the opinion that it had likely been smuggled away by a daring servant. Or perhaps even Queen Mariana and her daughter Maria Francisca had taken it and declined to turn it over to their much-despised prime minister.

But why had English highwaymen believed his father to be in possession of it? That was the mystery that haunted him always. They had made a deadly mistake, and he wished to know why.

Ambrose had made it the purpose of his life to find his father's murderers. Of course, to the *ton* he was the founder of the *Society for Advancing Criminal Knowledge*, or *SACK* as the members called it. Its outward facing purpose was to understand the criminal mind more thoroughly and to investigate and solve the most shocking of unsolved crimes.

Its inward facing purpose, though, the purpose he and just a few others understood, was the pursuit of information that might lead him to the man who'd shot his father in the heart. It had been only nine years ago, the trail may not have yet gone cold and the diamond might still be sought. Ambrose had built networks of informants all over England. Someday, somebody would bring him something that would lead him to the murderers.

While he waited for that satisfying day, he would carry on leading the society and catching criminals where he might.

Depsford hurried into his bedchamber with a newly-starched neckcloth. He had a decidedly pinched look on his face. The look that said something was amiss.

"What?" Ambrose said.

Depsford heaved a long and pained sigh. "Lady Featherstone has just arrived and settled herself into your drawing room. She's asked for tea, so…"

"So she plans to stay a while."

His valet nodded sadly.

Ambrose was rather inclined to nod sadly himself. Lady Featherstone was a dear old girl and he was exceedingly fond of her, rather like an aunt who was so admiring that one could not help but like her. She was also one of the longest running members of his criminal society, ever stalwart in bringing new members in.

Though, she did also bombard his house with sheets of paper containing conjectures, theories, things she'd witnessed that struck her as suspicious, and her own often amusing investigations.

Last summer, he'd received a letter from Brighton every other day, outlining how she got on with discovering the thief of some fishing nets. Alas, she never did solve it, though Ambrose still smiled over the idea that she'd accused the local physician of being the culprit. Then, just last week, she'd sent a request to look into an individual named Lord Luckstone.

She was certain to have arrived to hear what he'd uncovered regarding Luckstone. He'd not uncovered much.

No, that was not right. He'd not uncovered anything at all.

That, in itself, was very strange. There was something to know about everybody, and when there was not it was suspicious.

Depsford put the finishing touches on Ambrose's neckcloth and then handed him a small glass of brandy.

He downed it. His valet understood him very well—an extended interview with his dear Lady Featherstone would pass by far more pleasant while having a judicious amount of liquor circulating in his veins.

⇛⇒✕⇐⇚

BY GENTLE DEGREES, Prudence had woken her father and given him a cup of tea so that he might restore himself.

When she deemed him suitably awake, she handed him the letter that had so recently arrived.

As Lord Copeland took the letter and examined it, he became filled with a new energy. "Ah! Lady Featherstone has written back. And so quickly, too!"

Prudence waited patiently to be told who Lady Featherstone was and why her letter was so eagerly anticipated.

Her father tore open the missive and read. As he did so, he murmured, "Yes, yes, indeed, excellent."

He laid down the letter, appearing entirely satisfied.

"Father," she said, "I cannot bear the mystery longer. Who is Lady Featherstone?"

"She is a cousin by marriage. Of sorts. It was her father-in-law that worked with Maria Francisca to bring your dear mother to England from Portugal all those many years ago. It was she, when she was still only a princess, who arranged for your mother's care at the convent. There was some kind of family connection though I was never very clear what. Jóia was twenty-eight when she arrived and everybody assumed…well, they thought—"

"That she must be very much the spinster," Prudence said.

"Just so," her father said with a smile. "Until they met her, of course. There are few who are as vital as your mother was."

Of course, Prudence was well versed in the story of her parents' meeting. Lord Copeland, a confirmed bachelor, had been smitten. Her mother, a contented spinster, had been likewise. They had been exceedingly happy while she lived.

There had been some mystery as to her mother's family, but the earl had never pressed her on it. She'd gone by the maiden surname Ratavo though Prudence's father had never been entirely certain it was real. She'd been housed in a convent since she'd been a small child and it had been apparently hoped that she would make that her life, but she'd been steadfast against it.

Finally, and at the urging of English relatives, Maria Francisca had relented and removed her from that place. She was to come to England and begin a new life under the wing of Lady Featherstone's father-in-law. Prudence's father had no idea why his wife could not have made her life in her home country and the lady would never say, but it was apparently out of the question.

According to her father, her mother's introduction to English soil had not been welcoming. She and the old woman who accompanied her had been robbed before they were an hour off their boat.

She'd not come with extensive belongings and considered herself lucky that the highwaymen did not make away with the only thing of value she had—the gold locket that was just now around Prudence's neck. The gold locket that had been given to her mother by Maria Francisca.

"But Father, why does Lady Featherstone write to us now when I do not ever recall you mentioning her?"

"Ah yes, well, you know I am not a very great letter writer and have not kept up much of a correspondence with anybody."

Prudence suppressed the urge to smile. *Anybody* ought to be switched to *nobody*, if the truth were told. They received very few letters in a year that did not emanate from their own neighborhood, inviting them somewhere.

"Your mother was the great letter writer of the family. Though, I did think Lady Featherstone might remember me and agree to do us a service. She has and she will. She and a personage named Lady Heathway arrive on Wednesday."

"Here?"

Prudence's thoughts began to spin. What service would Lady Featherstone provide her father? But more importantly, two highborn ladies were to arrive, and stay, in two days' time? There was so much to be prepared!

"Lady Featherstone," her father continued, "has agreed to escort you through a London season. Is that not marvelous? Do you see? You will be free of Luckstone."

"A season? In London?" Prudence asked.

"Yes, of course, where else would one have a season?"

"But Papa, I could not leave you. I could not…"

"Now Prudence, do not upset yourself. I know what you think of. Your poor old father is getting very decrepit and you wish to fritter your youth away in looking after him. It will not do, though. I cannot rest easy until I know you are away from Luckstone and have settled with a gentleman worthy of you. All my days shall be pained until I know it so you will not do me a kindness by staying."

Prudence felt torn ten ways to Sunday. London. A season. Balls and parties and dinners. Dresses and gowns and shopping. These were things she had dreamed of.

But her father. How was she to get into a carriage and leave him behind? How was she to enjoy any of it when all she could think of was her father rattling round the house alone? It did not seem possible.

"But who would read to you at night?" Prudence asked.

Her father chuckled and said, "I suppose I could ask Jonas. After all, there have been many an evening when you've gone up early and we've sat together over a bottle of port. He's been with me over thirty years. We do not stand on ceremony much these days."

Prudence had not known, and it brought her some little comfort, but not nearly enough. Drinking port with the butler was not at all sufficient.

"In any case," Lord Copeland said, "I suppose there ought to be arrangements made for the ladies' comfort?"

Prudence leapt from her chair. "Goodness," she said, fleeing the room in search of the housekeeper.

CHAPTER TWO

L ADY FEATHERSTONE HAD ordered two carriages to take her and Lady Heathway to Copeland Hall. She had learned a few things from her trip to Cornwall with Lady Redfield to collect Lady Arabella.

One, she and Lady Redfield had set off without their maids and found themselves not as skilled as they'd imagined in looking after themselves. For most of the journey, they'd looked like disheveled fugitives. This time, their lady's maids would accompany them in a second carriage.

For another, a distance that might easily be covered in a day by a young person was not so easy for bones that had been walking the earth a good deal longer. They would take the trip in two easy and comfortable legs, halting overnight in Gravesend.

With these strategies, they would arrive in good order and not feeling as if their limbs had been shattered, as had been the case on their arrival in Cornwall.

Lady Featherstone's carriages arrived to Berkeley Square in good time. Lady Heathway's footmen hurried out with the luggage, followed by her maid. All were got into the second carriage with Meggy. Then, Lady Heathway's butler led the lady out the doors and to the carriage.

Lady Heathway got in and then opened her window to deliver some parting words to her household. "Mr. Ranston, you know what to do—deep breathing, no brandy, no gunfire, steady on."

Her butler nodded dutifully, not seeming at all surprised at these unusual pieces of advice.

Lady Heathway appeared satisfied, closed her window, and Lady Featherstone rapped on the roof. They were off.

As Lady Heathway's butler became a distant figure, Lady Featherstone said, "Mr. Ranston seems…more calm than he did when…well when…"

"When he attempted to shoot Grace off the side of the house?" Lady Heathway asked. "Yes, I suppose he is. The new kitchen maid has got him taking valerian."

"Oh, I see."

"By the by, did you know that Lady Redfield's butler, Hemmings, has determined to actually form that mysterious society of butlers we cooked up?"

Lady Featherstone had not known, though she *had* known that it was not she who had cooked it up. It had been the duchess and Lady Heathway, all to account for why Lady Redfield's butler had taken to dressing himself like a gentleman.

"Ranston has got an invitation to its first meeting. What about Danforth?"

"He's not said," Lady Featherstone replied.

"I told Ranston he might join if he likes, as long as it does not pressure his nerves. He hasn't fainted in the drawing room since he began taking the valerian and I'd like to keep it that way."

She would think so. She could not imagine Danforth collapsing in a heap in her drawing room.

Lady Heathway glanced round the compartment. Her eyes settled on Monsieur Vidocq's famed walking stick. "That goes with us, does it? Pray, do not accidentally stab me with the hidden blade."

"It is set in very securely and the top must be unscrewed to reveal it, so it is not at all prone to accident. Though, if we come upon highwaymen, you will be very glad I have it."

"Will I?"

"Now, we ought to devise our plan for the coming days, I propose we stay at Copeland Hall for two nights. That will be sufficient for Lady Prudence to pack and take her leave of her father. If we are importuned by this awful Lord Luckstone, we will…well, we will…"

"*I* will."

"Will what, though?"

"How should I know?"

"We must do something, I think."

"We will get Lady Prudence away, one way or the other."

Lady Featherstone nodded gratefully. She said, "I saw Lord Ryland yesterday. He has not been able to find out a thing about a Lord Luckstone. The man is like a phantom risen from the mist."

"His family has probably had him locked away somewhere— the man sounds deranged."

Lady Featherstone had not considered that possibility. It could very well be that the man was not in his right mind.

That could be exceedingly dangerous. A sane man weighs the risks to his person before taking an action, an insane man is only surprised when things do not end happily.

⋙✕⋘

LORD RYLAND SURVEYED his dining room. It was, as far as he knew, the largest dining room in London. He'd taken down walls to a music room and a library, moving his books to a new built library above stairs. He'd since had an entrance put in that led to the mews so that the room might be accessed without coming through the front doors.

The space was filled with square tables accommodating four persons, rather than the long single table generally found.

On the one night a year when he hosted his mystery ball, it was convenient to have the tables set up such, as two couples could work together and there was room for paper and graphite.

That was not why he'd designed the setup, though.

On every other day of the year, the doors to his dining room always remained closed, lest a visitor peek inside. Behind them, men and boys came and went and papers were piled high on tables.

This was the heartbeat of his operation. This was his network of information, always coming and going like long tentacles weaving throughout London and beyond.

The *ton* might also be interested to know that his valet Depsford and his butler Parker were part of the operation, both those gentlemen having certain connections in rather low areas of Town. Even the footmen, Robbie and Peter, could slip into any neighborhood and lend an ear, bringing back what they'd heard.

The servants' quarters contained a room specifically set aside for clothes of varying styles, most with shredded and stained cuffs, missing buttons, or carefully composed creases that would allow their wearer to seamlessly blend in with a certain milieu that considered crime a popular pastime.

The dining room was a place always humming, always moving forward, and the operation had caught out more than a few murderers, forgers, and kidnappers.

What he understood, as did everyone he employed, was that there was always somebody who knew something. If there were a murder in the vicinity of the Seven Dials, there was someone who had seen it. Those neighborhoods had eyes everywhere, lurking in the shadows. The difficulty was, the owner of those eyes would never step forward on their own. Where criminals tread, eyes snap shut and lips stay closed.

Only the identification of the witness, and then sufficient payment to allow them to tiptoe out of Town after giving over what they knew, would ever induce a person to talk.

Depsford approached and said, "There is still nothing on the name Luckstone, which makes me believe there is something to know. I've had a letter back from a contact in Lancashire, his alleged home county, and nobody has ever heard of him."

"So he is likely a fraud," Ambrose said. "Lady Featherstone has told me that she and Lady Heathway go to collect Lady Prudence Landry from an estate named Copeland Hall in Kent. This is the neighborhood where the man calling himself Lord Luckstone has placed himself, intent on marrying the lady."

Depsford rubbed his chin. "It don't make sense though. He can't keep the ruse up right through a wedding. What happens when the solicitors get involved to put together a marriage contract? Don't his story fall apart then?"

"One would think," Ambrose said. "However, you and I have often debated such a point, only to eventually realize that the perceived goal was not the goal at all and was in fact only a distraction. So, if Luckstone does not really imagine a wedding, what is he after?"

"I don't know," Depsford said. "But my lord, I hardly think Lady Featherstone and Lady Heathway are equipped to unravel it."

"No, they are not. I'd better go myself. I'll set off the day after tomorrow, as I will be taken up by the Morgan affair until then."

Depsford sighed and said, "The Morgans—in deep right up to their eyes."

⟫⟫⟪⟪

PRUDENCE HAD TAKEN to pacing the drawing room for the past hour. Lady Featherstone had sent a note ahead. She and Lady Heathway were due at any time.

Unfortunately, Lord Luckstone was due at any time too, as he had not yet made his daily call to the house. She prayed those two parties would not encounter one another on the drive.

Martha had taken a deal of care to dress her for the ladies' arrival. She wore her best muslin with a wide green ribbon tied round the waist, her only adornment her mother's beloved gold locket.

Lady Copeland had worn the locket always. It gave Prudence courage, just as it had her mother when she set out for England, accompanied only by an elderly housemaid.

The piece was unusual, in that it was more round than oval, it did not have a hinge, nor did it open. It had weight to it and her mother had said she thought it might be solid gold. The front was delicately engraved with vines and flowers and, if one looked closely, one could perceive the end of each vine was shaped as a hand with five tiny fingers, reaching for another hand like it.

It was engraved on the back. It said: *Os nossos corações vivem.* Our hearts live on. That idea always brought Prudence some comfort—the heart of her mother lived on in the locket.

Prudence rubbed it, as she often did, never certain if it were a nervous habit or for luck and protection.

Just now, she thought she really ought to be more like her father. He occupied himself with a game of Patience at the table that overlooked the back garden.

One of the footmen sped by the drawing room door, headed in the direction of the great hall.

Yes, it was the distant sound of carriage wheels. It must be Lady Featherstone, as Lord Luckstone always arrived on horseback.

"I believe they are here, Papa," Prudence said.

Lord Copeland struggled up from his chair and took the cane that leaned against the table. "Then let us go out to meet them, my dear."

LADY FEATHERSTONE HAD occupied herself on the journey by examining the mystery of the mistaken Lord Luckstone from every angle. Despite the effort, she could not make heads nor tails of the situation. Lord Ryland, when faced with a difficult case, often said that more information was needed, and she certainly felt that was true regarding this particular circumstance.

Lady Heathway had occupied herself somewhat differently. She had more than a few conversations that required little help from Lady Featherstone, all centered round the baby Lady Gresham was expecting. These conversations were rather pointed and circled round the idea that she would not find herself going on as Lady Mendleton had—head full of nothing but the baby and seeing advancements that were in fact not there.

Lady Heathway was determined to be a dignified great aunt and if her grandniece, and she was certain it *was* a girl, ever made the mistake of calling her *Bwandbaba* or anything like it, she would not be so idiotic as to tell anybody of it. She would be called Aunt or she would be called nothing at all until the baby had mastered her consonants.

Lady Featherstone did a lot of nodding through all of it, though she had her doubts. Penelope could be fierce when she was displeased, but underneath the bluster she had a rather soft heart. It was not every lady who was not at all discomposed to have a butler who had fainted on more than one occasion and had panicked to such a degree one fraught evening as to shoot a gun at the side of the lady's house. Lady Featherstone suspected Penelope would be exceedingly indulgent, no matter what she claimed now.

The carriage turned down a lane.

"Goodness," Lady Featherstone said. "This must be it. Yes, there is a fine house in the distance, it must be Copeland Hall."

Lady Heathway leaned her face close to her own window. "And not a deranged gentleman in sight. Excellent."

The horses picked up their speed, as horses tended to do. They always seemed to know when they grew close to their destination and wished to hurry so they might find themselves rubbed down and with a bucket of oats in short order.

Servants threw open the doors to the house, the carriage pulled up, and the earl and his daughter came out to greet them.

Lady Featherstone's breath nearly caught. Lady Prudence was lovely. Positively lovely. Her father's fair coloring and her mother's darker coloring had combined with stunning results. Her complexion was no pale English rose, but rather had a soft and sun-kissed look. Her hair was abundant and a charming tawny color that suited her complexion marvelously. And those eyes, those large and wide-set dark eyes. She was an entrancing original.

They were helped from their carriage and the earl stepped forward. "Lady Featherstone, Lady Heathway," he said, making a short bow aided by his cane. "My daughter, Lady Prudence Landry."

The girl curtsied prettily.

Lady Featherstone took the girl's hands and said, "My dear, you are positively enchanting."

Lady Heathway said, "Very charming."

The earl signaled his footmen to unload the second carriage, which had now come to a stop.

"Please do come in," the earl said. "Mrs. Rider will see you to your rooms to refresh yourselves and she will show your maids where they might find what they need. When you are ready, we will have tea in the drawing room."

Mrs. Rider had led the ladies above stairs while the maids sorted out whose luggage was whose.

Prudence felt herself breathe easier, as it seemed the moment of arrival must always be the most fraught. Lady Featherstone and Lady Heathway had been met and that fence had been cleared. They would find nothing amiss when they reached their rooms.

While the house had not had visitors to stay in some years, her father had not forgotten how it had been done so elegantly by

Prudence's mother. A basin of water cooled with ice chips taken from the icehouse, along with fresh towels and prettily wrapped soaps, would wash off the dust of the journey.

The ladies would find pitchers of fresh lemonade for their thirst. If they wished for something to eat, a glass box full of edibles charmingly arranged would suit any taste. There were biscuits, lemon lozenges, aniseed comfits, chocolate discs, and of course Cook's marvelous marzipan intricately formed in the shape of Copeland Hall.

As a fire would not be needed, the seating area had been shifted away from the fireplace and situated near the large windows and there were thoughtfully selected books and periodicals on a small side table. The ladies had been given rooms that overlooked the gardens and the park beyond, its gentle slopes dotted with old oaks and often the scene of a herd of deer peacefully grazing.

As if to bring the garden indoors, an abundance of fresh flowers decorated the room.

Lord Luckstone had so far not made an appearance at the hall, and for that Prudence was grateful. If he did come, she wished the horses and carriages to be gone off the drive and put away.

She did not wish him to know of their visitors. She could not say what he would do with the information, but she'd rather not find out.

Prudence was still not quite sure of what she thought of their visitors' purpose. A season in Town was a wonderful thing to contemplate, but leaving her father behind felt impossible. Remaining trapped in the house while Lord Luckstone darkened their doors each day also felt impossible.

She really did not know what would be the right course, or whether she would have any say in it even if she did settle on an opinion. She could at least look with favor upon how receiving visitors had seemed to boost her father's vigor. He'd just crossed the room and forgot his cane.

The ladies did not stay long above stairs and very soon they had come into the drawing room.

Jonas had brought in the tea service and Prudence poured the cups.

Lady Featherstone said, "Does Lord Luckstone continue on with this bizarre notion that you are engaged?"

"He seems to," Prudence said. "He comes every day, looking to be admitted. The footmen say he feigns surprise each time he is turned away."

"Feigns, indeed," Lady Heathway said. "What I fail to understand is where he thinks he'll get with this nonsense. He sees perfectly well that it cannot succeed. Is he quite right in the head?"

"Yes, is he?" Lady Featherstone said. "We did worry about that idea."

"That I cannot say," the earl said. "Though I believe he is less a madman and more a sharper of some sort. The type one might encounter at Newmarket, attempting to part people from their money."

"It is the talking," Prudence added. "He talks and talks, going round in circles and answering a question he has just asked. One can hardly follow him."

Lady Featherstone said, "There is some mystery to it and rest assured my mind is never quiet in the pondering of it. However, the first thing to do is to remove you from his sphere, which we would propose to do on the day after tomorrow."

In considering leaving her father behind and quite alone, Prudence's thoughts had been rolling this way and that like marbles set in motion.

They suddenly stopped in their places. She was certain of the right course.

"Lady Featherstone," she began, "your offer is so very kind and I am aware that my father has asked it of you, but I cannot leave him alone here. There is his health to consider, he will be trapped in this house, and it is not at all good for his spirits. And then…what might Lord Luckstone do next? He might be very angry. We do not find him predictable and so cannot guess how he might react."

"Now Prudence," the earl said. "I assured you I would be perfectly fine here. You are not to worry about me."

"How can I not?" Prudence said, very afraid that she was close to giving way to tears. "You are my entire family, Papa."

"Prudence—"

The earl was cut off from whatever he would say next by Lady Heathway. "My lord, this is in no way an insurmountable problem. You must come to Town too."

Since Lady Heathway had taken the liberty of inviting a person to what was in fact not her own house, it was fortunate that Lady Featherstone agreed with her.

"Indeed you must, Lord Featherstone will be delighted to have you. Really, it is the best solution. Prudence will take comfort in your presence and Lord Luckstone may ride to your doors here at all hours of the day and night and find nobody at home. Yes, that will suit very nicely."

"I am not certain I wish to impose upon you to such a degree," the earl said.

"It is no imposition, none at all," Lady Featherstone said.

"You must say yes, Papa," Prudence urged.

"Of course he will agree, Lady Prudence," Lady Heathway said, her tone all confidence. "His mind is just coming round on the idea."

"Well, I suppose—"

"There, you see?" Lady Featherstone said. "It is all arranged. We will set off the day after tomorrow."

This happy conversation was halted by the distant banging of the door knocker.

All eyes drifted toward the open drawing room doors. The footmen raced past in tandem while Jonas hurried behind them, taking up the rear.

"It is him? It is Luckstone?" Lady Featherstone whispered

softly, as if the dreaded man out-of-doors had unusually sharp hearing.

"I would hazard a guess that it is," the earl said, "as my footmen do not move quite as fast for any other person. They seem to take it as a personal badge of honor to turn him away."

Lady Heathway rose. "Nobody move," she said. She then stared determinedly at Lady Featherstone's walking stick and said, "Anne? If I may?"

Lady Featherstone handed over the stick and said, "You won't kill him, though?"

"Certainly not," Lady Heathway said. "He will only end preferring that I had."

"But my dear Lady Heathway," the earl said, "do not—"

"Never fear, Lord Copeland, I shan't be long."

With that, Lady Heathway strode from the room, her head held high as if she were Joan of Arc touring the streets of Orléans.

CHAPTER THREE

LADY HEATHWAY HAD disappeared down the corridor. The party looked at one another. Prudence had never in her life encountered such a personage as Lady Heathway. She hoped Lord Luckstone had not either.

She said, "We might repair to the music room. It has a view of the drive, in case…in case Lady Heathway requires assistance."

"Very good notion, Lady Prudence," Lady Featherstone said. "Though it has been my long experience that Lady Heathway rarely requires assistance. Even so, I would like to get a look at this fellow."

They rose, Prudence handing her father his cane, and made their way to the music room.

Once there, Prudence pulled back a curtain and opened the window an inch.

The scene before her was startling.

Lord Luckstone was off his horse and Lady Heathway was poking him in the chest with Lady Featherstone's walking stick. Jonas stood behind her, rather white in the face. The footmen appeared delighted.

"I do not know what sort of rogue you are, nor whether you are indeed a lord," Lady Heathway said. "If you are, you ought to be ashamed of yourself as your conduct is not that of a gentleman. If you are *not* the lord you claim to be, you had better board the first boat to the continent, lest you discover yourself in prison.

I am a powerful woman, Luckstone, and I have powerful friends in London. Even now, they are investigating your claims."

"But my dear Lady Heathway," Lord Luckstone broke in, "this is all a misunderstanding, surely you see it? Of course you do, I can tell you do. An elevated lady such as yourself would not involve yourself in what is, if you examine it, a strictly personal matter. No, I am sure you would not—"

"Stop your babbling this instant!"

Lady Heathway had paused her poking of Lord Luckstone's chest and unscrewed the top of Lady Featherstone's walking stick, revealing the blade. As for the lord, he appeared rather incredulous and, for once, Prudence thought, speechless.

Lady Heathway rested the sharp point of the blade against Lord Luckstone's neck and said, "Do you dare advise me on what I choose to involve myself in?"

"I do not say that, I only say—"

"Get back on your horse before I accidentally fall forward and the point of this blade pierces your windpipe. Do not ever darken these doors again. If I hear that you arrive in Town or in any other way harass Lady Prudence it will result in very dark days for you. *Very* dark days. You may not be aware, but my butler's gun is always loaded and he is not afraid to use it. He has rather limited self-regulation when provoked and I find you exceedingly provoking. Off with you."

Lord Luckstone was, for a moment, very still. Prudence thought he was silently debating which course of action must be the wisest, now that he was faced with a marchioness ready to slice his throat.

It seemed he could not see his way clear to battle the enraged matron. "Very well," he said. "As you wish, though I really think—"

"As I *demand*," Lady Heathway said darkly. "And I do not give a farthing for whatever thoughts may be staggering around in your uncouth mind."

Lord Luckstone's face had grown an alarming shade of purple, but it seemed he had finally run out of words. He mounted his horse and turned it.

Lady Heathway, for good measure, gave the horse a poke in its hindquarters, sending Lord Luckstone careening down the drive.

The lady screwed the top back on Lady Featherstone's walking stick, smiled and said pleasantly, "Excellent, that's done."

FREDERICK LUCKNELL, OR Lord Luckstone, as he'd been styling himself recently, bellowed for paper and pen. One of his men rushed in with the writing implements.

He scribbled furiously. He would send the letter by fast horse to London.

Clamarin—

Our strategy here has failed due to the interference of a marchioness who claims that my own claims are being investigated by powerful people. You said the earl and his daughter did not have powerful friends, and you were mistaken. I have no credible way of continuing on with this charade and the longer I stay the more I risk. I have had a blade to my throat and been threatened with prison or, if I do not make it to the safety of a locked cell, being shot by the harridan's butler. I will decamp forthwith to the Bull and Bear in Swanley and wait to hear from you. I will not show my face around London until we know more.

From what the old hen said, I gather she will take Lady Prudence to Town. You must find a way of ingratiating yourself into her circle.

Meanwhile, Paxton has decamped. He does not have faith in the long game toward that which we seek and wishes to go back to his old activities. I told him if he speaks of any of it I will blow his brains out.

I hope you have gathered at least some information from your attendance at Ryland's meetings, lest that prove a failure too.

L

PRUDENCE HAD BEEN rather shaken upon witnessing the scene on the drive between Lady Heathway and Lord Luckstone. Exceedingly gratified, but shaken nonetheless.

Over the next hours, though, her nerves settled and her spirits rose. After the encounter, they had all returned to the drawing room. Lady Heathway and Lady Featherstone were of such buoyant spirits and so confident of having dispatched Lord Luckstone once and for all that it was hard not to be carried along with the feeling.

Lady Heathway, in particular, was positively triumphant. She claimed such experiences, while not wished for every day, did something invigorating for the blood.

Lady Featherstone was just as proud of her walking stick, which had played its own part in the victory. Vidocq's famed stick continued its storied history, its blade having so recently touched the throat of a scoundrel.

The ladies had since gone up to change for dinner and Prudence was left alone with her father.

"There, my dear," the earl said. "It seems every difficulty has been whisked away. You and I will go to Town as guests of the delightful Lady Featherstone and I know you will meet many an eligible gentleman there. The distasteful Lord Luckstone has been driven off by the indomitable Lady Heathway."

The earl paused, then said softly, "Though I really feel I ought to have accomplished that myself."

Prudence knew very well that her father was feeling aggrieved that he'd come up short in not having driven off Lord

Luckstone. She did not think so, though. There would not be many like Lady Heathway, man nor woman. Further, she had begun to develop certain opinions regarding temperament, courtesy of Lord Luckstone. She was *glad* her father was no Lady Heathway.

"Father," she said, "speaking of the gentlemen I might encounter in London. If there is one thing these past weeks have shown me, it is that I would never be happy if I were to marry a man with a forceful personality. I really have become quite set on that point—I do not like to feel as if I am being run over."

The earl looked upon his daughter kindly. "You may choose as you please, Prudence. I trust your good sense not to connect yourself to a rotter, and beyond that you must follow your own inclinations. Just as my decisions were my own when I chose to marry."

"I know what I seek," Prudence said. "I do not *only* wish for a gentleman, but the gentleman must also be a gentle man. You have always been so, and my mother was treated with the utmost consideration. I do not ever recall you raising your voice or overpowering her with words or pushing her into anything."

"It was my honor to accommodate Lady Copeland in all things," the earl said.

Prudence suddenly smiled. "Even the salted cod at breakfast," she said.

"Ah yes, the salted cod. Bacalhau *à Brás*. It reminded her of her childhood in Portugal and I ate it in good humor with a smile. As best I could."

This genial exchange was suddenly interrupted. The sound of three brisk knocks on the front doors came barreling down the corridor and into the drawing room.

Somebody had come. Again.

It must be Lord Luckstone. Nobody in the neighborhood would be so inconsiderate as to call unexpectedly at such an hour. Only Lord Luckstone would do it.

The footmen fairly flew out of the drawing room. Jonas was

nowhere in sight, but he would have heard the banging and be making his way toward it from wherever he was.

Luckstone had been driven away, but he'd licked his wounds and recovered from Lady Heathway's threats. He'd decided to come back. There really was no stopping him!

Prudence and her father stared at one another. She felt an anger begin to boil inside her. Before, there had only been fear. Now there was a white-hot flame burning in her heart. She glanced around the drawing room for anything at all as helpful as Lady Featherstone's walking stick had been. She would beat Luckstone about the head if need be. She would make him go for the last time.

Jonas practically staggered into the drawing room. "The Marquess of Ryland, friend to Lady Featherstone, has arrived my lord."

A marquess? Who was he? Why had not Lady Featherstone mentioned him?

The gentleman in question seemed to have no patience for waiting in the front hall to see if he would gain entry or not and came striding in behind Jonas.

"Lord Copeland, Lady Prudence," he said with a short bow, "excuse my uninvited arrival but I felt it necessary. Lady Featherstone tasked me with making inquiries into a certain Lord Luckstone and what I discovered, or rather, what I did *not* discover, leads me to believe that there is a nefarious game afoot."

Prudence could see that her father stared at Lord Ryland with incredulity, as she did herself. He had blown in like a strong wind and stood, almost larger than life, talking about a nefarious game.

"I've taken you by surprise, I see that. Though, if we might dispense with pleasantries," Lord Ryland said, "I would have a horse from your stables and the direction of Luckstone's residence. My trunk is in my carriage if your footmen would look after it."

Prudence's father only nodded. He seemed incapable of doing

anything further, as she rather felt herself.

The lord was tall and dark-haired with broad shoulders. He was a beast of a man, though impeccably dressed despite traveling. It seemed to Prudence that it was not so much his person that was outsized, he had an almost overwhelming presence.

Lord Ryland turned to Jonas after the earl's nod to his request. "A horse, then? And you will point me in the direction of Lord Luckstone."

Jonas appeared as overcome as his earl and stammered, "Of course, my lord."

Lord Ryland strode out of the room as fast as he'd come into it.

Both Prudence and her father sank down in their chairs.

"He's rather frightening," Prudence said softly.

"Oh no, my dear, not him," the earl said slowly. "He has the power and vigor of a man in his prime, but he is nothing to fear. Lady Featherstone would not have brought him into our sphere if he was. Though, I am rather surprised she did not mention he would come."

"Perhaps she did not know?"

"If that is the case, if he has come on his own, then he must know something very dire about Lord Luckstone. I begin to think we must be grateful that he has inconvenienced himself to do it."

Prudence could not quite say she was grateful. She could not say what she was, precisely. Lord Ryland was the most handsome man she'd ever seen, but he was too…he was too much. His presence was too vigorous.

Was this what a London gentleman was like? If that were the case, how on earth was she to find her gentleman that was a gentle man? One who would come softly into a drawing room, not charge into it like a bull? One who would not make her feel as if she were being overcome?

"We'd better make haste to change for dinner," the earl said.

"Is *he* coming for dinner?" Prudence asked, staring at the spot that Lord Ryland had so recently occupied.

"I haven't the faintest idea, but he's brought a trunk, so I expect he's spending the night."

"What do you suppose he intends to do by going to Morris House to seek out Lord Luckstone?"

"I cannot say," the earl said, "but he is a marquess and seems in charge of his faculties, so we need not fear his intentions. I am sure Lady Featherstone will enlighten us further on his rather unexpected arrival."

AMBROSE HAD FOLLOWED the butler to the earl's stables and picked a horse from the rather meager selection. As far as he could tell, the earl only kept four carriage horses and a mare for Lady Prudence. It mattered little, for Morris House was not above two miles down the road. He would knock on Luckstone's door and see what the man would say for himself.

There would be only two possible stories the man could tell. One, there was some legitimate reason why Depsford's contact in Lancashire had never heard of him. Or two, he would stick to the story he'd been telling with no further elaboration.

If there was not some piece of information that might explain why he was not widely known, then Ambrose would be convinced that he was not a lord anybody and give him a warning to decamp.

As he trotted down the road, the dusk falling around him, he thought he ought to be only thinking of what he would say, how he would handle Luckstone.

And yet, his mind kept drifting back to the earl's drawing room.

Upon viewing Lady Prudence, he could see why a man might be driven by hook or by crook to wed her. She was unlike any other lady he'd seen.

Her hair was a lovely shade of brown, a very soft and glorious shade that was not quite chestnut. Her eyes were large, set wide, and very dark, her mouth full. But it was perhaps her coloring that was so alluring—her skin was warm and golden, as if she were perennially bathed in the light of an August setting sun.

He smiled at his musings, well aware that he indulged his own tastes. He had never been an admirer of what others held up as the glorious English rose. He found the over-pale looks of such a lady both cold and insipid. And, he could not ignore his near-revulsion when he could see a blue vein or two meandering round a lady's neck, poorly camouflaged by the translucence of her coloring. It reminded him of a corpse.

He pulled his mind out of the earl's drawing room and back to the matter at hand. The drive was just ahead and he planned to make quick work of Luckstone. *Then*, he could make his return to the pleasant environs of Lady Prudence.

Morris House was not as imposing as it might be, but it was substantial nonetheless.

There were no candles burning in the windows and he noted no activity. Perhaps Luckstone was out, gone to harass somebody else in the neighborhood.

If he were not at home, then Ambrose could at least leave him a note. The note would spell out precisely the situation—Lady Prudence and the earl had fallen under the protection of the Marquess of Ryland and inquiries into Lord Luckstone were being made. Assuming Luckstone was an adventurer of some sort, that ought to be enough to send him on his way.

Ambrose dismounted his horse and bounded up the stone steps, rapping the knocker sharply three times.

He stayed motionless and listened for the running footsteps of a footman, but he heard nothing.

The staff were all probably gathered round a card table in the servants' hall, drafts of ale in hand, enjoying a night off since the master had gone out.

He would not leave until somebody heard him and came to

the door. At a minimum, he would be shown in and given a sheet of paper and writing instruments.

He banged again.

And then again.

Ambrose felt his patience wearing thin. He shouted, "If one of you imbeciles does not put down your drink and answer this door I will break it down for you!"

He leaned his ear against the door and heard a quiet shuffling. Finally.

A small voice from behind the door said, "Who are you?"

"I am the Marquess of Ryland," he said, "and you had better open this door if you know what's good for you."

There was another moment of silence, and then the door swung open.

Ambrose had been looking straight ahead to see what footman the worse for drink had eventually roused himself to answer the door.

There was nobody there. Out of his peripheral vision, Ambrose noticed a head of hair below him. He looked down.

A boy stood there, gazing up at him as if he were the devil himself.

"Where is the butler?" he said sternly. "Where are the footmen?"

"They've all gone," the boy said tremulously.

"Gone where?"

"They didn't say."

"And Lord Luckstone?"

"He took them," the boy said sadly. "He took them all away and left me behind."

"Where did they go?"

"I'm not rightly sure," the boy said.

"And they left you behind?"

The boy nodded.

"But what are you supposed to be doing here?"

"I don't know!" the boy wailed.

Ambrose sighed. Clearly the little chap was in some distress. He sat down on the stone steps and motioned the boy to do the same. He handed him his handkerchief.

"Dry your eyes, crying will do you no good at all. Now, tell me everything you know."

The boy did as he was told and rather stoically blew his nose. "I done got hired in York and I was to keep the kitchen fire going and clean up and such, as Lord Luckstone don't want no maids about the place. I told 'em all, I said, I'll lower myself to it as I know I got to work my way up. I'm to be a valet someday."

Ambrose examined the boy's too-short trousers and his threadbare coat. "Are you?" he asked.

"Aye. I done studied the styles closely and I got a piece of fabric I use to practice the knots, I'm that good."

"And your name?"

"Thomas, my lord."

"How old are you, Thomas?"

"Eleven. I'm short for my years on account of thin victuals, but I'm old beyond my years on account of my ma and pa dead from the influenza these two years."

"And I suppose Luckstone has left you here to starve. When was the last time you've eaten anything?"

Thomas colored at the question. He said, "Well you know, my lord, they was in such a hurry when they upped sticks out of here that they left things as they were. I don't mind admitting that I helped myself to some ham." There was a long pause and then Thomas said, "Or all of the ham, if anybody wants to know."

"What will you do now, Thomas?"

"I'll starve. The ham's all gone."

Ambrose suppressed a long and labored sigh. He could not let the boy wither away alone in the house, though he hardly wished to take him on.

"I'm afraid I don't know what to do with you," Ambrose said. "I do not have any likely employment for an eleven-year-old would-be valet."

"Do you know the earl what lives down the road?"

"I do. I am staying there. At least, I think I am."

Thomas leaned over confidentially and said, "Lord Luckstone was forever talking about how decrepit he was and how he hobbled round on a cane and would fall over and crack his head open one of these days. I heard it all as I was cleaning up or fetching things. I feel like a man about to tip over ought to have a page. To fetch things. So he don't fall over."

"That well may be," Ambrose said, "though it seems unlikely, and I can hardly speak for him."

"You could speak for *me*, though," Thomas said, his look almost accusatory.

Blast the little blighter. Ambrose did not know what was to be done with the lad, but he could not leave him here.

"We'll see. Pack your things and be quick about it."

"I don't have no things," Thomas said gravely. "All I got is a comb in my pocket and the clothes on my back."

"Rather underdressed for a page-come-valet," Ambrose said wryly. "Stay here while I check the house. Luckstone may have left something behind that indicates where he's gone."

"I done searched the house from top to bottom. Not a farthing dropped or a note anywhere. Just the Morris's furniture. And the ham. And some bread and mustard. The ham and bread are gone now."

Ambrose nodded. He'd bet the lad did search the house thoroughly. If he'd been left in the same situation, he'd have done the same, hoping to come across some pounds and pence forgotten somewhere. "Very well. Let us go."

Thomas had leapt up and dashed toward the horse grazing on the lawn. Ambrose followed at a more dignified pace.

"I doubt he can carry us both," Ambrose said. "You'll have to walk the two miles."

Thomas stared toward the end of the drive and whispered, "I can try, in my weakened condition. If I fall down in a faint, keep on going! I won't be any trouble to you, my lord. If the wolves get me before I wake, it'll be a mercy."

"There are no wolves left in England," Ambrose said.

"I heard one of 'em screamin' like murder in the night," Thomas said.

"That was a fox," Ambrose said, picking the boy up and throwing him in the saddle.

Somehow, he'd arrived to warn Luckstone off and now he was walking home while the scruffy lad who planned on being the earl's page was on his horse.

CHAPTER FOUR

T HE DINING TABLE was awkwardly laid and nobody who sat at it was quite successful at pretending they did not notice the place that sat empty.

Would Lord Ryland dine with them? Would he not? Nobody knew.

When Lady Featherstone and Lady Heathway had descended to the drawing room before dinner, Lady Featherstone had been transported by the news of Lord Ryland's arrival.

She'd waxed on about how he was a man of action and to be counted on in dire circumstances. Prudence certainly agreed that he must indeed be a man of action, as she had yet to see him sit down.

Lady Heathway was rather sanguine to hear of the lord's arrival, though she seemed most approving of the idea that he would escort them on their trip back.

As he had come and gone so precipitously, nobody could be certain when he would return. They had delayed dinner as much as they dared, and they dared only what could be reasonably accommodated by Cook, lest she throw her apron down and walk out.

Once seated, they'd all made an effort at pleasant conversation, though Prudence was certain that every one of them had one ear listening for the return of Lord Ryland.

Now, they all nearly jumped as he appeared in the doorway

as if by sorcery. He strode in and said, "My apologies, Lord Copeland, Lady Prudence. Lady Featherstone and Lady Heathway, good evening."

Prudence was rather dumbfounded. He was changed for dinner and looked no more ruffled over his late arrival than if his valet had struggled with his neckcloth or some other household mishap had occurred.

"Lord Ryland," Lady Featherstone said with enthusiasm, "how good of you to come to us."

The lord sat down and said ruefully, "I know perfectly well that I was not asked and that I impose on Lord Copeland's hospitality."

"Not at all," the earl said. "Though we were wondering what happened on your visit to Lord Luckstone."

Wondering was putting it mildly, Prudence thought.

"There was no visit," Lord Ryland said, as the footmen brought him round a dish of sliced beef. "Luckstone and his household have decamped, destination as yet unknown."

Prudence felt all the tension leaving her body. He was gone. He was really gone.

It had been one thing to witness Lady Heathway drive him off, but there had been the lingering idea that he'd be back.

But now the news that he'd given up Morris House. That meant he was well and truly gone.

"I knew it," Lady Heathway said proudly. "He could not stand up against me."

"No doubt," Lord Ryland said. "There is, though, one other matter. He left a young boy alone there to fend for himself."

"All alone?" Prudence asked.

"Entirely. And out of food by the time I got there."

For all his glib talk, Prudence had known Luckstone was a cruel man. No other sort of man could attempt to force a lady into a marriage she did not want with no care whatsoever about what she *did* want. It should not surprise her at all that he'd so cruelly abandoned a child.

"Father," Prudence said, "we must do something for the boy. He cannot be left there—he must be so frightened! He has nothing to eat, and probably very few candles. We should send the carriage to retrieve him right away."

Before the earl could answer this interesting request, Lord Ryland said, "That will not be necessary. I took the liberty of bringing him here. We slipped in via the servants' entrance and I turned him over to your good housekeeper. She took one look at him and claimed she would throw him in a bath and scrub him down."

"How beastly to abandon a servant," Lady Heathway said. "One must work round their problems, rather than run away from them."

"I do not know what to do with him," Lord Ryland went on, "though he has a few notions of his own. In future, he imagines himself a valet. For now, he would wish to be Lord Copeland's page."

"My page?" the earl said laughing. "Wherever did he get such an idea?"

"Apparently," Lord Ryland said, "Lord Luckstone mentioned you frequently, and mentioned you employed a cane. From there, the boy's plans took flight. He imagines doing a lot of running and fetching."

"Well I—"

Prudence interrupted her father. "Do let us see him on the morrow, Papa. Mrs. Rider will have made him presentable and then we could see what might be done."

"Very well," the earl said indulgently. "We will have a look at him. I really do not imagine I require a page, but perhaps the stables could do with another hand."

Prudence nodded, though she had no intention that the young boy should be relegated to the stables. Further, she thought her father could do very well with a page. "Lord Ryland," she said, "we must thank you for your efforts, and for being so considerate as to rescue this poor lad that has fortuitously come into your sphere. Pray, what is the boy's name?"

Lord Ryland suddenly looked not as fierce or strong or…whatever he was.

"I am at your service, Lady Prudence," Lord Ryland said. "And the boy's name is Thomas."

Prudence felt herself blush at the idea that the lord was at her service, though she knew it was just a turn of phrase. She had high hopes that such silliness on her part would not be noticed. She had the sort of coloring that made it more subtle than it might be on some ladies. Her acquaintance, Miss Jellicoe, flamed like a roaring fire, where Prudence's own blushes more resembled embers.

"See what you think of the lad, Lord Copeland," Lady Featherstone said. "If you wish to take him on, there is plenty of room in the servants' quarters of my house in London. In any case, if Lord Ryland has thought him suitable to bring here, I am certain he *is* suitable."

"You give me too much credit, Lady Featherstone," Lord Ryland said.

"Nonsense," Lady Featherstone said. "I, of all people, understand your worth."

Despite the lord's protestations, Lady Featherstone went on to catalogue his worth. It seemed he'd founded some sort of society to unmask villains and criminals. Prudence was surprised by how much the lady knew about it, and then further surprised to hear that she was a longstanding member of it.

"Lady Prudence, we meet weekly during the season and I am certain you will wish to attend," Lady Featherstone said. "Lord Copeland, you will also find the meetings quite interesting."

Prudence was not at all certain she *would* wish to attend, but if it were of great interest to her hostess, then of course…

"Lady Prudence and Lord Copeland may not find the same delight in examining mysteries that we do ourselves," Lord Ryland said.

"Lord knows I do not," Lady Heathway said.

"I rather like a mystery," the earl said. "In my youth, we used to play Catch the Rogue. Our governess would make up cards relating to a crime, such as who stole the last biscuit. Then we'd all be given cards, but only one of them was called the rogue. We'd interrogate each other until we could uncover the villain."

The earl paused, then said, "Though now that I think of it, it may have been only a rather ingenious idea to occupy us and keep us quiet for an hour."

"A rather charming idea," Lady Featherstone said. "I certainly will employ it when I have my own grandchildren. Oh, and I nearly forgot, Lord Ryland hosts a ball every year and the accompanying supper follows with a mystery to be solved. Always coming with a very great prize."

Lord Ryland smiled indulgently at his friend. "Lady Featherstone has prevailed for two seasons running."

"My brooch and my cane were both won," Lady Featherstone said, gazing down at the green gem pinned to her bosom.

For a moment, Lady Heathway's eyes traveled up to the ceiling, as if she demanded an explanation from the heavens regarding the brooch. Then she said, "Lady Prudence, do you bring a maid to Town?"

"I shouldn't think so," Prudence said. "Martha does the duty here, but she is to be shortly married and will not wish to be away. She's to marry my father's valet and they will take over his father's farm, so he will not wish to go either."

"Meggy will suffice for us both, I think," Lady Featherstone said. "A valet can be hired in Town for the earl."

The conversation then turned to clothes. Or rather, the conversation turned to Lady Featherstone and Lady Heathway discussing various modistes and planning how to go forward with a wardrobe for Prudence.

The men smiled and nodded though they could make nothing of it.

They had been seated for some time after the last course and Prudence found herself grateful that her father had insisted that she act as hostess these past years. She was confident the time had come.

She rose to lead the ladies to the drawing room.

HAVING THROWN OFF the name Lord Luckstone, Lucknell took a room in his own name at the Bull and Bear. He was unknown at that particular inn, but he was impeccably dressed as a gentleman and had been used these many months to carry himself in the bearing and accents of a lord. That bit of playacting had come in handy. The staff of the inn bowed and scraped as if he were a prince.

He had paid off the men that had attended him at Morris House, a collection of criminals from York who would either be paid or slice his throat. Except, of course, for Paxton, who had left of his own accord, and that urchin who he'd directed to stay at the house and make it look lived in. The longer it took for anybody to realize Lord Luckstone was gone, the better.

The best room of the inn was given him and, as he'd had to wait for it, he presumed some poor fellow had been driven out of it.

Now, he sat in a private dining room, eating the best of the inn's beef.

The door opened and a boy hurried through it. "This just come for you, Mr. Lucknell."

Lucknell took it wordlessly and handed the boy a coin. He was not particularly enthusiastic about handing out coins everywhere, but a lord would do it and so must he.

After the boy left, he tore open the letter.

L—

Our letters must have crossed, as I wrote to you to warn you that you were being looked at. Unfortunately, who was doing the looking was Lord Ryland himself. Lady Featherstone, who is a rather stalwart member of the criminal society, has somehow taken an interest in Lady Prudence and asked Ryland to investigate your claims of an engagement.

Since discovering that, I have found out that Ryland travels to Kent to join Lady Featherstone at Copeland Hall.

I was of course relieved to hear that you'd decamped and presume you are now safe at the Bull and Bear, well before Ryland's arrival to Copeland Hall. He is not to be toyed with, nor will he be fooled easily.

Assuming that happy circumstance, I do not believe all is lost. Lady Featherstone will bring Lady Prudence here, and as Lady Featherstone never misses a criminal society evening, I have every hope she will bring the young lady along. I will do my best to ingratiate myself to her and we will see where we can go with it. In the meantime, I continue to be trusted with organizing files and reports, so nothing that is known to Ryland remains unknown to me.

At this moment, do not come to London. Not yet. Go back and find discreet lodgings somewhere nearby the earl's neighborhood and watch the house. With only the earl in attendance, the staff may be cut. Your plan to tiptoe into the house as Lady Prudence's intended, giving you time and access to look around, may have fallen through. But, now might be the ideal time to search the premises by tiptoeing in at the dead of night.

I am certain we have unraveled the mistake of the old Lord Ryland's attack and that we know now where the diamond has been all along.

There are likely safes and locked boxes in multiple rooms— if you intend on gaining entry to the house bring your tools to get them open.

We will get that diamond yet.

I have not seen hide nor hair of Paxton and so I suppose he really is gone for good. I do not like it. The three of us are the only men who know all. I wonder if his lamentations about the unfortunate demise of the old Lord Ryland were only playacting, and he now goes after the diamond himself. Why should his conscience bother him after all these years? You should have disposed of him when you had the chance, but as he's out there somewhere, we must stay alert.

C

Paxton. Clamarin was right, he should have killed him. But there had been too many people in Morris House, too many witnesses.

He did not know why Paxton had suddenly developed a conscience. He did not think it playacting, though. The man had started to have nightmares and would wake everyone with his screaming. Why bother with that sort of performance? If he wished to go after the diamond himself, or he simply wished to go back to highway robbery as he'd said, he could have slipped out in the night and been gone.

No, Paxton had wrestled with himself. Only God would know why.

Lucknell shivered just the smallest bit. He did not know if it came over him because Paxton was out in the world and might betray them, or if it were the thought of God. He did not like to wonder about God, and he certainly hoped that God was not wondering about him.

Lady Featherstone looked round the drawing room with a feeling of supreme satisfaction.

She admitted to herself that she'd felt no little amount of trepidation on coming to the rescue of the earl and his daughter. But it had all come out so satisfactory!

The girl was just what she would have wished for—well-mannered, gracious, considerate, well-spoken, a doting daughter, and all of those pleasant attributes wrapped up in a very charming countenance.

Lord Luckstone, or whoever he really was, had been driven

off by Lady Heathway, in partnership with Lady Featherstone's own walking stick. Whether she ought to give most of the credit to Lady Heathway or whether it must go to her own walking stick…well, she did not believe Lady Heathway would have got very far without the use of that particular weapon.

Lord Ryland had made a surprising and very gratifying appearance to the house, though she had not asked it of him. It was a testament, she was sure, to their long-running collaboration in the *Society for Advancing Criminal Knowledge*. The doings of SACK, as those familiar with the society called it, had long been her primary interest.

The Society of Sponsoring Ladies had certainly been an interest too, but there was something so compelling about a mystery to be understood. Lord Ryland felt the same and now he could not help but to race to the scene when there was danger lurking near her.

Soon, they would all repair to London, and there she would act as Lady Prudence's mama.

The idea fairly gave her chills. There was so much to do, so much to arrange, but she reminded herself that her friends would be there to help.

Just now, she would enjoy the moment. The gentlemen had long since come into the drawing room from their port. Lord Copeland slept peacefully in his chair, having dozed off an hour ago. Lady Prudence played softly on the pianoforte, while Lord Ryland helpfully turned her pages for her.

Lady Featherstone was touched by what she saw at the instrument and it occurred to her that she'd never viewed Lord Ryland in such a domestic scene. It seemed to suit him somehow. It was as if Lady Prudence had brought out a softer side of the lord.

Perhaps there was something to hope for in that direction?

Lady Featherstone leaned toward Lady Heathway and said, "What do you think?"

"I think I am bone-tired and I pray that a breakfast tray will be sent up to me in the morning and I will not be expected to drag myself downstairs to the breakfast room."

"No, what do you think about Lord Ryland and Lady Prudence?" Lady Featherstone asked.

Lady Heathway regarded the couple. "Anne," she said, "every season, poor Lord Ryland is our first idea. Every season and every girl, somebody inevitably says, '*What about Lord Ryland?*' We are never right."

"It might be right this time, though. I have a feeling about it. My instincts, as you are no doubt aware, have been heightened over the years that I have participated in the lord's criminal society."

"Have they?"

"Indeed yes. Look how he bends over her. Look how he is so attentive at turning her pages while she plays."

"He is being polite, as well he should be, having crashed into the house uninvited."

"I am sure I am right," Lady Featherstone said.

"I am sure that I am going to bed," Lady Heathway said. "Lord Copeland has been asleep this past hour and I find that I envy him."

Lady Featherstone was not at all put off by Lady Heathway's naysaying. After all, her nickname in society *was* Lady Naysay.

As for herself, she could see that there was something promising beginning with her own eyes and her own instincts. She would nurture it in whatever way she could.

Goodness. The very idea of Lord Ryland becoming her son-in-law. Well, not technically a son-in-law, but something very much like it!

⇛⇚

PRUDENCE HAD ARRANGED for breakfast trays to be sent up to Lady Featherstone and Lady Heathway, as she was certain matrons such as those did not take breakfast in the breakfast room like ordinary mortals. As she was not certain what they preferred, they were to receive everything the kitchens had on offer. If they were not drawn to the savories, then certainly they would not be able to resist Cook's honey cakes.

Prudence had come downstairs on the late side of things herself, though it was not her usual habit. She was generally up with the sun, but this morning she had dillydallied and delayed.

She did not wish to meet Lord Ryland in the breakfast room, particularly not alone.

The evening before, he'd put himself forward to turn her pages as she played and he'd leaned over her so close that she could detect the scent of him. It was earthy, but clean, very like the forest after a heavy summer rain. There was even that moment when she'd felt his warm breath pass lightly across the back of her neck like a faerie's touch at dusk.

It had been both alluring and frightening. He was a devilishly handsome man, but he was far too *much* man. She'd had to concentrate to keep her fingers steady on the keys.

Her discomposure was not because a gentleman turned her pages. No, that had been done for her often enough.

Both Mr. Swindon and Mr. Cahill were assiduous in putting themselves forward for the task, and sometimes seemed near an argument over who would do it. But, whoever prevailed and appeared beside her, it was of no more consequence than a moth beating its wings about her shoulders. Mostly, she hardly noticed anybody was there.

She could not help but notice Lord Ryland though. He was very there. He made Mr. Swindon and Mr. Cahill seem as boys, though they must all be close in age. He seemed older, though he was not, he seemed taller, though he was not, he seemed…

Well. Lord Ryland seemed very…unsettling.

When hunger had finally driven her downstairs, she'd been relieved to find her father in the breakfast room with Lord Ryland.

They had been talking of estate management and Prudence had been happy to let them get on with it.

The only thing that shook her was when Lord Ryland had casually said, "I trust you slept well, Lady Prudence."

She had nodded and put all her attention on her eggs. It seemed very personal for him to wonder how she'd slept. Had he thought about her sleeping? That was even more personal!

They'd had so few houseguests over the years that Prudence was not at all certain if it were a usual question. Her father did not seem alarmed by it, so perhaps it was.

Still, the idea that he'd wondered about anything that might occur after her bedchamber door was shut…

Now, they were gathered in the drawing room. Her father had laid out plans for an expansion of the gardens and the addition of a hothouse and a fountain, while Lord Ryland leaned over him examining them.

Lady Featherstone and Lady Heathway had heads together over a list of items that must be purchased for her launch in society. Prudence thought both ladies were very generous in their estimations, though she was not wholly convinced that a parasol in every color was in fact needed. Further, twenty-two pairs of gloves seemed highly excessive.

Lady Featherstone had been resolute in the idea that it was her purview to purchase what was needed, despite the earl's objections. Poor Lord Featherstone likely had no idea what expense he was about to be put to.

There was a soft knock on the drawing room doors and they opened, showing Jonas coming in with a boy.

CHAPTER FIVE

THE BOY LORD Luckstone had left behind at Morris House was led into the drawing room by the butler.

Prudence felt a wave of shame over her selfishness. She'd all but forgotten the poor mite in considering her own feelings over the past day.

He seemed very young indeed. Lord Ryland had said he was eleven years old, but he looked closer to eight or nine. He'd been dressed in somebody's castoffs, and while they were clean, they were decidedly too big.

"My lord," Jonas said, "this is Thomas, who was brought to us last evening and has been intent on emptying our larder ever since."

Thomas, seeming not at all affected by Jonas' hints about his appetite, ran to Lord Copeland and bowed until his head nearly touched the floor.

"Stand up and let me look at you," Lord Copeland said kindly.

"I'm not much to look at, my lord," Thomas said, straightening. "But I'm fast on my feet. You want something, I'll run for it. It'll be in your hands before you can blink."

"I am sure that is true. Though, I am not at all sure I require a page," Lord Copeland said.

Thomas got a faraway look in his eyes and said softly, "It's the end for me then. I'll be off to the workhouse now. No, don't try to stop me! My dream of someday becoming a valet is over and I'll take my rightful place among the wretched and down-trodden."

"No need to go that far, I am sure," Lord Copeland said.

"Never you mind it, my lord," Thomas said gravely. "I'll join me ma and pa, what starved in the workhouse afore me."

"You told me your parents died of influenza," Lord Ryland said.

Thomas looked dolefully at Lord Ryland. "They starved, and *then* they got the influenza. I'll likely go the same."

"I'd not be surprised if they weren't dead at all," Lord Ryland said drily.

Thomas took this moment to dramatically faint onto Lord Copeland's lap.

Jonas hurried forward. "My lord," he said, "if the boy is weak, I can assure you it is not for lack of food. He's put away more than a full-grown soldier on the march!"

Lord Ryland put an arm underneath Thomas and raised him from Lord Copeland's lap. Thomas hung limp in his arms, his eyes closed.

"I do not believe there is a thing wrong with this little blight-er," Lord Ryland said.

"Well, that may be so," Lord Copeland said thoughtfully, "but he seems very keen for a chance."

Thomas' eyes then remarkably flew open. "I won't let you down, my lord. You have my word." He then proceeded to wriggle out of Lord Ryland's grasp, miraculously recovered from his recent state of unconsciousness.

"Jonas," Lord Copeland said, "make arrangements for the boy to travel with us to Town. Find some clothes, perhaps somebody in the village has a set that could be tailored to fit?"

Jonas gripped the boy by the shoulder and muttered, "By the way he eats, we'll be buying a new set every week."

Thomas did not dispute this theory and went happily enough with the butler.

"I am afraid you've got yourself rather a handful," Lord Ryland said.

"I am certain of it," Lord Copeland said good naturedly. "If he does not have a future as a valet, then perhaps he might find success on the stage. He is a rather wonderful actor."

"It was very good of you, though, Papa," Prudence said.

"Well," the earl said, "we will see."

AMBROSE SAT IN Lord Copeland's library, staring at the pile before him.

Whenever he traveled, whether it were near or far, Parker and Depsford kept him apprised of the society's doings via a packet of letters. They had done no less now, though he was only to be away for two days in Kent.

He was usually happy to get them. The society, and his hunt for his father's murderers, had become the focal point of his life. There had been no other thing that took precedent. There were distractions from time to time, but his mind and heart were always led back to the society.

In this moment, though, the letters felt more like a chore. He sat at the library's desk, facing a bank of windows that overlooked the garden. The ladies were out strolling its paths while he thumbed through a stack of notes. He would very much like to be out there with them.

Ambrose tore open the correspondence and scanned it. The Morgans were well and truly done up, both arrested and imprisoned. They were a married couple who preyed upon those who were desperate to climb society's ladder.

He posed as a viscount, while *she* posed as his sister. They had defrauded a gentleman who'd made his money importing goods and who'd held a burning desire to marry his daughter to a lord. That desire had clouded the man's judgment and stopped him from asking questions that should have been asked. Most particularly, why he was not to have his own solicitor represent him in the contract negotiations and why the dowry was to be transferred so far ahead of the wedding.

The Morgans had collected that very handsome dowry and disappeared. Ambrose had found them, though, when they'd booked passage to America. Had one more day gone by, they would have been out of reach forever.

News of their capture was the only news of any consequence.

He bound the packet up with string and contemplated Lady Prudence.

She looked very charming in her straw bonnet, cutting daffodils and placing them in a basket.

On the whole, they were an exceedingly pleasant family. He'd quite enjoyed his conversation with Lord Copeland after dinner the evening before. He was a man of good sense, but not so hemmed in by sense that he could not be generous.

The earl had directed his butler to give out glasses of the wine had at dinner when he returned to the servants' quarters, being of the opinion that it was well-earned when there were guests to look after. Considering the quality of the wine served, it had been generous indeed.

Having spent most of his adult life peering behind facades and gathering histories, Ambrose had found himself inquiring into Lord Copeland.

He'd asked about the late Lady Copeland and the earl had been most happy to speak about her.

The lady had been born in Portugal and then found herself raised in a convent upon her parents' death. Lord Copeland was not at all clear on why there were no relatives to take her, but he did know that Queen Maria Francisca had been instrumental in making contact with the old Lord Featherstone, the current Lady Featherstone's now-departed father-in-law. The lady and Lord Featherstone were connected…well, he was not clear how. It was one of those typical loose connections made by following the meandering byways of a family lineage.

In any case, the old Lord Featherstone had agreed to receive her. As she was already twenty-eight, he'd presumed she would end a spinster. Jóia, as that had been her name, turned out to be not very spinsterish at all. London had been at her feet, despite her age, though she had not been over-affected by it. As gentlemen turned somersaults and attempted all sorts of derring-do to catch her eye, Lord Copeland did the sensible thing. He talked to her.

They were married not three months later.

Of course, at the mention of Portugal, Ambrose's mind instantly drifted to the Lisbon Diamond. The diamond his father had been killed for. He had, over the years, become too suspicious by half, seeing connections everywhere when often they did not exist.

Lord Copeland's wife had been named Jóia, which meant jewel in Portuguese.

Coincidence?

Yes, that was exactly what it was.

His younger self would have been certain there was a connection, but his more experienced and wiser self had learned that if one sought connections, they were practically falling from the trees. He had made some mistakes in a few of his investigations in those early days and those mistakes had led him down dead-end paths. One plus one equaled two only when the *ones* in question had a clear and factual relationship to one another.

Out the window, Jóia's daughter, Lady Prudence, was off on her own, diligently clipping bunches of daffodils.

He threw his pile of letters down and headed for the door.

PRUDENCE HAD BEEN forcing herself to put her full concentration on gathering flowers for the house. It had long been her responsibility to do so, though the task could have easily been done by a housemaid. She found her mid-morning walks through the shrubberies a most excellent way to begin the day.

This day, though, her meanderings were not as peaceful as they usually were. Lord Ryland was in her father's library and staring out the window quite a bit. Why was he looking out into the garden when he really should be attending to whatever work he'd set for himself? It was very discomposing, as if she were being spied upon.

As she determined she would not steal one more glance toward the windows, he suddenly appeared beside her.

"Lady Prudence," he said, in his deep voice.

Prudence nearly lost command of her basket and a few of the daffodils slipped out and fell to the ground.

Lord Ryland picked them up. "May I carry your basket?" he asked.

Though he asked it, he did not in fact wait for a reply. His fingers brushed her own as he took possession of it.

"Thank you, my lord," Prudence said.

He put back the daffodils that had fallen to the ground and said, "Why does not a maid assist you in the operation?"

Why did he wish to know that? It seemed a personal sort of question.

"I only say," the lord went on, "that it is more convenient for two people to do the job."

"I prefer to come out on my own most mornings," Prudence said. "The maids often chatter too much, they break the spell of a morning garden."

"Ah, and here I am worse than a maid," Lord Ryland said. "If a lady wishes for peace in the garden, she hardly wishes for a gentleman to come crashing into it."

"No, I did not mean that…" Had she been insulting? She rather thought she had, at least a little. Though, Lord Ryland seemed more amused than anything.

"I think I know what you meant," the lord said. "This is a

decidedly feminine domain and I often feel as a bull breaking out of its pasture and stomping through where I do not belong."

"I am sure you are well able to conduct yourself in a garden, Lord Ryland."

"Perhaps. I do have them on my estate, as they seem to be a requirement. Though I much prefer the walks I've laid out at my house in Ramsgate. There, the wildflowers and grasses seemed more suited to me and I do not fear trampling a lady's daisies."

Prudence had no answer to that as it seemed very apt. A man like Lord Ryland *would* be more suited to wild coastal scenes than a tame English garden.

She'd clipped a few more daffodils and handed them to the lord, though her basket had grown quite full and she really ought to stop.

"Ah, there you are," Lady Featherstone said, coming round a corner. "Lord Ryland, how kind that you carry Lady Prudence's basket for her. Very accommodating. Lady Heathway has gone inside, she says the sun is all well and good, but the shade is better."

For some reason, Prudence felt very put on the spot, as if there were something to explain about Lord Ryland holding her basket.

She said, "I am sure we should go in, too. I have gathered quite enough flowers for Mrs. Rider's use."

They turned to walk the path that led to the stone steps back to the house. Prudence took the lead while Lord Ryland and Lady Featherstone fell behind her.

"Lady Prudence," Lady Featherstone said, "I cannot tell you how much you shall enjoy Lord Ryland's mystery supper. There is a ball first, of course, but then the real fun begins."

"I am sure," Prudence said, "though I have no particular skill at solving mysteries."

"Oh, but you will come up to it quick, I think. You seem a clever sort of girl. And then, Lord Ryland does always make it so interesting."

"You flatter me, Lady Featherstone," Lord Ryland said. "My small entertainment is just one of a thousand during the season."

"Small entertainment indeed," Lady Featherstone said. "It is *the* event of the year."

Lord Ryland laughed, rich and deep. Prudence could almost feel it in her bones.

"Lady Featherstone," Lord Ryland said indulgently, "it is the event of the year for *you*, as you have proved yourself victorious on two occasions. I do not envision it the event of the year for a young lady, though."

"Oh I think you are wrong, Lord Ryland," Lady Featherstone said. "But it occurs to me, as Lady Prudence has not had much experience with solving mysteries, that she ought to accompany me to the SACK meetings."

"Only if she wishes it," Lord Ryland said. "If so, she would be very welcome. Very welcome indeed."

What on earth were *sack* meetings? Prudence did not know. She began to think there was quite a lot about what went on in London that she did not know.

"There now, Lady Prudence," Lady Featherstone said gleefully. "You have heard it for yourself. You are not merely welcome to attend, you are very welcome indeed."

"I am grateful for the courtesy," Prudence said, though she did not have the least idea what the courtesy was, and the courtesy somehow felt too much.

Blessedly, they had come to the steps. She turned and held her hand out for the basket of flowers. Lord Ryland handed them to her.

"Well," she said, "I had better get these to Mrs. Rider before they wilt."

She hurried up the steps, leaving Lady Featherstone and Lord Ryland behind.

AMBROSE WATCHED LADY Prudence run up the steps with her basket of daffodils. He almost got the feeling that she was less concerned with the state of her flowers and more concerned with running away from him. It was as if she had been cautious of being alone with him in the garden, though they were in view of every window on the south side of the house.

He paused, thinking of how recently she had been harassed by a gentleman. Or if not a gentleman, then one who had posed as a gentleman. It had perhaps made her wary of gentlemen in general.

"She will be the toast of the season, I think," Lady Featherstone said.

Ambrose nodded, as he gave the lady his arm to climb the steps. Lady Featherstone was probably right, though he could not like it. Lady Prudence and her father had long lived in this small neighborhood, going nowhere and seeing few families. They were both, in their ways, naïve to the ways of the wider world. Had they not fallen prey to a fraudster and failed to discover a way to get rid of him beyond hiding in the house?

And yet, what would be the effect when a lady such as this walked into a ballroom? As far as he knew, she would have a suitable dowry. She had a suitable background. She'd had a suitable upbringing. All the necessary particulars were in order. There was nothing to weigh but her looks, and those were spectacular, and her temperament, which was pleasing.

She would be a magnet, drawing men to her. Some would be reputable, some would pretend they were but probably were not. Then some, as he knew from his own poking around, were downright disreputable, though they might be accepted everywhere.

Those men who held secrets were admitted to every drawing room until their shame was a secret no more.

There were those in debt up to their eyes, there were those whose dairy maid had a son who looked suspiciously like him, there were those who treated an old aunt abominably or refused to pay school fees for a cousin. There were those who preyed on women in need of money and there were even those who would end beating their wives, should they ever convince a lady to accept them.

"I will be very careful of her, of course," Lady Featherstone said. "I will count on my sharpened instincts to keep her away from anybody not quite up to snuff. The ladies of the society always do worry about such characters. For example, Mr. Vance is so genial, he really can be so charming, though the fact remains that his grandfather was in trade."

Good God, she was worried about Vance? Vance was one of the more reputable gentlemen in Town. Clean as a whistle and the sort that wore his character on his sleeve. Vance was precisely who he made himself out to be, and *that* was who she worried about?

As dear as he found Lady Featherstone, Ambrose did not trust her instincts for a farthing. He was still perplexed over how she'd managed to win one of his mysteries, never mind two of them.

At the SACK meetings, she was almost counted on to be wrong. If Lady Featherstone's ideas went one way, everybody else in attendance about-faced and went the other way. Except for Mr. Clamarin, of course, who was unflagging in his indulgence of the lady.

Certainly, Lady Prudence's protection could not be left to Lady Featherstone's rather dizzy theories and summations.

"Lady Featherstone," he said, "I would put myself forward to assist you in ensuring that Lady Prudence does not come under the influence of the wrong people."

The lady seemed delighted with the idea. "Do you? Oh yes, of course you do. Just as I thought. Lady Heathway will be happy to know that she was wrong with a capital W."

Ambrose had no idea what Lady Heathway had to do with anything. But then, Lady Featherstone's thinking could be so disordered that it was probably useless to attempt to work it out.

⇒⟩⟩⟩⟩⟨⟨⟨⟨⟨⇐

PRUDENCE HAD HANDED over her basket of flowers to Mrs. Rider and then repaired to her bedchamber. Her face felt hot and she had an urgent wish to be alone.

She sat by the windows overlooking the recently walked garden and fanned herself.

She was acting so stupid! No, she was *feeling* so stupid. She had run up the steps to the house, leaving Lord Ryland and Lady Featherstone behind, as if she were fleeing a murderer.

Why? What had he done but carry her basket? Why was she so frightened of him?

Or not frightened, exactly. Both drawn and repelled. She wished to be both in his vicinity and away from him.

What could be more stupid than that?

Prudence had often credited herself with good sense. She might not have the classical good looks of a Miss Jellicoe, or the elegant seat on a horse of a Miss Ramsey, or even the neat stitching of a Miss Wallace. But she at least had sense.

So she had thought. She supposed it had been easy to think so when she had been cloistered at Copeland Hall and sense had been rarely called on. Things were arranged at the hall and they went on peaceably.

Now, the arrival of a gentleman, hardly an earth-shattering occurrence, had sent her nerves jangling. It was extremely stupid, there was no other word for it.

It was one thing to be discomposed by Lord Luckstone, anybody would have been. But to be equally fluttery over Lord Ryland, who posed no danger whatsoever?

And yet, he did seem dangerous, in some way.

There was a sharp rap on the door. A rather sharper rap than Martha's would be.

"Yes?" she said.

The door swung open and Lady Featherstone came barreling

through it. "There you are, Lady Prudence. I could not delay in apprising you of a recent development."

Lady Featherstone sat herself in a chair by the hearth and made herself comfortable. "As you know, I will be your guiding hand through London. If I may say so, I am well-equipped for the job."

Prudence was certain she must be, though she could not guess where the conversation was going.

"Naturally, though, two heads are better than one," Lady Featherstone said. "And, well, such a head as that…"

The lady had drifted off, as if Prudence was meant to know what it was she said.

"I am sorry, my lady?" Prudence said.

"Lord Ryland, of course!" Lady Featherstone said, appearing delighted with herself. "He positively insists on being my partner in the scheme. *He* will watch out for you too."

"Will he?" Prudence said, a small finger of dread winding up her back.

"Oh yes. He is very handsome, do not you think so?"

"Well, I—"

"No! Never mind. It is too soon for *that!*"

Lady Featherstone hopped up just as fast as she'd sat down. "Now that's settled, I'd better be off to see Lady Heathway. She ought to know as soon as possible that she was wrong with a capital W. She won't like it, but it cannot be helped."

The lady was off in a swish of silks, the door closing behind her.

Prudence fanned herself vigorously. She had to get hold of herself and stop being stupid. If a person, whether it be Lady Featherstone or some lord or other, wished to look out for her, then certainly that was their own affair.

She would not think of it. Or she would at least try not to think of it.

CHAPTER SIX

LADY FEATHERSTONE HAD found Lady Heathway the precise same way she'd found Lady Prudence—by rapping on her door and charging in uninvited.

She found Lady Heathway directing her maid in the packing, as they would set off for London on the morrow.

Lady Featherstone took in the operation and thought Lady Heathway had packed enough for this short trip to be able to successfully reside in the palace during coronation ceremonies. There certainly was enough jewelry involved to turn a princess' head.

Lady Heathway, noting Lady Featherstone staring at her cases of jewelry, said, "They are all paste, except for the pearls. I had copies made years ago. If they are stolen, the jest will be on the thief."

"Very clever, Penelope," Lady Featherstone said. "And yet, you have not been clever in one thing. What do you think? Lord Ryland has put himself forward as Lady Prudence's protector."

"Very gallant, I'm sure," Lady Heathway said.

"More than gallant," Lady Featherstone said. "He has a real interest, I have seen it with my own eyes. He did insist on carrying her basket in the garden."

"Did he propose while he was doing it?" Lady Heathway said, examining a pair of gloves.

"It is too soon for that, as you well know. Now come, Penelope. Admit you were wrong with a capital W."

"I'll do no such thing."

And so they went on for some time, Lady Featherstone insisting on an admission of wrong with a capital W and Lady Heathway swearing she would never do it.

They were finally interrupted by Lady Heathway's maid slamming a case shut with vigor and sighing loudly.

"You see, Anne?" Lady Heathway said. "Even my maid thinks it is nonsense."

"Time will tell the tale," Lady Featherstone said with conviction. "Time is the teller of all tales."

"Is it?"

PRUDENCE HAD BUSIED herself all day in preparing her father and herself for their departure the following morning and ensuring the household understood how to carry on while they were away.

It would be a new experience for the staff, as they had never before been away, but Jonas appeared well able to manage it. There would be extra days off given out and shortened working hours, as otherwise the staff would go mad dusting, cleaning, and polishing, but with no inhabitants to appreciate their efforts.

The dinner that evening had come off rather well. Cook had already taken receipt of supplies necessary for a week before she'd been apprised that they would go. She prepared the very best of it and Lord Copeland was well-pleased.

The conversation at dinner had not been as laborious as Prudence had thought it might be. Between Lady Featherstone's speculations and plans for the London season, and Lady Heathway's speculations about her soon-to-arrive granddaughter, there was not much silence to fill.

There was, of course, that one awkward moment.

Lady Featherstone had told the earl of some entertainment or other that he was certain to find amusing. Her father had explained that with his gouty foot and his penchant for falling asleep early, he was doubtful of attending very many events at all. He would be quite happy to remain at home and trust in Lady Featherstone to squire his daughter round the town.

Lady Featherstone had been delighted by his faith in her good judgment. Then she'd added the news that Lord Ryland had put himself forward to act as a chaperone too.

It had been more than awkward actually. At least, for Prudence it had been. She'd felt Lord Ryland looking at her intently, as if he wished to divine her thoughts on the matter.

Her father had been approving and said, "That is very gracious, Lord Ryland. Very gracious and much appreciated."

Fortunately, the subject had not been left to linger, as Lady Heathway took to explaining the glories of Barlow Hall. They were to take the lady there and spend the night before proceeding into London. Her nephew, Lord Gresham, had been apprised by letter of their arrival.

Lord Ryland briefly wondered aloud if he ought not go straight to London, as Gresham would not be expecting him and Lady Gresham was so close to her confinement.

Lady Featherstone had quickly overruled him, though it was not her own relative's house they traveled to. She was convinced that after what Lady Prudence and the earl had suffered at the hands of Lord Luckstone, they required Lord Ryland's protection on the road.

Lord Ryland had seemed to take that idea seriously, though Prudence could not imagine that Lord Luckstone would be lying in wait for them somewhere.

For that matter, her father seemed highly approving of the scheme too.

And so, it was settled. Lord Ryland would travel in their own caravan of carriages.

In the drawing room, Thomas, her father's recently employed page, stood dutifully by his chair, ready to fetch anything and everything. Jonas had managed to find him clothes that fit better, including a rather jaunty looking navy jacket.

Dear Lord Copeland did send Thomas on some errands, no doubt only to keep the little fellow occupied.

Her father could not keep his eyes open for long however, and once he was asleep, Prudence suggested that Thomas ought to go and get his own sleep.

The boy had refused and stood stoically by the earl's chair until he woke and went up to bed. Thomas had followed her father out of the room with a certain air of dignity, as if he were following a king retiring from his court.

Prudence had followed soon after, claiming she had some last-minute packing to attend to. It was all nonsense, she had been packed very early in the day.

She'd left Lady Featherstone and Lady Heathway playing piquet and Lord Ryland reading a book from her father's library.

Though the lord had been reading the entire time after dinner, Prudence had often felt his eyes were upon her. It had been a relief to get to the sanctuary of her bedchamber.

Now, Martha came in to help her out of her dress. It would be the last time she would do so. As Prudence had assumed, the maid had no wish to go to London. She was engaged to be married and would not be separated from her beau.

Prudence had arranged with her father to pay both Martha's and Mr. Cadmon's wages through to the end of the year, though they would be long married by then, and to add a ten-pound gift on top of it to help the young couple get started. John Cadmon had acted as her father's valet for some years, but now he was poised to take over a farm from his own father.

"Well?" Martha said, brushing out Prudence's hair. "Would you hear my opinions or no?"

Prudence smiled. Martha had long been in the habit of watching people carefully and then informing her if they were good or bad, generous or stingy, truthful or liars and so on. Remarkably, she was generally right.

The moment she'd set eyes on Lord Luckstone she'd informed the earl that he was a sharper, not to be trusted.

The earl had been quite taken aback to hear another lord described so. She had been proved right, of course.

Her father had asked Martha how she knew so quickly, before seeing what he would do. Martha had said, "The air feels heavy when he approaches, and I don't suppose anybody would miss those shifty eyes. They don't settle anywhere, but flit this way and that like they don't know where to land."

Just recently, Miss Wallace had been diagnosed with a mean spirit and a wish to cause trouble.

Prudence had found it hard to believe until she paid closer attention. Then she realized that Miss Wallace, though always seeming so demure and bent over her sewing, often somehow managed to say something that cast doubt on another person. It was always opaque, along the lines of, "Poor Miss Jellicoe, I cannot imagine what they say is true. At least *I* will not be guilty of passing on unfounded gossip. I will say nothing of it."

One was left to wonder what mysterious thing had been said, and to have a vague feeling that it must be very terrible.

"I know you will tell me your opinions whether I wish to hear them or not," Prudence said now. "Though as it happens, I do wish to hear them."

"It's like this," Martha said, "Lady Heathway is a prickly sort by nature. She don't mean nothing by it, but if you say up she'll say down. Like most prickly sorts, it's a brittle shell she wears over a marshmallow heart and her feelings are easily hurt. She won't show it though, not for all the world."

Prudence nodded.

"Now, Lady Featherstone is quite a different matter. She's more the happy type what hasn't had a lot of burdens placed on her. She's the type that can confuse wishing for believing. She gets distracted by ideas. If she likes an idea, then the idea seems true. For all that, though, I like her. She always means well."

"And?" Prudence asked.

"And what? Oh, I see. You want to know about Lord Ryland."

"I assume you have an opinion," Prudence said. "I have never known you not to."

Martha paused her brushing. "I'm not sure I do. He's deep, that one. He's not shifty like Luckstone, not at all. He's upright, but he's guarded. I can't say what's behind it. He's old beyond his years, for some reason."

Prudence agreed, he did seem older than other gentlemen his age.

Martha shrugged. "I can't entirely make him out, but you'll be safe around him. That I do know."

That was more than Prudence knew. It was not that she imagined there was anything downright dangerous about Lord Ryland. Certainly, he was everything a respectable gentleman should be, and her father had formed a rather high opinion of him.

It was just…well, she supposed it was just that she was being stupid.

"Only think," Martha said, finishing the last of Prudence's braids, "you'll soon be in London, mixing with the great muckety-mucks of the place."

Prudence rose. "And you, Martha, just think, before you know it you will be a married lady."

She opened a drawer and took out a brown paper package tied in white ribbon.

"You didn't never get me another present?" Martha said. But of course Martha knew that was precisely what it was. She took it and tore through the paper.

The package contained five yards of a very finely weaved cotton, roller-printed with delicate flowers in Turkey red, and a yard of Brussels lace. It would make a wonderful wedding dress, and then could be made serviceable for church and trips to the village.

"Aye, this will do very well. Very, very well. John Cadmon will have his breath taken from him on viewing me."

Prudence laughed. "Do make sure he has enough breath left for his vows, though."

Martha nodded. Then her expression grew serious. "You know, miss, how I do get a feeling about something from time to time. Not just people, but things that will come to pass?"

"I do, and dearly hope you never mention it to the vicar lest he think you possessed by the devil."

"It runs in my family, my ma always had the same. I say only this: there's some in London who…well they don't wish you harm exactly. It's that you might be in the way of something they're wanting to get to."

Prudence shivered. She really never knew whether she ought to believe in Martha's feelings or not. Though, this one was particularly ominous.

"In that particular matter, trust in Lord Ryland. Lady Featherstone, cheerful soul that she is, will be no use whatsoever."

"But you do not say I am in any real danger?" Prudence asked.

Martha ran her hand along the fabric that would soon be her wedding dress. "I believe it will all come right in the end. You're meant to be going where you're going, and it will all come right. That's the important thing."

AMBROSE REGARDED THE boy sitting across from him in the carriage, who had somehow got himself hired as the earl's page. Lord Copeland would ride with his daughter and so Thomas had been foisted on him. The newly-minted page ought to be riding with the lady's maids, but those two females had whispered to their mistresses, and somehow it was not to be. Ambrose supposed they'd campaigned that it would be too crowded and hatboxes would be crushed, or some nonsense.

He'd almost refused, ready to insist the boy go with the maids. But then, Lady Prudence had thanked him for his kindness. And well, what could he do? Once a lady thanked a gentleman for a kindness, it was as good as done and there was no going back.

The chap was just now officiously straightening his cuffs and gazing out the carriage window with his chin up, eyes hooded and seeming slightly bored with what he saw. His expression looked for all the world like lofty condescension, as if he were the young heir to a duke. Lord Copeland was right in his assessment—the lad was a gifted actor.

"I was wondering, Thomas, what is the whole catalogue of lies that you have told so far? For instance, I am fairly certain your parents are not dead."

Thomas nodded graciously out the window to a farm boy on the side of the road who watched slack jawed as the carriages passed by. That farmer's boy would likely return home and tell his family he just saw a mighty young lord and his older valet.

"My lord," Thomas said, "news of my parents' death weren't rightly a lie, as they *ought* to be dead. Me ma takes in laundry and she'll happily drown a person getting too close to her wash buckets. Me da takes the money she brings in and drinks it at the tavern. What two people ought to be deader than that?"

Ambrose did not weigh in with an opinion on the question, though he thought that story, at least, had the ring of truth. Through his various investigations in the poorer neighborhoods, he had run into like situations. It was a miracle that children like Thomas ever survived at all.

Of course, he did not think bad temper and bad habits the exclusive purview of the poor. There were plenty of people with deep-lined pockets that went on in the same condition. However, money cushioned all things. If a lord made brandy his primary pastime, it would have little impact on the sons away at school or daughters raised by governesses. The situation became a deal more dire when the family lived in one room and the threat of starving was forever hanging over their heads.

"I said to 'em one evening," Thomas went on, "as they were beatin' each other about the head, that they ought to be dead as they was just taking up space in the world. They ran me off after that."

"I see," Ambrose said. "And that's how you came upon Luckstone."

"Aye, one of his men hired me and we lingered for a while in York and then off we went to Kent. My eyes was opened, don't you know. I looked about meself and discovered there's heaps of jobs working for his nibs what don't require much work at all. I found an old cloth in Morris House and started practicing my knots for when I'm a valet."

"You mean you stole a cloth you found."

Thomas ignored that statement and leaned forward. "Your own knot could use some sprucing up."

"Do not even think about it. I tied it myself, but I shall soon be back in the grips of my own valet. Now, I have one other comment. When I found you at Morris House, you claimed you were on the brink of starvation. I've since discovered that Luckstone had left you there *that* day. Hardly an extended privation."

Thomas threw his chin up. "He was gone *four* hours."

"You had a ham."

"Only for the first hour. The other three hours, I was wasting away."

"No more lies," Ambrose said.

Thomas shrugged and went back to looking out the window like the heir to a dukedom he was not.

Ambrose considered him. He was a very wonderful actor, as evidenced by his dramatic faint onto Lord Copeland's lap and his various falsehoods. He seemed to have steady nerves. He might be useful.

"Thomas," he said sternly, "I will put you on a retainer of one shilling a week to be my eyes and ears in Lady Featherstone's house."

At the mention of money, Ambrose had the boy's full attention. "*Two* shillings, and I'll be your eyes, ears and nose."

"I don't need your nose."

"Don't you?" Thomas said. "Sometimes, a fella's eyes and ears don't see nothin' in particular, but he can *smell* something gone wrong."

Ambrose quietly sighed and said, "Two shillings and I am being robbed. I only agree to it because I am concerned for Lady Prudence's safety."

Thomas chuckled and said, "Safety. 'Course that's the interest."

Ambrose stared at him, the stare he'd so often used to break a recalcitrant witness.

The smile dropped off the boy's face.

"If you see anything suspicious, any hint of Luckstone, I am to be informed. I would also like to know if there are any particular gentlemen calling regularly so they can be properly looked into. Write a note and send it with a footman. Lady Featherstone sends them to me every other day so nobody will think anything of it."

Thomas squirmed a little on his seat. "As to that, my lord. I always find that a face to face is a better way to go about things."

"So, you can't write," Ambrose said.

"Could *you* write if your ma was tryin' to drown you in a wash bucket and your pa was tipplin' at the tavern?"

Ambrose supposed there would have been little time for lessons in that congenial atmosphere. "You'll have to come in person then. I'll give you the address and you are to come in through a door located halfway down the mews. You are to ask for my butler, Mr. Parker, or my valet, Mr. Depsford. If neither are available, ask to be directed to Mr. Clamarin, as he is generally about the place."

"So Depsford fancies himself a valet, does he?"

"That's enough, you little blighter."

PRUDENCE WATCHED THE countryside pass by her window. She'd never been anywhere beyond the confines of her own neighborhood and each new vista held a certain charm. A farmer's field might be similar to others she had seen, but it was not precisely the same. A small wood was very like their own, but it had its own peculiar charms. They had just passed through a shady lane that had a stream running alongside it, graced with weeping willows that looked as if they'd been there since the beginning of time.

Most importantly, she and her father were leaving their problems with Lord Luckstone behind. If the man ever decided to return, he would not find them at home.

The morning had dawned bright and the ladies had been downstairs promptly, though Prudence had wondered if either Lady Featherstone or Lady Heathway were naturally early risers.

There had been a flurry of confusion in the setting off, all around who ought to ride with whom.

Lady Featherstone and Lady Heathway wished to be accompanied by Prudence, but that would have left her father alone. It was briefly considered that the earl could be accommodated too, making four in one carriage, until Prudence pointed out he would need room to prop up his gouty foot from time to time.

Lady Featherstone then suggested that Lady Heathway ride with Lord Copeland in another of the carriages, but then Lady Heathway pointed out the impropriety of two unrelated persons of opposite genders alone for an extended period.

Prudence did not think either of them would get up to much, but she supposed appearances must be maintained.

In the end, everybody would go as they'd come. That left Thomas, who surely should have gone in with the maids.

Somehow, those two women had dodged it by pointing at hatboxes and frowning.

Lord Ryland had been left to take him and Prudence had thought it very generous, though he had not looked delighted.

"I suppose poor Lord Ryland is having his ear talked off just now," her father said. "Whenever that boy and I are alone, he rattles on like an old aunt. His parents have died eight different ways so far."

"It was very good of you to take him in, though, Papa. You have a soft heart."

The earl smiled. "Your mother softened it for me. And she gave you a soft heart very like her own, too. I will caution you that London is not known for being full of soft hearts, though. It can be an intimidating sort of place."

Prudence thought of the carriage just now clip-clopping behind their own. "I suppose Lord Ryland is typical of a London gentleman," she said.

"Is he? Oh, I don't know. Lord Ryland does not strike me as a man who means to be intimidating. He has a more forceful presence than I do myself, but I think he can be relied upon. It was exceedingly gracious of him to put himself forward in looking out for you."

Prudence supposed it had been gracious. Though, it made her uncomfortable all the same. Lord Ryland always seemed to be looking at her. Now, he would keep looking at her.

She really would have to develop more sense, more of a backbone. She was going to London, where it did not sound as if there were room for ladies finding themselves nervous over a person looking in their direction.

Prudence had never felt a case of nerves over somebody looking in her direction before. It would be highly inconvenient to begin now.

What had her mother always said? Coragem é encontrada no coração. Courage is found in the heart. She really must find it, and soon. She was becoming disgusted with herself.

They had been traveling for some hours and had now made several turns off the main thoroughfare. Suddenly, the road widened and a monstrosity of a house came into view.

"Goodness," Prudence said, "look at that."

CHAPTER SEVEN

THE EARL PEERED out his own carriage window at Barlow Hall. "*Goodness* would be the right word for it. Lady Heathway has told no tales about the place."

The hall was a monstrosity of gray stone with long wings slightly curved and branching out east and west. It appeared an oversized crane poised to take flight over the countryside. Lady Heathway had said there was even another wing running north, but as they approached from the south, that could not be seen.

It had an almost medieval look to it and there were stone balconies all along the upper floors. One could almost imagine Guinevere appearing on one of them.

The evening before, Prudence had been rapt by Lady Heathway's tale of Grace Yardley and her sickly mother driven out of the place and sent to live in the dilapidated dower house after the viscount died, and then how Lady Heathway had managed everybody so expertly.

Apparently, Lady Barlow had been cured and Miss Yardley was now Lady Gresham, married to her nephew and back into her ancestral home. Though, Prudence was not entirely clear what had happened to the gentleman who'd inherited the estate, as it had not been Lord Gresham.

A stream of footmen came pouring out the doors, along with the butler and housekeeper. They were followed by a gentleman Prudence assumed must be Lord Gresham.

All the parties were speedily got out of their respective carriages and Prudence and the earl were introduced to the lord of
the house. Everybody else seemed well-acquainted with one
another. In particular, Lord Ryland and Lord Gresham seemed
old friends.

Lord Gresham led them inside and Prudence heard him directing the butler to bring tea into the east drawing room. It was
her first experience of a house that had more than one of those
rooms. She could not believe it to be very common.

They entered and found a middle-aged and delicate looking
lady reclining on a fainting couch.

"Lady Barlow," Lady Heathway said, striding over to her.
"You do not fade back into your old habit of malingering, I
hope?"

"Lady Heathway," Lady Barlow said, "I am only resting after
my vigorous walk with Nurse Maddington. I like to come out
ahead, you know, and at this point we are nearly at a run. It is
exhausting."

"Excellent. And Grace? How does she do?"

Before Lady Barlow could answer the query, the lady herself
entered. There could be no mistaking it was her, as the lady was
heavily pregnant.

"Dear Lady Heathway," she said, kissing the lady's cheek,
"how good you are to come."

"Of course I've come."

"And Lady Featherstone, how wonderful to see you again
too."

"You are radiant my dear," Lady Featherstone said.

"Of course she is radiant, she is my niece by marriage, after
all," Lady Heathway said. "Now, Grace, here is Lord Copeland
and his daughter Lady Prudence."

Prudence curtsied. Lady Gresham said, "You are both most
welcome to Barlow Hall." She leaned confidentially toward
Prudence and said, "I understand you are a project, as was I. I
wish you a glorious time in London and all the happiness in the

world."

Prudence was both taken aback by Lady Gresham's directness and charmed by it.

"We intend that everything is to go smoothly for Lady Prudence's launch," Lady Featherstone said. "Very smoothly. This time everything is to go smoothly."

Prudence did of course get the idea that perhaps not every project *had* gone smoothly, though she did not know the particulars.

"Do sit down, Grace," Lady Heathway said. "You make me nervous standing about in your condition. Our little girl is not ready to arrive so soon."

Lady Gresham laughed and said, "Ah, you remain convinced it *is* a girl."

As they moved off to a quiet corner, Prudence overheard Lady Heathway say, "Whatever happens, on no account will we allow my grandniece to call anybody *Bwandbaba*. I absolutely put my foot down on that point."

"Heaven help us if it is not a girl," Lord Gresham said laughing.

"I quite agree with Lady Heathway," Lady Barlow said. "Girls are, well, they are…easier."

"Are they?" Lord Gresham said, not looking at all convinced.

The butler came in, leading two footmen with the tea trays. Lady Barlow roused herself and said, "I will pour. Grace will be too taken up with Lady Heathway's arrival to manage it. Lord Copeland, how do you take it?"

"Very sweet, I'm afraid. Four sugars if you do not mind."

"I do not mind at all. I quite agree with you, in fact," Lady Barlow said. "As far as I'm concerned, tea is only a convenient vehicle for sugar and would have little to recommend it on its own."

Between inquiring of Lord Ryland how he liked his tea and pouring for her son-in-law, Lady Barlow and the earl lapsed into a rather in-depth conversation about their respective sweet tooths.

Prudence smiled to herself as they found total agreement in their appreciation of a good savoy cake.

Prudence gazed round the room. Lord Ryland and Lord Gresham were in conversation together, though Lord Gresham's eyes did a lot of drifting toward his wife.

Lady Gresham was enjoying the attentions of Lady Heathway.

Lady Featherstone, who sat by her side, said, "It is a wonderful picture of marital felicity, is it not?"

"Indeed it is," Prudence answered. She was really very charmed by the scene.

"Just think," Lady Featherstone said, gazing at Lady Gresham, "that shall be *you* in not too long a time."

For some reason, Lady Featherstone's words had more of an effect than she probably meant them to have.

All along, when Prudence had considered marriage, it had been a vague sort of idea that had ended in a church.

Now, she was observing what she might become. What her life might be like.

It was rather thrilling.

Lady Featherstone's eyes traveled across the drawing room to settle on Lord Ryland. "Someday soon," she said, "you will marry your own lord."

Prudence smiled but did not answer. She was fairly sure Lady Featherstone hinted at something. She hinted at *somebody*.

Surely not.

Lady Gresham had risen, and she approached the tea tray. "My dear guests, despite the size of the house, we do not stand on ceremony here. By now, your maids will have unpacked for you and you may retire whenever you like to rest and refresh yourselves. The gong is rung at seven forty-five and we dine at eight."

SITTING IN THE drawing room after dinner, Ambrose would like to claim he was actually reading the book in his hands. However, he was not. Turning a page occasionally for effect was about all he'd managed.

Lady Barlow, the earl, Lady Featherstone, and Gresham had settled to whist. Lady Heathway and Lady Gresham had heads together, reviewing all that had been purchased for the soon-to-arrive baby.

Lady Prudence played softly on the pianoforte.

It was not often that he had a wistful feeling come over him, as if something vital were just out of reach.

He liked the life he'd built for himself. Though sometimes…

Sometimes, as he watched this friend or that marry and start a family, he wondered if he would regret ignoring that side of life.

It was sensible to ignore it, that he knew. All his attention must be focused on hunting down his father's murderers. And, if he could not do that, he could at least focus his energy on outwitting the criminal element and bringing them to their knees when he could catch them. How many tragedies in the making had he stopped, thereby saving some family from agony? He did not know, but it had been many.

In any case, he could hardly bring a lady into his house in Town. Not with having given over the dining room as his base of operations. Not with all sorts coming and going. It was no place for a lady.

He would have to marry eventually, if only to get an heir. But he had something to accomplish first.

And yet, the scenes he'd taken in today had hinted at what he missed. Gresham's drifting eyes, never staying away from his wife for long. The quiet contentment of a game of whist between people who liked one another. Lady Prudence elegantly running through a rather poignant Irish air on the instrument. These were things his house did not have.

It all spoke of peace. It was peace, though, that he'd never find until he could avenge his father's death with a hanging.

Sometimes, he could almost hear his father talking to him from beyond the grave. *Get on with it, Ambrose. Find the villains.*

Gresham's butler quietly entered, carrying a silver tray with a letter.

Ambrose had not expected the man to walk toward him with it, but he did.

"My lord," he said, "this just arrived by a courier."

Nobody took much interest in his receiving the letter, but for Lady Featherstone, who would guess at its being SACK business.

She glanced at him as he opened it.

My Lord,

One of ours was able to catch up to a York man who had gone with Lord Luckstone to Kent, having met the fellow in that town. After sufficient pressure, we have discovered the following: Luckstone's real name is Lucknell.

Lucknell is suspected of relieving gentlemen and ladies of their purses on lonely roads and may be the author of other unsavory activities, particularly during the races at Newmarket. He appears to be part of a trio who have long worked together, though this man says he only knew the other two as Mr. C and Mr. P.

Lucknell corresponds regularly with Mr. C, now residing in London, though the fellow claims he does not know the address. It is not certain what happened to Mr. P—it seems he was having some sort of mental breakdown and then disappeared.

As for the others, Lucknell hired a collection of men to accompany him to Kent, though none of them was clear what sort of scheme was afoot. They began to think him mad in his pursuit of a lady who would not admit him to her house.

Whatever game was being played, it very suddenly ended and they were all paid and sent on their way. That's all for now,

Depsford

It came as no surprise that Luckstone, or Lucknell as he was actually named, had used an alias or that he was a fraud. But there was still no explanation for what the man was attempting to do. Even his accomplices had not understood the scheme.

That he had an associate in London was a new concern. After Lucknell had fled Kent, where had he gone? Had he gone to that associate and was in Town even now?

Ambrose was certain Lucknell would not carry on attempting to pass himself off as Lord Luckstone. The man was well aware the game was up on that gambit.

Might he try something else, though?

Whatever Lucknell had been after, whether it had been Lady Prudence in marriage or something else Ambrose could not yet see, the man had been engaged in what he called a long-swindle. It was the type of scheme that required time, not the lightning fast *give me your purse and I'm off* crime. It required organization, determination, and an outlay of money. The prize in a long-swindle was always substantial.

Perhaps it had something to do with the earl's estate. Ambrose believed the estate to be entailed, though he was not aware of any heir close by. There must be one somewhere, else the title at least would die out. But perhaps Lucknell had thought he could get round things through marriage to Lady Prudence?

Ambrose could not see how, but that did not mean it was not possible. If there were one thing he understood about the criminal mind, it was that it was wildly inventive and always thinking up new ideas.

Though he had his eyes on the paper in his hand, Ambrose was never unaware of what occurred around him. Just now, Lady Featherstone was creating a travesty at the whist table, likely distracted by wondering what the letter communicated.

He stood and said, "I am sorry, I must answer this letter for the morning and so I will retire. I bid you all good night and, Lady Gresham, please compliment your cook."

With that, he bowed and left the room. There would be no need for letter writing, he would be in London on the morrow.

There was a need, however, for a plan.

A rock-solid plan.

It was all well and good to employ Thomas as his eyes and ears in Lady Featherstone's house, but Lady Prudence would be often out of the house. There must be eyes upon her at all times, lest Lucknell make a second run at his prize.

Ambrose would also set a watch on the earl's house in Kent. If Lucknell were aiming for the estate, he might well take the opportunity of an empty house to slip in and fish around for papers and documents that might help him in his cause. Proofs such as that were often sought, as the forgery of one or the disappearance of another could make it extremely difficult to extricate oneself from a fraud.

Now that Lucknell had disappeared, he would not be easily found again. Ambrose's only chance to catch up to the man was to be there when he made an approach.

Lady Prudence must be protected.

LADY GRESHAM HAD very graciously urged the party to stay on for a few days at Barlow Hall, but nobody wished to impose upon the lady at such a delicate time. Aside from Lady Heathway who would stay and did not view herself as the least imposition, the rest of them would depart before noon.

Prudence had woken to Lady Featherstone's maid, Meggy, slipping in with a cup of tea. The maid was of the opinion that a cup of tea was necessary before a lady could even think of dressing.

It was an odd idea, but Prudence welcomed it all the same.

She was not the only person up, as it happened. She took her tea to the windows overlooking the back gardens. On account of the third wing on the house, the gardens were divided into two sides, with the long north wing running between them.

On the east side, Lord Ryland was pacing the paths with some determination, as if he wished to get the operation over with. When they had met in her own garden, he had fashioned himself a bull charging in and that seemed apt at that moment. Fortunately, the paths were wide enough that he was not likely to trample Lady Gresham's flowers.

An even more surprising scene was on the west side of the gardens. Her father and Lady Barlow made their way forward slowly, her father employing his cane and the lady stopping to pick a flower here and there.

Prudence could not guess what they talked of, unless it was a further examination of the qualities of a fine savoy cake, but they seemed to be enjoying themselves. She could not hear their laughter but could see it well enough.

She supposed she should not be surprised. They had partnered at whist the evening before and done quite well. Lady Barlow had that reserved and calm quality that the earl tended to admire.

Prudence thought traveling, though she had worried it would be hard on her father, was having quite the opposite effect. He seemed more lively since they'd set off.

She certainly could not remember when he'd last walked their own garden.

Now, they were in the carriage and on their way. Goodness, they were on their way to London.

The carriages started down the drive, with much waving back and forth between those who would stay and those who would go.

Since Lady Heathway would stay on at Barlow Hall, Lady Featherstone had joined them in their own carriage. As a usual thing, when Prudence and her father went in the carriage together somewhere, they might speak or they might be content in silence.

Lady Featherstone seemed to have no use for silence.

The carriage door had not been closed a minute before she

began to catalogue the first hurdle to be cleared in London.

"The ladies of the society will of course come to the house to be introduced to you on the morrow. Except Lady Heathway, naturally, as we've just left her behind. That is rather fortuitous, I think. Two of my friends can be rather…intimidating. Lady Heathway is one of them, as you've seen. The duchess would be the other one. Well, you know what a duchess is like."

Prudence actually did not know what a duchess was like, as there was not one living in her neighborhood.

"She pronounces her opinion on a thing as if she were the queen herself. She likes things noble, or to decide if they are noble."

So that was what a duchess was like.

"Then there is Lady Redfield, now she is of a different stripe altogether. She only wishes for everybody to be happy, so she shan't frighten you at all. Lady Easton is rather more stern, but she will not give you trouble as long as you are on time. If you are late, well, that is a different matter."

Prudence and her father glanced at each other.

"Then of course there is Lady Mendleton. She is the one with the very advanced grandbaby. You probably heard something about the subject from Lady Heathway. The baby has taken to calling Lady Mendleton *Bwandbaba* and Lady Heathway is wildly against it. It seems to be her new white soup."

"White soup?" the earl inquired.

"Lady Heathway is entirely against white soup. I'd never dare serve it to her."

After seeing Lady Heathway defeat Lord Luckstone with a walking stick, Prudence had some idea that the lady was unusual. Now, it seemed all of the ladies belonging to the society were unusual. For that matter, Lady Featherstone's keen interest in crime was unusual too. Aside from Lady Redfield, who sounded like a more typical sort of lady, they all seemed a bit eccentric.

"So that's the ladies," Lady Featherstone said. "Now, I shall tell you all about Lord Ryland's *Society for Advancing Criminal*

Knowledge. We regular members call it the SACK."

With dizzying speed, loops, backtracks, and speculations, Lady Featherstone proceeded to relay a case the SACK had recently examined. It seemed a lady had discovered a pearl necklace missing. All the servants were interviewed to no avail and just when the case appeared hopeless, the necklace reappeared.

"So it ended happily," the earl ventured.

"Ended?" Lady Featherstone asked. "My lord, the mystery has only doubled. Who took it *and* who put it back?"

Prudence imagined the necklace had been misplaced and a servant had run across it—slipped behind a dressing table or something like it. That poor servant would have been terrified to report the discovery, lest they be connected to the supposed crime.

Though, she did not think that such a simple explanation would suit Lady Featherstone, who was just now speculating on the existence of a crime ring specializing in pearl necklaces.

Prudence glanced out the window as Lady Featherstone catalogued her list of suspects belonging to the criminal enterprise, the poor lady's maid at the top of the list.

They were passing through Swanley, by an inn called the Bull and Bear. The door to the inn was opened by a boy, and a man strode out. A man she recognized very well.

She blinked her eyes, feeling as if she were suffering from a hallucination.

She was not. It was him.

"Luckstone!" she cried.

CHAPTER EIGHT

U PON PRUDENCE'S CRY, Lady Featherstone ceased her ramblings and flew across the carriage to her side. They had passed the inn and she leaned her head out to look behind.

"That tall one?" she asked.

"Yes," Prudence said softly, pressing herself against the leather of the seat as if she would disappear into it.

He was everywhere. He could not be lost or avoided.

Lady Featherstone grabbed her walking stick and rapped on the roof. The carriage slowed and then stopped. Before Prudence could imagine what the lady meant to do, she was out of the carriage and heading toward the inn.

The earl slid across his seat to peer out the window after her. "What on earth…" he said.

Prudence looked back out herself. Lady Featherstone was charging toward Lord Luckstone with her walking stick raised. "Luckstone!" she shouted.

Lord Luckstone looked up in surprise. He only hesitated for a moment, then set off in a run behind the inn.

Lord Ryland, appearing to understand the situation at once, had leapt from his own carriage and set off after him, passing by Lady Featherstone at a fast run.

Just as quickly as the carriage had stopped, all three were gone from view and disappeared behind the inn.

Prudence and her father stared at each other. The earl recovered himself first. He leaned out the window and said to the coachman, "Bring us into the yard of the inn. I must get Lady Prudence inside to a safe location."

"Do you think we are in danger, Papa?" Prudence asked.

"I take no chances, my dear," the earl said. "Has he followed us to this neighborhood or is it only by happenstance that we encounter him? I trust Ryland to find out, but in the meantime…"

Prudence nodded. As the carriage made its turn to go back to the inn, she thought that for all Lord Ryland's oversized presence, she was rather glad he was there. What would they have done if he had not been?

"I trust Ryland will protect Lady Featherstone," the earl said. "Though to go chasing off like that…these ladies are not…well, they are not the sort I have ever encountered."

The carriage pulled into the yard and was met by the owner of the inn himself. Mr. Jenkins was immediately apprised of the situation and had a variety of emotions about it. It seemed that Lord Luckstone had been staying there under the name Lucknell and had not yet paid his bill.

The earl cut off the man's lamentations. "A secure room, if you please," he said sharply. "And while you are at it, send some servants after my friends to determine if they can be of assistance. One of them is a middle-aged lady, and I do not imagine she's got very far."

Prudence was taken aback at her father's forcefulness, and rather reassured by it. Very little could bring out a sharpness in him, but it seemed this had done it.

They were escorted to a private dining room with windows facing the back of the inn. Beyond the small garden, there was a field of wild grass and then a thick wood. There was no sign of anybody. Had they all gone into the wood?

It seemed dark and dangerous.

A servant brought in a tea service while another one stood officiously at the door, having been ordered to secure the room.

Thomas came bounding in, pushing past the rather ineffectual guard. "Lord Ryland gave me strict orders to stay in the carriage, but I know my duty. An earl's page don't go cowering in the face of danger."

He came to stand by the earl's side.

Prudence had stayed at the window, searching the scene for any signs. Suddenly, she saw a flash of blue silk at the edge of the wood.

Lady Featherstone staggered out of it, leaning heavily on her walking stick, her bonnet askew.

"There is Lady Featherstone!" Prudence said. "I will go and help her in."

"Go nowhere, Prudence," her father said. "Thomas, go out and help that lady inside."

The boy peered out the window. "Right you are, my lord."

Thomas set off at a run and was out the back garden and across the field in a trice. Prudence watched anxiously as the boy reached Lady Featherstone and held out his arm. She leaned on it gratefully and they made their way back to the inn.

But where was Lord Ryland? Had he caught up to Lord Luckstone? If he had, what had happened?

The dark wood gave no clues to anything.

It was not more than a few minutes before Thomas helped Lady Featherstone into the room.

"My dear lady," the earl said, "do sit down and I will pour the tea myself. I really do not think you should have gone running off like that."

Lady Featherstone worked to catch her breath and made an unsuccessful attempt to straighten her bonnet.

"I believe you are right, my lord," she said rather breathlessly. "As it happens, I am not very fast on my feet and what with tree roots tripping me up…"

Lord Copeland handed the lady a cup. "Did you see any sign of Lord Ryland?"

"He passed by me before we reached the wood. I did not see either him or Lord Luckstone again before I turned round."

AMBROSE HAD RESIGNED himself to the idea that the short journey to London would feel long indeed. Thomas had once more been put in his carriage, though he had not the first idea why. Lady Featherstone's carriage was going empty and he ought to have been in there.

Of course, there would be nobody to talk to in that lady's carriage, and the boy liked to talk endlessly.

He was just now telling the tale of how he'd been lost in Barlow Hall for some hours the night before and had found himself in a frightening sort of place. According to Thomas, there was room after room, all dark and empty.

After he'd finally made his way out, he was told he'd wandered into the abandoned barracks of the north wing. It seemed a viscount of old had raised and housed an army, all to settle a dispute over the rights to a stream.

Ambrose had no idea if any of it was true, or only the boy's fevered imagination.

"He was that determined to have the stream and don't you know he got it too—"

Thomas had suddenly thrown himself at the window.

"That's Luckstone," he cried.

Ambrose had looked, though he'd been certain it was just another flight of fancy from the young rogue. That was, until he saw Lady Featherstone striding after the man, waving her walking stick, and shouting, "Luckstone!"

"Blast," he said, rapping on the roof. "Stay in the carriage."

He'd leapt out and followed the pair. Luckstone, or Lucknell as he was really named, had run behind the inn while Lady Featherstone attempted to follow him.

Ambrose easily passed Lady Featherstone, shouting at her as he went by. "Go back!"

She'd answered, "Lord Ryland, that man is Lord Luckstone!"

Lucknell had reached the edge of the wood and disappeared into it.

The man could not escape him. Ambrose, along with Depsford and a few other men, regularly trained in the park in the early mornings. They would run a mile, rest for a few minutes, run another, rest, and then run a final mile.

It had long been his observation that, even in a young man, strength and fitness were not a static state and must be maintained. He knew from experience that most gentlemen did not bother with it, or only bothered to exercise on a horse or in a boxing ring. Most gentlemen became winded fairly quickly.

Lucknell would be no different.

The wood was dense and there was only a weedy footpath to follow. Ambrose could see signs of a recent passing—trampled grass, broken branches. Of course, it *was* a path and therefore used by others so anybody could have left those signs. However, what he did not see was any evidence of a veering off the path.

Luckstone would take his chances running, rather than hiding.

Where did the man propose to go? Surely, all of his things were left back at the inn. He would have only whatever money was in his pocket.

That would likely be enough to get him to London, and he had an associate there. He must be just now calculating how to elude his pursuers and get on a road where he might find a conveyance out.

He must be stopped before he did so.

Up ahead, Ambrose saw more sun coming through the trees than he'd seen since he'd entered the wood. The flora was thinning and he was coming out the other side. Where was Luckstone?

Before he could answer that question for himself, he heard a large crack and his head exploded in pain.

LUCKNELL HAD OFTEN heard of those who were dogged by bad luck. In his circles, it was speculated that luck one way or the other would attach itself to a person and color their every move.

Ansel Mayer was usually held up as an example. Tried for murder and hanged for it, but the scaffolding broke before his neck did and he had to wait two days for it to be rebuilt. Hanged twice—it didn't get unluckier than that.

And now, his own luck had turned. He'd been meant to be well away from the earl and his daughter, now that Lord Ryland was making inquiries about him and the deranged Lady Heathway had threatened to slice his throat.

He'd considered himself well away. When he'd first heard that matron at the inn's yard call out "Luckstone," he'd only felt confusion. He did not know the lady, but somehow she knew him. Or at least, who he'd pretended to be.

Then his eyes took in the scene on the road in front of him with sickening speed. Lady Prudence and her father in one carriage. Thomas, the boy he'd left behind at Morris House, in the other.

Worse, a very powerful-looking gentleman leapt out of the carriage that housed Thomas and came straight for him. He did not know the gentleman, but for some reason he had Thomas with him. Whoever he was, he was in pursuit.

Lucknell had not stayed in the dark regarding the gentleman's identity for long.

Just as he'd reached the edge of the wood, he heard the matron call out.

She'd called him Lord Ryland.

Understanding it was Ryland in pursuit sent energy coursing through him. He could not be caught by Ryland.

Legs pumping, he raced through the wood, his mind working just as fast to find a way to elude his would-be captor.

He could hear Ryland behind him and, no matter how fast he ran, the man seemed to be gaining.

Lucknell knew from Mr. Clamarin that Ryland could run for miles at a time. *He* could not, however.

Hiding wouldn't save him either. Ryland was too skilled at tracking.

He had to disable the man. He had to buy time, it was his only chance.

Lucknell spotted an old oak ahead of him, its base littered with heavy branches taken down in a storm.

He raced to it, picked up a substantial bough, and climbed up with it. Inching out on a sturdy limb six feet over the road, he had just got himself in place as Ryland came into view.

As the man ran underneath him, Lucknell swung the branch down, making good contact with his head.

Ryland had stood there for a moment and Lucknell began to be terrified that he'd not managed to fell him.

But then, he'd dropped to the ground and he'd not risen.

Lucknell had climbed down from the tree and cautiously approached, fearful that the man might open his eyes at any moment.

He kicked him hard, ready to run if necessary.

Ryland did not move.

Satisfied that he would be no more trouble, at least for a while, Lucknell grabbed Ryland's ankles and dragged him into the brush so he would not be found.

He had got the time he needed to get away.

And so he did, traveling over hill and dale. He made his way to St. Paul's Cray and took a seat in a coach for London.

There had been so little time to reflect when he'd been in the midst of making his escape. There was time now, though, as he anxiously waited for the coach to depart.

Would they look for him here?

And most worrying, had he killed Ryland? Whether he did or did not, the consequences were dire. If Ryland were dead,

Lucknell was a murderer and his identity was known. He'd used his real name at the inn! If Ryland were not dead, then it was Ryland himself to fear, as he'd never stop hunting for him.

He was beginning to think that his idea of going to America someday was not a bad one.

Not yet, though. He and Clamarin would finish what they'd started all those years ago.

⫸⫸⫸✕⫷⫷⫷

PRUDENCE HAD WATCHED the search party set off over an hour ago, though she was rather terrified to discover what they would find.

That afternoon, Lady Featherstone had been certain that Lord Ryland would return promptly, either with Luckstone in tow or without him.

As the minutes, and then an hour had ticked by, that prediction seemed rather less certain.

Lady Featherstone called for the magistrate, a local gentleman named Sir Jonathan Ralston. Sir Jonathan had sent men in different directions to watch the roads and then he'd organized a search party.

He was a calm and careful man, and it was Sir Jonathan's opinion that no harm had come to Lord Ryland. He speculated that the lord was likely loath to give up his pursuit and had ventured far afield.

Nevertheless, they would search the wood and they would inquire at the farmer's cottage on the other side of it to determine who, if anybody, had been seen.

"I put my faith in Sir Jonathan's opinion," her father said. "Lord Ryland is a man of sense and is sure to have avoided any real danger."

"Just so," Thomas said.

Lady Featherstone paced the room. "One would hope.

Though, Luckstone, or Lucknell, as I think the innkeeper said his name was, must be feeling desperate. After all, he ran from *me* before he ever even saw Lord Ryland and he was apparently willing to abandon his possessions to get away."

"What might he do?" Prudence asked.

"Who knows?" Thomas said, though Prudence had directed the question to Lady Featherstone.

"It's hard to say, desperate people are never very rational," Lady Featherstone said.

"No, they ain't," Thomas confirmed.

Lady Featherstone turned to the boy. "Did you ever see the man with a pistol in his possession?"

"A pistol!" Prudence said.

"Hard to say," Thomas said. "Some of them York men he hired had 'em, some didn't. I never did see his hands on one, though that don't mean he didn't have one tucked away somewhere."

"We haven't heard any shots, at least," Prudence said.

"I know *I* haven't," Thomas said.

"If he owns a pistol, I doubt he's got it with him," the earl said. "He was likely going out for a stroll and would not bother to take it, having no idea he might have need of it."

Thomas nodded gravely. "Clever thinking," he said.

"Thomas," the earl said quietly, "it is not necessary to comment on everything that is said."

"Also clever thinking, my lord," Thomas said.

Prudence had stayed by the windows. Surely the men must come back soon. The sun was beginning its descent and they could not very well search in the dark.

What had happened to Lord Ryland?

In the glow of early evening, she saw movement at the edge of the wood. And then men filing out of it.

Prudence watched until the last man was out. None of them were Lord Ryland. They had not found him.

"They are coming back," she said quietly.

As Lady Featherstone raced to the window, Prudence sat down heavily. She had an overwhelming feeling that something terrible had happened. Was this what her prescient maid Martha felt when she looked into things that would come to pass? There were no words to it, just a feeling.

But then, how could anything have happened to such a man? He was…well he seemed indestructible.

They waited in a dreadful silence until Sir Jonathan came in to see them.

The expression Sir Jonathan wore when he entered did nothing to alleviate the heavy sense of doom that had settled round Prudence's shoulders.

"Lord Copeland, Lady Featherstone, Lady Prudence, we have found Lord Ryland and moved him to a farmhouse that stands nearby the wood. He was badly injured, I'm afraid. Knocked on the head and left for dead. We found no sign of Lucknell, who I surmise is long gone."

"But Lord Ryland is not dead?" Prudence asked.

"No, he is not, but he remains unconscious. I have sent a man to fetch my own physician."

"Surely, Lord Ryland would be better cared for here at the inn?" the earl said.

"We dared not move him any further than was necessary," Sir Jonathan said. "The farmhouse is a small one and not well fitted out, but the couple who own it are sensible people."

"He will need a nurse," Lady Featherstone said, "I will go to him."

"Are you experienced as a nurse, Lady Featherstone?" Prudence asked.

"Experienced, well, I would not go that far…"

"I am, though," Prudence said. "Surely I must go."

Two years before, her neighborhood had been struck down by a particularly virulent influenza. As her household fell to it, Prudence had kept her father well away from everybody as she was certain he could not survive it. She'd isolated him in his rooms and only she brought him food.

As for herself, she'd felt poorly for a few days but not so terrible that she need take to her bed.

It was well that had been the case. As one housemaid improved, another footman worsened. The doctor, treating many households at once, only arrived sporadically. She'd been run off her feet, but she'd pulled everybody through it.

"Prudence," the earl said, "I am certain the farmer's wife has things well in hand."

"But Father," Prudence said, "Lord Ryland is not the farmer's wife's responsibility. He is ours and has been struck down on our account."

"Truer words…" Thomas said softly.

The earl gave his page an irritated glance. Then he said, "I suppose you are right. Though, perhaps wait until morning. The sun will set in no time."

"Then we must go quickly," Prudence said. "Sir Jonathan, will you lead us there?"

Sir Jonathan looked to the earl, who reluctantly nodded. "Very well, though we must go now. The wood will have grown dark already, much longer and we will not be able to make our way through it. Going by road would take us far out of the way, as the entrance to the farmer's land can only be reached by narrow country lanes to the north."

Prudence went to her father and kissed his forehead. "We shall be fine and you will have Thomas by your side."

"How comforting," the earl said, casting a wry glance at his page.

"Just so," Thomas said, nodding gravely.

"Let us not dillydally," Lady Featherstone said. "We must be off!"

CHAPTER NINE

Ambrose had woken to find a rather substantial matron staring down at him. He struggled to sit up. "What…who—"

"Calm yourself," the matron said, pushing him back down. "I got enough problems without havin' a petulant lord on my hands."

"Petulant? Where am I? How did I get here?"

The matron crossed her arms. "You're at Small Brook Farm and you got here by a bunch of the magistrate's men taking my front door off the hinges and using it to collect you in the wood, where you'd got yourself into some kind of palaver. 'Parently, somebody knocked you on the head and dragged you into the brush. My man is still working on gettin' the hinges back on and it's none too convenient."

As the lady, if he would go so far as to name her a *lady*, talked, Ambrose began to remember. He'd been chasing Lucknell. And then a crack on the head. The villain must have laid in wait for him and then left him for dead.

"Sir Jonathan was to fetch the doc for you," the matron said, "and I got high hopes he says you can be up and out of here."

"Madam," Ambrose said, examining her stained apron that convivially matched her stained hands, "your hopes could not possibly exceed my own."

"Couldn't they now?" the matron said. "You're in me bed, where will me and my man sleep if you're crowdin' the place up?"

Ambrose could not fathom where she or her hapless husband would sleep, nor did he care. He only hoped it would not be himself sleeping in this wretched place.

"Inconvenienced, is what I am, and I don't suppose I'll be paid for my trouble either. Also, I ain't *madam*, me own da named me Fancy and I married a Geleder."

He had a headache and Fancy Geleder was not likely to make it any better.

"I suppose you'll be wantin' ale. Sir Jonathan said if you were to wake you should have it. 'Course he didn't bother sayin' who would pay for it."

Ambrose only stared at her.

"Look at me haughty all you like," the woman said. "But it ain't me what's so unpleasant as to cause people to hit me over the head and leave me for dead."

Ambrose was not too sure about that. Surely, Mr. Geleder must have thought about it from time to time.

"I've got a mind to snip the buttons off your coat to pay for your keep."

With that genial threat, Fancy Geleder stormed out of the room.

Ambrose looked around him. It was a small and bare sort of place. There was only the bedstead, a side table, a set of drawers, and a washbasin. The small window had curtains pulled closed, but they were of a thin material and he could see through them that the sun was setting.

He must have lain in the wood for hours before he'd been found.

How had he been found, though? The enchanting Mrs. Geleder claimed it was the magistrate's men who had brought him here.

Lady Featherstone must have called them in. She would have known something was not right, if not because he did not return, but because he did not send a messenger as to why.

Consistent communication had always been a tenet of any SACK investigation—one hand could not act without knowing what the other was doing. Lady Featherstone had studied the manual for years, she could practically recite it from memory.

Ambrose laid his head back down. He could not call today's operation a success. Lucknell had been within his grasp and had got away.

The man had also proved himself far more dangerous than Ambrose had thought. He'd imagined him a fraudster with a care for his own person—trying his luck and then running when it seemed he would be caught out.

Now, he understood that Lucknell was capable of more than that. He'd left his pursuer for dead in the woods.

And why had Lucknell been here in the first place? In those early days of his career, Ambrose would have jumped to the conclusion that Lucknell had been following Lady Prudence. That was unlikely, though. If he had known the lady and her father were in the vicinity, he would not have allowed himself to be spotted.

No, the man had been making his way to London by a circuitous route, on the off chance somebody was looking for him. It was a reliable criminal strategy—never go the way a sensible person would go. Defy expectations.

Lucknell had likely detoured, possibly through Dunton Green, before coming to Swanley.

If Lucknell had known that Lady Prudence and the earl would make their way to London, and there was always the off chance he had a servant in his pocket, he would not have expected to see them at Swanley. There was a faster route to the north. After all, *they* had only come this way to take Lady Heathway to Barlow Hall.

Ambrose suspected it to be only a fortuitous meeting. It was the most likely scenario and was so often the case.

He'd noticed that nearly every new member to the SACK came in violently opposed to coincidence. Nothing was to be a coincidence. However, the world was full of them and the law of parsimony reigned over them all—the answer was nearly always the one that required the fewest leaps of logic.

Lady Featherstone still wracked her mind for a solution to the missing and since returned pearl necklace case. As she strained to reach for a solution, she'd even speculated that there might be a crime ring specializing in pearls. He'd concluded long ago that it had been inadvertently lost, and then inadvertently found. It was the answer requiring the shortest leap.

As he waited for the ale that Fancy Geleder would grudgingly bring him, or the scissors she would take to his coat buttons, he heard the low hum of voices down below. He supposed the doctor had come and he also supposed Mrs. Geleder was complaining to him.

THE PARTY THAT was to escort Prudence and Lady Featherstone through the wood and on to the farmhouse was got going as quickly as any group of people could be organized.

There had been a delay as Sir Jonathan sent one of the inn's servants for rushlights to help light their way through the wood. Then another delay as Lady Featherstone insisted on retrieving her book of investigative notes from the carriage, in case there was anything to document about the attack.

Finally, they'd set off, the sun hanging low on the horizon.

Prudence could only silently commend Sir Jonathan for insisting on the rushlights. It was dusk outside, but once they'd entered the wood it seemed closer to midnight.

She walked behind Lady Featherstone, that lady assisted by a strapping lad named Matthew who lit her way and grabbed her arm whenever she was in danger of tipping over. Which had been a few times already.

The wind was picking up, portending a storm, and the leaves

rustled over Prudence's head as if they were being shaken by the heavens.

Ahead of Lady Featherstone, Sir Jonathan had paused. "We discovered Lord Ryland just there," he said, indicating an area of heavy brush to his right. "We would have walked right past him if young Matthew had not sharp eyes and spotted the tip of his boot."

"Excellent work, my boy," Lady Featherstone said, tripping over another tree root and being caught before she hit the ground. "And further excellent work keeping me upright."

"We'll get you there in one piece, my lady," Matthew said cheerfully. "I'll carry you if it comes to it."

"Gracious, let us hope not," Lady Featherstone said.

It was not long after passing the spot where Lord Ryland had been left that they came to the far edge of the wood.

"The farmhouse is just there," Sir Jonathan said. "I'll take you in. Mrs. Geleder is a sensible woman, though…well she is what she is."

Prudence did not think that a very ringing endorsement. Nor did she take comfort from the farmhouse's appearance. It was a two storied stone cottage and seemed very old indeed. It was likely to be drafty and damp and lacking any modern sort of convenience. She dared not imagine the plumbing situation, if there were any plumbing situation at all.

They found Mr. Geleder at the front door, reattaching its hinges. Prudence presumed they'd taken it down to carry Lord Ryland to the house.

"Sir Jonathan," he said, tipping his hat. He looked suspiciously at Prudence and Lady Featherstone.

"Mr. Geleder, this is Lady Featherstone and Lady Prudence Landry. They are friends of Lord Ryland and have come to nurse him."

"We ain't the inn, you know," Mr. Geleder said. "We only got the one bed."

"We will manage, Mr. Geleder," Lady Featherstone said.

"Manage, will ya?" Mr. Geleder said with a snort. "Go meet my wife and then get back to me 'bout that."

"What's the ruckus now?" a storming voice bellowed from inside.

An imposingly built lady appeared in the doorframe, dwarfing her rather slight husband. That husband nodded knowingly at Lady Featherstone, as if to say, "I warned you."

"Mrs. Geleder," Sir Jonathan said, with the smallest of sighs. "Lady Featherstone and Lady Prudence, come to nurse Lord Ryland."

"Aye, have they? Here," she said, thrusting a cup into Prudence's hands. From the smell of the liquid sloshing round it, it was a very stale sort of ale.

"Thank you," Prudence said, for wont of anything else to say to this behemoth of a woman.

"He's up the stairs," Mrs. Geleder said. "You can't miss him, we only got one room up there."

"I'll be off before the rushlights burn out or get doused in the rain that is surely on the way," Sir Jonathan said. "The doctor should arrive in the next hour or so and I will come and check on things in the morning."

"Oh I see," Mrs. Geleder said. "We're to be turned into a veritable hackney stand, with people coming and going at all hours, all because a lord decides to go wandering round the woods and gets himself clobbered."

"Yes, well, good evening," Sir Jonathan said, hurrying toward the relative safety of the wood.

If there were not a job ahead of her, Prudence might very well have turned and followed Sir Jonathan. As it was, she must stay. The lady had grudgingly stepped aside to allow them entry.

"Onward, Lady Prudence," Lady Featherstone said, lifting her skirts and marching forward.

They found the stairs easily enough, as the lower floor of the farmhouse was just one room decorated with two threadbare chairs in front of a smoldering fire. An iron pot sat on the embers, cooking something that smelled rather ghastly and perhaps consisting of a good amount of cabbage.

They left Mrs. Geleder slamming cookware around that pleasant location and climbed the stairs. As the lady of the house had suggested, they easily located Lord Ryland. There was no corridor, just the stairs ending in the room.

The lord was laid out on the bed, his neckcloth undone and his shirt torn. He seemed pale and weakened, though he struggled to sit up at their approach.

"Lady Prudence, Lady Featherstone, what on earth do you do here?"

"You are awake, very good news indeed," Lady Featherstone said. "We came as soon as we heard. We are to nurse you back to health."

"I do not require—"

"We have met Mrs. Geleder," Lady Featherstone said in a softer voice, in case that congenial lady overheard what was said. "You do not want that lady supervising your care."

Lord Ryland sank back on the rather thin pillow. "Her given name is Fancy, if you can believe it, and she's mulling over cutting off my coat buttons for the inconvenience of my arrival."

"She's sent you this," Prudence said, approaching the bed. "I believe it is ale."

"Ah yes," Lord Ryland said, taking it from her. His hand brushed hers and Prudence shivered as if the room had gone cold.

"She wonders who will pay for it," the lord added.

"I am not certain anybody should pay for that swill," Prudence said.

Lord Ryland laughed and then clutched his head. "She gives me a headache."

"Lucknell has given you a headache," Lady Featherstone said. "Now, drink the swill as it will likely be all we will get in this abode and I will go down and face the dragon. She must have a medicine chest somewhere as I suspect she's had to patch up that poor husband of hers on occasion."

With a swish of her skirts, Lady Featherstone was gone, bravely descending to go toe to toe with Fancy Geleder.

"You should not have come," Lord Ryland said.

"Of course I should have," Prudence said. "Luckstone, or rather *Lucknell*, is my family's problem and now we have made it yours. Why does he follow us? What does he want?"

"I do not believe he followed you, else he would have hid himself more carefully. I believe he took a circuitous route, as did we, setting us on a collision course that nobody could have foreseen."

Prudence nodded. She had not considered that possibility.

"As for what he wants," Lord Ryland said, "perhaps nothing. It could be we have seen the last of him. We cannot assume so, though, as we do not understand what game he played in the first place. I suspect he makes his way to London to join an associate there. I cannot say if he has another move in mind, nor what it would be."

Prudence did not answer, but she felt as if she might never be rid of Lucknell. It felt as if he might always be around the next corner.

Now that he'd attempted to murder Lord Ryland, what else might he do? She had not thought that either she or her father were ever in any physical danger, but after this…

"Do not allow your thoughts to be consumed by it," Lord Ryland said. "You will be well protected in London. I will personally see to it."

Prudence stole a glance at the beast of a man so recently brought low by a knock on the head. His presence had seemed overpowering, but now…now that she'd begun to fear she really did need protecting…it was rather comforting to lay the task at Lord Ryland's door.

As well, lying prone as he was, he did not seem as overpowering as he had done.

"I will admit that I am glad of it, Lord Ryland. I could not imagine how Lucknell thought to succeed when I did not know he could be violent. Now, though, you do not think he might…"

Prudence had trailed off. The lord looked at her expectantly.

"Well, what if he were to try a kidnapping to ruin my reputation and force me into a marriage? Something of that sort?"

Lord Ryland very suddenly slammed the cup in his hands on the rickety side table beside the bed. "That will never happen," he said forcefully. "I will not allow it to happen."

Prudence had jumped at the outburst and found herself both frightened and comforted. Mostly comforted. She might not understand Lord Ryland entirely, but she believed him. He would never allow such a thing to happen.

They both heard the telltale creaks of the stairs drifting up.

Lady Featherstone's bonnet came into view, and then her whole person. She said, "That woman has nothing useful whatsoever, or if she does, she won't give it over. I was hoping for some laudanum for your headache but she doesn't even have willow bark for a tea. How do these people stagger on together? In any case, the doctor's carriage has just now arrived and he ought to be up shortly."

AMBROSE LISTENED TO the howling wind and beating rain assaulting the lone window of the room. He was not at all tired, though it was late and the candle burned low. Lady Prudence and Lady Featherstone were asleep, sitting on the floor with their backs against the wall and only covered by a thin blanket.

It was a shameful situation. The earl would go mad if he knew his daughter was just now sleeping on a floor. He'd argued and argued against it, proposing that it be he who took the floor and the ladies take the bed. He'd even struggled to get up, though he'd fallen backward from dizziness.

Neither Lady Prudence nor Lady Featherstone would be at all moved and together they were a stone wall of resistance.

It was an embarrassment that he, as a man, should rest in a bed while they made do with the floor.

They should not have come.

Though, he was rather touched that they had.

He rolled over on his side and regarded Lady Prudence. Her hair was mussed and her cheeks flushed with sleep. She looked exceedingly charming.

Ambrose was certain he should not be looking at all, but it was very hard to drag his eyes away.

The doctor had come and gone and, unlike the wonderful Fancy Geleder, he *did* have laudanum. That tincture had gone a long way to easing his headache.

In fact, it had gone some way to alleviating his worries, too, as laudanum was so prone to do. It was a substance one must always be careful of, as it could easily lull a person into ignoring problems that ought to have full attention. More than a few young gentlemen had gambled themselves into oblivion by taking laudanum and feeling as if the next bet must come through.

According to the doctor, the knock on his head did not seem too severe. Though, he advised that Ambrose remain where he was for at least a few days.

That, of course, was out of the question. He would depart this place at first light on the morrow. There was no possibility that he'd subject Lady Prudence to this environ further than that. And of course, Lady Featherstone too.

He could not forget what Lady Prudence had said about Lucknell. That he might try something drastic like a kidnapping. It was an outside possibility, *very* outside, but it was not impossible. As long as it was not impossible, he would guard against it.

She certainly needed to be in a more secure location than this lonely farmhouse.

Lady Prudence shifted, her hand reaching up to the necklace she wore. She murmured something foreign. It sounded like, "Couragay elcontrada no corasue."

He did not know what it meant. It certainly was not French. Her mother was Portuguese, so he assumed it was from that language.

Whatever she'd said to herself, her hand fell and she went into a deeper sleep.

He ought to get some sleep himself, rather than watching a charming lady sleep all night. It was ungentlemanly and to no purpose.

It was probably the laudanum.

PRUDENCE HAD NEVER in her life seen a patient make more trouble than Lord Ryland. The doctor had made it clear that he was to rest, precisely where he was, for at least a few days. She had girded herself to manage Mrs. Geleder until at least Monday.

That was not to be, however. Against all advice, including her own and Lady Featherstone's, he would insist on rising. He would not, under any circumstances, allow two ladies to sleep on the floor for another night. As soon as he'd heard Sir Jonathan's carriage arrive, he'd struggled to his feet.

Prudence could not fault him for his chivalry, and it *was* chivalric as she could see well enough that he was not entirely recovered. But he really ought to have bowed to the doctor's orders!

He had not been at all steady and had even tripped on the last stair. Fortunately, or unfortunately depending on who was looking at it, Mrs. Geleder was at the bottom of the steps and cushioned his fall.

Now, Fancy Geleder shouted a string of oaths, Lady Featherstone was attempting to help Lord Ryland to his feet, Prudence hurried down the stairs behind, and Sir Jonathan knocked on the door.

Lady Featherstone got Lord Ryland upright, while Mrs. Geleder rolled away and leapt up like a gymnast with the circus. Prudence hurried toward the door.

"Sir Jonathan," she said, "we are all a bit topsy-turvy here at the moment."

Sir Jonathan took in the scene and slowly nodded.

"Topsy-turvy my eye," Mrs. Geleder said. "I been inconvenienced from here to Sunday by these silk-dressed daisies and what do I get for my trouble? To be assaulted in me own house."

Lord Ryland, who appeared less than abashed by this condemnation, reached into an inside pocket of his coat. He handed Fancy Geleder a crown and said, "Though I give this to you, if there were true justice in the world, *you* would pay *me*. You are a harpy of the first order and I shall pray for your poor husband."

"Well I never…" Mrs. Geleder said, snatching the coin.

"I imagine there are a host of things categorized under what Mrs. Fancy Geleder has never," Lord Ryland said sternly. "Showing civility no doubt topping the list!"

Though Prudence really did not see the sense in arguing with a person such as Mrs. Geleder, she could not help but be a little amused by Lord Ryland's wrath. There was a certain wit to it.

"Am I to take it then," Sir Jonathan said, "that you will not be staying, Lord Ryland? I had thought the doctor advised—"

"Let us depart this fourth circle of hell forthwith," Lord Ryland said.

Prudence covered her mouth to stifle a laugh. The fourth circle was greed, though it was unlikely Mrs. Geleder was aware of that fact.

"Yes, indeed, we'd better be off," Lady Featherstone said. "We really cannot turn back now, I do not think."

"Very well," Sir Jonathan said. "Though I warn you it is a longer trip than you would imagine. We must travel to the west before connecting to a road that takes us south again and then east. It will take us an hour at least. Unless of course, you would consent to go by litter through the woods."

"Certainly not," Lord Ryland said. "I am perfectly capable of walking."

This, of course, was not true. Lord Ryland was still clutching the doorframe to keep himself upright.

"Lord Ryland," Prudence said, in a voice she would use to scold naughty children, "you will not go lurching through the wood unsteady on your feet. You'll only risk another fall. Now, it is either the carriage, or a litter, or the hospitality of Mrs. Geleder. That must be the final word on the subject."

Mrs. Geleder looked deeply affronted at the notion that her guests might not depart after all. Lady Featherstone murmured, "Well said."

If Lord Ryland could look anything that approached abashed, he did so now. "I certainly do not wish to cause anyone alarm."

Sir Jonathan paused, then he said, "If I might suggest, Lord Ryland, why do not you relocate to my house? It is not much further afield than the inn and certainly it will be more comfortable."

Lord Ryland was already weaving toward the carriage. "No, though I thank you for the courtesy. Lucknell's rooms must be searched and I intend on being there."

Sir Jonathan had nodded and Prudence was grateful he was not inclined to argue the point. As far as she could see, Lord Ryland could be very stubborn when he liked it.

In fact, she was rather surprised he'd not put up more of a fight about walking through the wood. Though, it would have been ridiculous—he'd just managed to stagger to the carriage.

And so, they were to say a final adieu to Mrs. Fancy Geleder and make their way back to the inn.

CHAPTER TEN

THOUGH AMBROSE HAD been determined to part with Fancy Geleder in all haste, he could not say the carriage ride had been at all comfortable. Everything seemed to be moving too much and his eyes had trouble keeping up. He'd finally closed them and forced himself to imagine he was on one of his boats off the coast of Ramsgate to account for the toing and froing.

If there had been anything at all to recommend the trip, it must be the worried glances from Lady Prudence, which he'd found exceedingly gratifying. She seemed to take an interest in whether he lived or died and he was glad of it.

Of course, there had been others who'd taken an interest in his health over the years. The marriage mart of London was the most robust market in the world and the *ton's* mamas were more skilled at moving the inventory than any fishwife.

He'd easily escaped their nets, however, as he'd never been much tempted by the bait dangled in front of him.

He was a little tempted now, though.

Lady Prudence was lovely and he had begun to see that she was made of sterner stuff than he'd imagined.

She seemed so delicate, and yet she'd slept on the floor with nary a complaint. As he thought of other ladies he knew, well, what a scene they might play out now. The grievances and lamentations! Their skirts were stained, they hardly slept, they must look a fright…

Lady Prudence said nothing like it and looked the entire opposite of a fright. Her hair was not as tightly regulated as it had been the day before, but the softening really had a charming effect.

And then, she had all but ordered him into the carriage. He had not minded being bossed about the least little bit.

They'd reached the inn after what seemed like an eternity. He could not immediately depart the carriage. Or, as he explained, "I shall be perfectly fine once the swaying stops."

Lady Prudence had said, "Oh dear, the swaying *has* stopped."

She'd seemed alarmed when he explained that it would soon stop in his eyes too.

He'd then been forced to rest, though how he was to rest with Thomas being sent to fetch anything he might need was a mystery as the boy never stopped talking.

He had at least wrenched a promise from Sir Jonathan that Lucknell's rooms were not to be searched without him.

Sir Jonathan had been very civil about it and had gone off to find the earl and suggest they have refreshments.

Now, after some hours and his balance improving, they had entered Lucknell's rooms. Quite a few people had entered, as Lady Featherstone refused to be left behind, and then the earl wished to come, and that brought Lady Prudence too. And of course, nowhere the earl went was to be devoid of Thomas.

The state of Lucknell's rooms must say something about the man himself. It was disorganized and had trunks open everywhere with no seeming reason as to what was in them. It spoke of an individual having departed a place in a hurry, and one who did not employ a man to keep things in order.

It looked very much like Lucknell had grabbed what he owned and shoved it all into cases before setting off and had not bothered to attempt to straighten it all out. There had been ample time to do so, as he knew Lucknell had been in residence for three days, but he'd basically ignored the problem in front of him.

It was disorderly and showed a lack of attention to detail,

which was a detail Ambrose would file away about him.

"If I might suggest," he said, "we should do this methodical-ly."

"If *I* might suggest," Sir Jonathan said, "Lord Ryland, do take the chair. I do not suppose the doctor would wish you to be on your feet for any length of time."

"I am perfectly fine," Ambrose said.

"Lord Ryland," Lady Prudence said, "please do as you are asked. It is only sensible. We can bring you items to examine."

She said it in that scolding tone she'd employed earlier and it was rather adorable. He supposed he should not cross her if she were so determined.

"Very well," he said, sitting down with some relief.

"We will start in different corners," Sir Jonathan said, gazing round at the disorder of the room. "Search every pocket of every coat, flip through books for hidden letters, that sort of thing. Once all the cases are emptied, I will examine them for concealed compartments."

"Correspondence would be particularly helpful," Ambrose said.

"Aye," Thomas said, "though you won't find much unless they're old. He never did write letters when we lived in Morris House, 'cept the occasional to his friend."

"What friend?" Ambrose asked. "What is his name?"

Thomas shrugged. "He only ever called him Mr. C. He's a fella that was there in York but he went on his merry way. He didn't work for Lucknell, they was more like brothers. Lucknell talked to him as equals, just like he did with Mr. P."

"Who is Mr. P?" Ambrose asked, wondering exactly how many associates Lucknell had.

"Oh him? He was the one that used to wake up screamin' in the night. Always something about how it was a mistake."

"What was a mistake?"

"How should I know? He never got that far afore Lucknell woke him and told him to shut it. He disappeared one day.

Maybe he's in Bedlam, gone stark raving mad on account of nightmares."

"What did these three talk about?" Ambrose asked, ignoring Thomas' hopes for Mr. P.

"Around me? Only vagaries. Everything was said like they knew what they meant but didn't want anybody else to know it. They talked a lot about 'the thing we seek.' We all knew we were going to Kent for somethin' but didn't know what. I won't lie, I was pretty surprised to find out the thing was Lady Prudence, as I thought it might be a pile of gold or something of value."

The earl grabbed Thomas by the scruff of his neck. "Do you imply that my daughter has no value?"

Thomas wriggled out of his grasp.

"Papa," Lady Prudence said, laughing, "do let him be. You know what he meant."

The earl did let the boy go. Thomas straightened his coat. "It's all right, Lady Prudence. My lord just didn't ken that I meant you were *priceless*."

Lady Prudence shook her head in amusement. She had a way with the little rogue, did she not?

"Aha," Sir Jonathan said, picking something out of the grate. "He's burned a letter, but part of it still remains." He took it to Ambrose and they laid it on a table.

Most of the letter had been consumed in fire and what was left was smudged, but he could still make it out.

Lord Ryland himself. Lady Feather

somehow taken an interest

claims of an engagement

Whoever had written this letter, and he presumed it was one of the mysterious associates, he had somehow known both he and Lady Featherstone were involved in Lady Prudence's difficulties with Lucknell. Ambrose might have thought the information had come from simple observation—somebody had seen him arrive to Copeland Hall.

Except, the information was traveling the wrong way. This was a letter Lucknell had received, not sent.

Most likely. There was always the off chance that Lucknell had written it and then decided not to send it.

"We need examples of his handwriting to rule out that he wrote this himself and then changed his mind about putting it in the post," Ambrose said.

"I know what his hand looks like," Thomas said. "Every day, he left lists of things I was supposed to be doing. I don't know why he thought I could read them."

"Did he think it because you *told* him you could read?" Ambrose asked.

"Probably," Thomas said. He climbed over the bed to Ambrose's side and peered at the shred of a letter. "That's not him. He makes big loops and curlicues like he were the King of England making a proclamation."

So that was confirmed. The letter was from an associate, who had somehow known Ambrose would go to Kent before Lucknell knew it. It must be the associate currently located in Town, as the one named Mr. P had departed Kent very recently.

That was disturbing. The only people who knew of his trip were those associated with his own house. All of them knew of his destination, he'd not kept it a secret, and he had dozens of men coming and going every day. As soon as he got back to Town, he would confer with Depsford and Parker on what to do about it.

Not much else was found, other than to confirm Thomas' assessment of Lucknell's handwriting through various notes tucked in pockets, generally signatures on receipts for laundry and such.

Lady Prudence had found a few such bits as she diligently searched. Ambrose could almost feel her distaste over handling Lucknell's things, though she bravely carried on with it.

Lady Featherstone made progress very slowly, as each new item she encountered seemed to suggest a theory.

Ambrose was hard-pressed not to sigh when she held up a small stick pin topped with a pearl as if she'd discovered the Holy Grail.

Did it not suggest a connection to the crime ring specializing in pearl necklaces that she believed to exist due to the case of the lost and then found pearl necklace mystery?

By the end of the afternoon, and thirty theories later, Ambrose had almost begun to think fondly of Fancy Geleder, her ramshackle farmhouse, and the dose of laudanum the doctor had given him. He had a headache.

PRUDENCE GAZED OUT the window at London. She had never imagined so many people could be living in such close quarters. She had known it as a factual sort of thing, but to see it was altogether something else.

After they'd searched Lucknell's rooms and Sir Jonathan had taken possession of his catalogued belongings, the decision had been made to depart for Town the following day.

The decision had been made mostly by Lord Ryland, though everybody else thought he ought to rest at least another day.

The lord was determined to get home and something in his manner told her he thought they might be in danger by staying.

This was further confirmed when they'd gone out to the carriages that morning. From somewhere, Lord Ryland had hired six men on horseback to accompany their carriages.

Prudence had been certain they were armed.

It was frightening to think that one might require that sort of protection.

But then, it was also something else. She was touched, and she felt safe under Lord Ryland's protection.

He was a forceful and stubborn sort of man, not the sort she favored. But then, when one needed a defender those qualities came in very handy. It was very strange to be both put off and drawn in.

They had made the journey safely, with men on either side and Thomas keeping Lord Ryland company in his own carriage.

"Here we are, turning into Russell Square. Goodness, it seems ages since I left it. Now my dear, you must rest this evening as tomorrow will be full of things to do. The duchess will have arranged her modiste to arrive first thing. Though," Lady Featherstone said, a flash of concern overlaying her features, "I will put my foot down on brocade if she seems to be going in that direction."

"Brocade?" Prudence asked.

"The duchess does rather favor it for herself," Lady Feather-stone said. "We all did, I'm afraid, two seasons ago. But then some of us heard that the queen thinks the duchess looks like a walking pair of curtains and so we gave it up. Nobody's had the nerve to tell Theodosia, though."

Prudence saw her father press his lips tightly together in an effort not to laugh.

"Never fear, I will parry that sword if it comes to it. I won't have *my* girl trouncing round in brocade."

Prudence was rather grateful for that, as she did not particularly favor the material.

"Then of course," Lady Featherstone went on, "we will have the ladies arriving, and no doubt we'll have a stack of invitations to sort through. The ladies were in such confidence of Lady Heathway's ability to drive off Luckstone that they will have told everybody in Town that you are to arrive."

"Goodness," Prudence said softly.

"On the following day," Lady Featherstone said, "we will have a criminal society meeting at Lord Ryland's residence. That is always fascinating and, Lord Copeland, I do hope you will consent to come. I understand that you do not wish to go wandering round a rout, but these meetings are intellectually stimulating."

The earl nodded though Prudence did not put much store by it.

Lady Featherstone said, "Though, I have never been able to convince my lord of it. He'd rather be at his club. White's, I am certain he'll put your name forward."

"I have been a member these twenty years, though I have not been there in person almost as long," the earl said. "I shall be delighted to walk those old halls again."

"Ah, there is Danforth coming out to meet us."

The butler opened the door while footmen ranged round him ready to assist. "Welcome home, Lady Featherstone," he said.

He looked approvingly at Prudence and Lady Featherstone said, "Yes, Danforth, you have guessed correctly. We have rescued Lady Prudence and brought her here. We also bring Lord Copeland, her father. You will see to sleeping arrangements? Oh, and Lord Copeland brings his page, he'll need to be put somewhere."

At the mention of Thomas, the boy leapt out of Lord Ryland's carriage as it pulled up behind their own.

Danforth had helped Lady Featherstone to the sidewalk, and now Prudence herself.

He made an attempt to help the earl, but Thomas pushed past him. "No need for that, my good man," Thomas said. "I'm the Earl of Copeland's particular page."

Lord Copeland said, "He is my *only* page and there is nothing particular about him other than his particular lack of manners."

This scolding washed off Thomas like water on oil cloth and he winked at the rather nonplussed Danforth.

"Help them all in, Danforth," Lady Featherstone said. "I must have parting words with Lord Ryland. Criminal society business."

Danforth nodded knowingly and led them indoors, leaving Lady Featherstone marching toward Lord Ryland's carriage.

Prudence climbed the steps resisting the urge to look behind her. She did so hope the journey had not overtired Lord Ryland or given him a setback.

Though, it would hardly be appropriate to inquire.

LORD FEATHERSTONE'S HOUSE was the last on the south side of the square and very bright and airy. It was fairly new-built, having been designed by Lord Featherstone. He had certain ideas that could not be accommodated in their last house in Town. Lady Featherstone said he'd worked with the builder for above two years before a brick was laid.

Among other wonders, such as an ironing room, a laundry room, various storerooms, and the largest wine cellar ever seen, there was an elaborate ladies' retiring room adjacent to the ballroom. It consisted of a long corridor of private apartments equipped to allow a lady to relieve herself, or just rest on a velvet sofa and then fix one's hair at the looking glass.

This was shown to Prudence on arrival, and the housekeeper had even offered to show the earl though he very sensibly declined. That, though, was not the greatest of the surprising accoutrements to Featherstone House.

Attached to each bedchamber was a small, tiled room housing a copper bath with an open pipe sitting at its head.

Somewhere up above, there was a room walled and floored in double brick and vented to the outdoors that housed a copper tank of water that could be heated.

Assisted by gravity and through a series of pipes and the handles that opened and closed them, heated water could be directed to any of these bathing rooms.

Lord Featherstone employed what he termed a 'bath boy,' whose only job was to look after the system and make certain the fire was doused at night. Even the servants were given leave for a hot bath once a week.

One might only send word that one wished for a bath and wait for a maid to come and say that it was ready. Turning the handle delivered the water.

It really was extraordinary.

Lady Featherstone claimed that Lord Featherstone often found his joints sore in his middle age and that the baths were restorative. Prudence's father had nodded in agreement and she had the idea that he would take advantage of this luxury at the earliest possible moment.

She had not been wrong—Lord Copeland had bathed before dinner and seemed much the better for it.

He and Lord Featherstone found an enjoyable hour after dinner discussing the finer points of hot water. Lord Featherstone even went so far as to reveal that he had a collection of salts from various parts of England and he would send to Lord Copeland that which might be most effective for the gout.

The two gentlemen had found a commonality between them that would cement their friendship.

Prudence was encouraged to retire early as Lady Featherstone wished her to be rested for the activities to follow on the morrow. She did so, and gratefully, as the past few days had worn on her.

She was both thrilled and nervous to find herself in Town. First, it had been a far-off place she would not likely see anytime soon, then had come the idea that she would go. Now, though, she was actually here.

Prudence was well aware that she'd come on serious business. She must set the course for her future through marriage. There was no other course to choose from.

There was no idea that she would not marry, as her circumstances would be rather dreadful. Her father's estate was entailed, and not happily.

She had never met the earl's heir, as they were not on friendly terms. Lord Copeland said he was a flagrant gambler who'd spent his own fortune and now waited hopefully to come into another one. He would not take well to being saddled with a spinster daughter.

Her dowry was sufficient, generous even, but it would not

support an independent household for a lifetime.

She had known all of this for quite some time, but she'd pushed it to the back of her mind while they had been going on quietly at Copeland Hall.

Now, though, she was in London for a season. Now something must be done.

If Lucknell had done her any favor, he had at least taught her what she did *not* want from a marriage. She did not want to be run over, her every opinion subsumed by a husband as if she'd never had any of her own at all. She did not want her weakness as a woman exploited.

If she chose carefully, though, she could avoid that dreadful circumstance. She would favor gentlemen who did not show that inclination. *Gentle* gentlemen. Mild gentlemen. She would wed a gentleman who did not make her feel overpowered.

As she thought of all these qualities, she could not help but think of the opposite—Lord Ryland.

He was honorable and decent and had taken great steps to protect her. But he was also…overpowering. He was a lion, when what she sought was a lamb.

At least, sometimes he was overpowering. He had not seemed so when he'd lain injured. But then, most men with a head injury probably would not seem overpowering. They would have been tamed by illness, at least temporarily.

She would look for that gentleman who was tamed, though no illness had struck him. She would look for that man who was tame in temperament.

If there were any niggling doubt to this course, it must be her experience with Mr. Ackins from her own neighborhood. He was very tame. Timid, even. A veritable spring lamb trying to find its legs. His mother had hinted at his regard for Prudence, though Mr. Ackins, himself, had never had the temerity to do so. Prudence did not like him. She found him tedious, with all his stammering and handwringing.

Well, just because she wished for a tame man did not mean

she would like all of them. She must only find one she did like, perhaps one who did not wring his hands so much.

Who was he? Where was he?

Meggy finished brushing her hair and Prudence said, "Meggy, I am a goose. I am far too much in my own thoughts, though I have not even met him yet."

"Met who?"

"Precisely!"

CHAPTER ELEVEN

Ambrose had called a meeting in his upstairs library as soon as he'd returned from Swanley.

His head pounded from the journey, but it could not wait. There was somebody coming and going from his house who was in contact with Lucknell. If this mystery individual were not one and the same as the associate Lucknell had met in York and now surely sought out in London, he was connected to them both somehow.

It was impossible to know yet if they dealt with two people or three people or thirty people.

Depsford had looked askance at his neckcloth as soon as he'd entered the room. As well he should, Thomas had practiced on it during the journey in the carriage and, for all the boy's ideas that he would become a valet, he'd not quite got the knack of it yet.

Parker, his batman from his army days and now his butler, was entirely expressionless over his rumpled clothes. Parker never gave away anything unless he meant to, and he rarely meant to.

Ambrose laid out the situation, as far as he knew it.

"Perhaps we can use this to our advantage," Parker said. "If there is a spy among us, then *we* determine what information that spy carries away. By sending false information, we may set a trap."

"Agreed," Ambrose said, "but we don't know what to bait it

with. What are they after? We cannot lure until we understand what bait would be taken."

"So it is not Lady Prudence he wants?" Depsford asked.

"Not exactly. At least, I do not believe so," Ambrose said, rubbing his aching temples. "I believe it to be something *about* Lady Prudence, or some connection to her. Possibly the estate, though I cannot work out how."

Parker poured him a glass of brandy and handed it to him. "We'll set some men to watch Copeland Hall in case there are goings-on there. Though, we don't really know what we look for."

"Whatever he's after," Depsford said, "he did attempt to engage himself to Lady Prudence. It seems to me that it would not be convenient for his plans if she were engaged to another. We might send out that information and see if it prompts him to act."

Ambrose looked at his valet as if he'd lost his wits. Depsford had a whole host of useful skills, but understanding the *ton* was not one of them.

"We cannot put out that she's engaged," he said. "That sort of news would spread like a fire through a dry forest and then what? It comes to her notice and she is in distress over it, *and* immediately denies it. That, coupled with the story put round her own neighborhood by Lucknell, that they were engaged and now he's disappeared, would earn her the moniker of either jilter or jilted, depending on society's mood. In any case, who was the gentleman you planned on dragging through this mire?"

"I was thinking of you, naturally," Depsford said.

"It's a ghastly idea, and not one we will pursue. Until we think of a better one, Lady Prudence must be protected at all times. Set a watch on Lady Featherstone's house. I want to know who goes in and how often. When she leaves the house, she must be followed. Put Robbie and Peter on it."

Parker sighed. As he did not give anything away unless he meant to, he meant to be understood. Ambrose was well aware that it would be an inconvenience, as Robbie and Peter were his most experienced and reliable footmen.

However, Robbie and Peter were also some of his most reliable spies when unobtrusive was sought. They both looked younger than they were and had boyish, innocent-looking faces. Dressed as the sons of merchants, they disappeared from view. They simply were not seen even when they were seen.

"Perhaps we won't need to invent that Lady Prudence is engaged," Depsford said. "After all, she's a young lady come to Town. That's what they come for, right? I assume she's a looker and comes trotting in with a good purse, which is the whole recipe as far as I know. If she gets herself engaged for real, we must be on high alert for any movement from Lucknell."

"A looker? Trotting in? The whole recipe?" Ambrose said, barely containing his outrage. "You are speaking of a lady. An earl's daughter. Furthermore, Lady Prudence will *not* do you the favor of engaging herself, so put that thought out of your mind."

"Then what's she come here for?" Depsford asked, appearing exceedingly puzzled.

"She's come here for…she arrives to…escape Lucknell," Ambrose said.

"But he left her neighborhood afore she did," Depsford pointed out.

Parker patted Depsford on the back and said, "If a man finds he's been digging himself a hole, the sensible thing is to put down the shovel."

"Is that one of your poetic ways of telling me to shut it?" Depsford asked the butler.

"Yes. Yes, it is."

Ambrose dismissed them both, bickering as they went, and stayed at the desk with his brandy. Depsford really could step out of line in spectacular fashion.

The idea that Lady Prudence would swiftly engage herself. Well, it was…he did not know what it was. He just did not like it.

THE MODISTE SENT by the duchess had come and spent the morning with Prudence and Lady Featherstone, while Lord Featherstone had taken Lord Copeland to White's to reintroduce him to his old club.

Much to Lady Featherstone's relief, Madame LeGrange did not once suggest a brocade.

Rather, with Prudence's particular looks and coloring, pastels in light silks and satins for evenings, fine muslins for daywear. Various jackets and coats would be made, including a selection of spencers, though according to Lady Featherstone, Lady Heathway was entirely against them.

A new riding habit in dark green and a host of slippers and shoes were added to the list.

Madame LeGrange was not a shoemaker herself, but she traced Prudence's foot and would consult with the right man for the job, as she knew what fabrics and colors must be used.

The cuts and styles for everything were to be simple and modest, suiting an earl's daughter who has just come to Town.

There had been some discussion of jewelry, as Madame LeGrange was of the opinion that those accoutrements were integral to the finished look of any dress.

Lady Featherstone had been enthusiastic and offered to turn her entire box of jewels over to the project, though Prudence had insisted that she only wore her mother's gold necklace.

Madame LeGrange had not seen the charm of it, but Prudence had refused to budge on that point. The necklace gave her comfort and so it would stay on.

Now, the modiste was long gone and Lady Featherstone's friends had arrived. At least most of them had. Lady Redfield, the duchess, and Lady Easton already had their tea. Lady Mendleton was, presumably, running late.

"Now, Lady Prudence," Lady Easton said, "you'll want to

always turn to us when the question of a young gentleman arises. Depending upon the advice and guidance of your elders is only sensible."

Prudence nodded. "Of course, my lady. I am very grateful for any hints that may be given me."

Lady Easton seemed satisfied. "She is very different from Caroline. I believe she *will* take advice and guidance."

"Caroline was Miss Upton and is now Lady Bertridge," Lady Featherstone said to Prudence. "She was Lady Easton's girl. Very spirited."

"Very," Lady Easton said darkly.

"Yes, now that's settled," the duchess said, "how did you get on with my modiste, Madame LeGrange?"

"Oh very well, thank you, ma'am. She was very helpful."

"She is, is she not?" the duchess said. "She has a particular way with brocade that few can match."

Prudence did not answer that idea, as she was already aware of Lady Featherstone's feelings about brocade. And that the queen thought the duchess looked dressed in curtains.

"I do hope you will have the opportunity to meet my dear Arabella," Lady Redfield said. "She is a cousin, but as her parents are dead, I have really stepped in as her mama. She is recently married to the duchess's son, Lord Blackwood."

"I condoned the match," the duchess said, as if there might have been a different outcome if she had not. "Peregrine's happiness and my own are as one."

"Does he write regularly, then?" Lady Redfield asked anxiously. "I have not received a letter from Arabella in over a fortnight."

"How often does not signify," the duchess said.

Prudence took that to mean not so very often, which did not surprise her. It would be an unusual young lord indeed who maintained a frequent correspondence with his mother.

"Peregrine and I have always had a meeting of the minds," the duchess said. "I know his mind without a physical letter in my hands."

"Goodness, how do they get on, then?" Lady Redfield asked. "Last she wrote, Arabella said they'd taken in a herd of ailing horses from a circus that had shut down."

"They get on…very well," the duchess said. "Now, we have business at hand. Who is it for Lady Prudence? What gentleman do we put forward for consideration?"

"I was thinking of Lord Ryland," Lady Easton said.

"As was I!" Lady Featherstone said. "Lady Heathway says we always do think of him, but this time I feel we have hit the mark."

"Ryland," the duchess said, "yes, he would do very well. Further, Lady Prudence has the advantage of already being introduced to the gentleman."

Prudence felt the conversation was like a runaway carriage. It just kept careening forward though she would wish it to stop.

"We are going to a criminal society meeting at his house on the morrow," Lady Featherstone said.

"The society," the duchess said. "Is that really the right venue for Lady Prudence's first outing?"

"But it is at Lord Ryland's house and he specially asked for her to be brought there," Lady Featherstone said hopefully.

"That is something, in any case," Lady Easton said.

"What do you think, Lady Prudence?" the duchess asked.

The ladies turned toward her, though they had just been discussing her as if she were not there. They were rather highhanded, though how to disabuse them of their ideas?

"I am very much appreciative of all your care and plans," she said slowly. "However, Lord Ryland and I…well, we would not suit, I am afraid."

"Why ever not?" Lady Easton asked.

"Yes, why not?" Lady Featherstone said.

"It's his looks, isn't it? Is he too tall? Or do you prefer a light-haired gentleman?" the duchess asked. "Please do not say auburn, as my son is already taken and there are not many with that fine coloring. The Tudor coloring, you know."

"No, it is not his hair color," Prudence said. "It is just that I would prefer a more…mild gentleman."

"Mild?" Lady Easton asked.

"Do we know any mild gentlemen?" Lady Redfield asked.

As the ladies pondered the question, Danforth opened the drawing room doors and said, "Lady Mendleton and her granddaughter, Miss Daisy Louisa Stapleton."

Prudence presumed this was the very advanced baby that seemed to irritate Lady Heathway so much. She was surprised Lady Mendleton had brought her, as she did not think it the done thing.

Her surprise was entirely surpassed by the rest of the ladies who sat round the tea table. Lady Easton set her teacup down with a clatter. The duchess slowly turned her head. Lady Redfield whispered, "Goodness."

"I am sorry I am late," Lady Mendleton said, leading the little girl in by the hand. "Daisy and I have been riding in the carriage."

Daisy was a solid little creature, fairly drowning in white muslin ruffles. She staggered along, none too steady on her feet, as toddlers were wont to do.

Lady Mendleton walked the girl to the table and said, "Now Daisy, this is the Duchess of Stanbury, Lady Easton, Lady Redfield, and Lady Featherstone. And this must be Lady Prudence. Do the pretty curtsy you've been practicing, my dear."

"No!" little Daisy shouted. She then wrestled out of her grandmother's grip and grabbed at the table, taking Lady Easton's teacup in her chubby little hands.

"Do give it over, Daisy," Lady Mendleton said.

Daisy took this request as some sort of game and gleefully staggered away with it, the tea making its inevitable way down the front of her muslin.

The end result surprised nobody, except perhaps Lady Mendleton. Daisy dropped the cup on the marble floor, it shattered, and the child wailed.

"Oh dear," Lady Mendleton said, rushing over and sweeping her up and away from the fragments of porcelain. "Nanny!" she shouted.

A stout woman who had seemed to be waiting in the hall for just such a moment, hurried in and took the child.

It was not a moment before Miss Daisy Louisa Stapleton's wails were a distant echo.

"Well, *Bwandbaba*," the duchess said with asperity.

Lady Mendleton sat down as if nothing untoward had occurred, while footmen hurried in to sweep up the broken shards and bring Lady Easton another cup.

"She has left her first year behind. It is a hard age, though Daisy goes through it bravely," Lady Mendleton said. "What have I missed?"

AMBROSE HAD TAKEN special care with the setup of this particular society meeting.

The meetings gathered together individuals who wished to understand the criminal element better than they did, along with those who worked for him every day.

At least, those who worked for him that were presentable enough to mix with the *ton* attended.

There were, of course, some of his peers that only came for the originality of the evening, or who wished to frighten themselves, but those never came more than once or twice.

There were also, occasionally, a mama and daughter—the mama believing it to be a unique opportunity to push a daughter to his notice. They too did not often return, as they found so little success.

The meetings examined and attempted to unravel unsolved crimes. Ambrose was surprised at how often they actually did so, or at least came up with a theory he could pursue. More than one murderer had met his maker on account of forty or fifty people putting their heads together.

Lady Featherstone would bring Lady Prudence and, as he knew there was somebody who would attend that was associated with Lucknell, he would have eyes and ears everywhere. Who watched her?

Of course, everybody who worked on society business had been well-trained. They might not give themselves away so easily. On the other hand, they would not know that Ambrose had found that piece of a letter in Swanley. They would not know that he looked around at his own organization.

He would place Lady Prudence and Lady Featherstone at his own table. Depsford would lay out the crime, his valet having a skill for the dramatic. A barber had been murdered with his own tools and Ambrose was certain he knew who had done it, but he would be interested to hear the various theories.

He suspected he would hear quite a few theories, as he was to be next to Lady Featherstone. He would round out his table with Mr. Clamarin, that fellow having a unique patience for Lady Featherstone's mental wanderings.

At least his head had cleared. The dizziness that had plagued him had gone when he woke that morning and he felt like his old self again.

Depsford had brought him his coat and helped him into it as he prepared to descend.

He examined it critically. "Have I not worn this one to death? Has not the dark blue I ordered arrived yet?"

"It has," Depsford said, "though I was holding it back for a more elevated occasion."

"Don't be ridiculous, I'll wear it."

Depsford fetched the coat. "This sharpening up wouldn't be laid at Lady Prudence's door, would it?"

"What?"

"I only say, in all the society meetings we've had, this is the first time you've worried about your coat."

"You don't know what I worry about," Ambrose said gruffly.

As it happened, he *had* thought of Lady Prudence when he'd

examined himself in the glass. Depsford had a very annoying habit of peering into his thoughts.

Though, why should he not attempt to be presentable when a lady would be present? There was nothing unusual in it.

"Well, I may not know what you worry about," Depsford said jovially, "but I do know that I'll take special care with your neckcloth just now."

Ambrose did not answer the jibe. The man was enraging.

PRUDENCE COULD NOT say she was particularly enthusiastic about attending Lord Ryland's criminal society meeting.

For one, she was not that interested in examining crimes. She'd really rather not think about them.

For another, she was both repelled and attracted to Lord Ryland. It was not at all comfortable how many times the picture of him lying in Mrs. Geleder's bed flashed in her mind.

He'd seemed so approachable and docile then. He had no end of complaints and was stubborn as anything, but not particularly threatening.

Lord Ryland had been a lamb then, but he would have proceeded with his recovery. He would be back to a lion by now. A masculine and overpowering lion.

Despite her wishing to be going nearly anywhere else, she was determined to put a good face on it. Lady Featherstone had been so kind, all the ladies had been so helpful to both her and her father, that she would not for the world appear ungrateful.

In any case, she was to represent her father too, as the earl had declined to come.

He blamed it on his gout, though Prudence had the idea that he'd simply prefer to be at home enjoying his new favorite pastime. She had heard him tell Thomas to find the bath boy and order a tubful of water hot as Hades for him—he was determined to try some of Lord Featherstone's salts.

Lady Featherstone had filled the carriage with conversation as they made their way to Berkeley Square. Apparently, she was one of the longest-running members of the society. She knew absolutely everybody and aside from Lord Ryland, she was a particular collaborator with a certain Mr. Clamarin.

That gentleman was a wealthy landowner from the north and he had further to recommend him that he so often found Lady Featherstone's theories intriguing.

The carriage slowed and Prudence peeked out the window. Lord Ryland's house on Berkeley Square was fine indeed. It was large and built of pale stone. The builder had made generous use of windows that overlooked the square, affording a view of the plane trees that shaded it. Prudence supposed it *would* be very grand. Lord Ryland was a marquess, after all.

"I always feel a sense of anticipation when I arrive to these doors," Lady Featherstone said. "What will we encounter? Who can say!"

Prudence smiled and nodded as a footman opened the door. What else could she do—the lady's enthusiasm was contagious.

"Robbie," Lady Featherstone said to the footman. "Have you got any clues for me?"

Prudence was surprised that Lady Featherstone was on a first-name basis with one of Lord Ryland's footmen. Robbie himself did not look very surprised, though.

"All I know, Lady Featherstone, is you're to examine the case of a murdered barber-surgeon. My own guess is that it's the wife, trying to pin it on a grieving husband."

"Excellent!" Lady Featherstone said, slipping Robbie a coin.

Prudence was certain that their unusual arrival only portended more strange things to come.

She was not disappointed in that guess. She had not seen anything like Lord Ryland's dining room in her life.

At least, Lady Featherstone called it a dining room, though it had little resemblance to that area of a house.

There was no dining table as such. Rather, there were small square tables scattered about. Further, the room itself was enormous. It could not possibly have been built that way and must certainly be two rooms combined. She would have even thought it an oversized ballroom, had she not seen one as she passed it in the great hall.

Just now, footmen were running back and forth, escorting a surge of people to their tables.

The crowd seemed to be from all walks of life. Some were dressed very finely, others might be merchants of some sort. There was a hum in the room, as people recognized and greeted one another. A sense of excitement too.

How odd that there would be so many people interested in hearing about a murder.

"Lady Featherstone," a male voice said from behind them.

Prudence turned to find a smiling gentleman.

"Mr. Vance," Lady Featherstone said. "I do not believe I have seen you here before."

"No, nor will you likely see me again," Mr. Vance said. "I bring my great aunt who is in Town visiting a friend and was determined to come."

Mr. Vance looked enquiringly at Prudence.

"Mr. Vance, this is Lady Prudence Landry. She stays with me in Town."

Mr. Vance bowed. "Lady Prudence. I hope we can meet again at a more genial occasion where there might be dancing."

"This is genial!" Lady Featherstone nearly cried.

"My apologies, Lady Featherstone," Mr. Vance said. "I did for a moment forget how skilled you are at the sport of solving mysteries. Alas, I am not so gifted."

"Well, I suppose you must be forgiven then," Lady Featherstone said, mollified by hearing of her skill.

"Might I suggest you join the table with my aunt and me? She would be thrilled to be in company with the storied Lady Featherstone. I have told her about the brooch *and* the walking stick."

Prudence looked to Lady Featherstone to see what she would say. From behind her, a deep voice said, "Lady Prudence and Lady Featherstone will be at my own table."

CHAPTER TWELVE

LORD RYLAND HAD come up behind Prudence.

Mr. Vance nodded. "Ryland. I should have known; you keep the best company for yourself."

"It is *my* society meeting, after all." Lord Ryland motioned for a footman and one came running. "Peter, show Mr. Vance to his table."

Mr. Vance gave Prudence a wry smile. "Until we meet again, Lady Prudence." He bowed and went off laughing with the footman.

Whatever he was, he was a rather jovial fellow. Lord Ryland, though. Why must they be at his table? Why must he be so forceful about it?

"I should have realized, Lord Ryland," Lady Featherstone said, "that you would wish us by your side."

The lady seemed delighted with the idea, though Prudence was certainly less so.

Lord Ryland nodded and collared another footman. "Benjamin, escort Lady Featherstone and Lady Prudence to table number one."

They were whisked off by the footman and taken to a table situated at the head of the room. Lady Featherstone sat down and shook out her skirts with an obvious sense of relish.

"Mr. Vance seems genial," Prudence said. She was eager to have a discussion on anything other than murder.

"Genial? Oh yes, he does always have that going for him. He's invariably jolly. He's to be a baron, too. Sadly, his grandfather was in trade."

"Is that significant?" Prudence asked. She did not see how it would signify—Lord Merkell of her own neighborhood had arrived at a title through his father's service to the crown and nobody thought anything about it. Her father said a gentleman must be judged on his behavior.

"The duchess finds it exceedingly significant," Lady Featherstone said.

Before Prudence could inquire more about it, they were interrupted.

A man in his early thirties, of average looks and height but neatly and well-turned out, bowed. In a rather soft voice he said, "Good evening, Lady Featherstone."

"Mr. Clamarin! There you are. Do allow me to present Lady Prudence Landry. She stays with me this season."

Mr. Clamarin bowed. "Lady Prudence."

"Her father, the earl, has come to us too, though he does not attend the evening."

"The earl," Mr. Clamarin said.

It seemed to Prudence that there had been a flicker of surprise that crossed Mr. Clamarin's features, though she could not account for it.

"Mr. Clamarin," she said.

He sat down and they exchanged pleasantries. Prudence found herself liking him. He was rather soft-spoken and gentle in his opinions. He was not forceful like Lord Ryland or laughing and jolly like Mr. Vance. His temperament reminded her a little of her father.

As Lady Featherstone was distracted by the line of well-wishers that had formed to pay homage regarding her victory of last season, Mr. Clamarin said, "I wonder if you find a real interest in the society or whether you have only been carried along by Lady Featherstone's enthusiasm."

Prudence instinctively felt she could be truthful with Mr. Clamarin. "I am afraid I do not find great interest in it. I'd really rather not think about a murder."

Mr. Clamarin nodded thoughtfully. "I would suggest thinking of something else—recite a poem in your mind or something like it. You will not be required to advance your own theory." He glanced at Lady Featherstone indulgently. "There will be enough theories floating round this table."

Prudence found the advice very considerate. A more forceful man might have attempted to sway her opinion with all the reasons she *ought* to be interested. Mr. Clamarin appeared satisfied that she'd developed an opinion for herself and would accept it.

"If there is any recompense at all," Mr. Clamarin said, "Lord Ryland does see to it that rolling carts of sweets and savories do come by regularly and you might have any sort of drink that you like. Lady Featherstone is always very fond of the Canary."

"I hope tea will be on offer?" Prudence asked.

"Yes, of course. I do prefer tea myself."

A dinging upon a glass stopped their conversation. Most of the guests had been already seated and those who were not drifted back to their places.

Lord Ryland said, "Welcome to a new season of the *Society for Advancing Criminal Knowledge* meetings. As we've done in prior years, we will examine unsolved murders, high-value forgeries, and high-profile kidnappings to attempt to determine the culprits. As always, my valet Depsford will give you the facts of the case as they are understood."

Lord Ryland sat down next to Prudence and she could practically feel the heat of him. Why could he not be just...less? Why could he not be more like Mr. Clamarin? Softer spoken, and shorter, and not quite so broad-shouldered?

Lord Ryland's valet began reciting the facts of the case as if he were an actor on a stage. He was full of animation in describing how the poor barber-surgeon had been discovered dead in his own parlor.

When the valet got to the pattern of blood splashed across the floor, Prudence took Mr. Clamarin's advice. She began to picture her books of Shakespeare in her mind's eye and selected her favorite.

She put all her concentration on the words as she recalled them—

Now, fair Hippolyta...

As time went on, she moved through Shakespeare's *A Midsummer Night's Dream*, only occasionally finding her attention pulled to Lord Ryland's valet and the horrible facts of a murder.

Full of vexation come I, with complaint

Those words became mixed in with the idea that the murder weapon belonged to the victim himself.

Mercifully, the valet ended his recitation. As he did so, people all across the room reached for the paper and graphite provided on the tables and footmen began to wheel carts around to offer refreshments.

As Lord Ryland himself sat at their table, a cart arrived speedily. Prudence and Mr. Clamarin asked for tea and selected various cakes and biscuits. Lady Featherstone requested the Canary, just as Mr. Clamarin had predicted, while Lord Ryland took a glass of claret.

Now that they were no longer an audience but were meant to be collaborating on a solution to a murder, Prudence could no longer hide inside her play.

"I think the wife wanted to get rid of him all along, did she not have bruises?" Lady Featherstone asked. "He was a brute and she waited for her opportunity. When she realized that Mr. Farthey was mad with grief over the death of his wife and blamed the barber, the stage was set. She killed him and allowed Mr. Farthey to take the blame."

"What do you think, Lady Prudence?" Lord Ryland asked.

"Me? Oh I am certain Lady Featherstone must be right. I am afraid I do not have the head for this sort of work."

Lord Ryland did not appear entirely satisfied with that answer, though Prudence hardly knew what else to say. Who was Mr. Farthey? She had apparently missed that gentleman's appearance in the tale.

"Mr. Clamarin?" Lord Ryland asked.

"I find Lady Featherstone's theory intriguing," he said. "Unfortunately for the wife, Mr. Farthey, as it turned out, had a solid alibi for the time of the murder. Though, I wonder…"

"What do you wonder about, Mr. Clamarin?" Lady Featherstone asked, scribbling notes on her paper.

"His alibi was given by Miss Farthey. What might a sister do to protect a brother?"

"Good gracious!" Lady Featherstone cried. "It was Mr. Farthey all along."

"I believe so," Lord Ryland said. "There are plans in the works to interview Miss Farthey separate from her brother. Then we shall see."

A footman approached the table and called Lord Ryland away, as some table or other looked for clarification on one of the clues. Lady Featherstone, satisfied that she'd solved the case, looked about her and waved to acquaintances.

"Ah, there is Maribelle Montrose," Lady Featherstone said. "She's been away two seasons and won't have heard of my victories. I will just go over and say hello."

The lady patted her beloved brooch, arranged her walking stick and made her way across the room.

"I am afraid you have found this distressing, Lady Prudence," Mr. Clamarin said.

"I will admit that I have, though I did take your advice to distract myself as much as possible. I was silently reciting *A Midsummer Night's Dream*."

"A fine play indeed. Do not take your aversion to these matters as a weakness," Mr. Clamarin said. "It only speaks of finer feelings." He paused, glancing round the room. "You see, for most who attend these meetings, the victims of these cases are not real. It is only a story. That is why they are able to show so much equanimity."

Prudence nodded. She was certain he was right. "But Mr. Clamarin, how are you able to contemplate these things, if you also realize that the people involved were real individuals?" Prudence asked.

"I feel it not a pleasure but a duty," Mr. Clamarin said. "My estate's housekeeper was struck down by a murderer and I watched the ripples of grief roll out through my family, the servants, the village, and relatives of the lady all across England. You see, a murderer does not just take one victim, but many. I vowed that I would do something to work against it, and so this is what I do."

Prudence was struck by Mr. Clamarin's ideas. She could not understand why all these people thought the evening's activities were entertaining, but she could at least understand Mr. Clamarin's motivations.

And so, the evening went on. It felt rather endless to Prudence, though she did find comfort in Mr. Clamarin's calm and steady presence. Lord Ryland was often called to another table and Lady Featherstone was like a queen on a summer progress, flitting from table to table and deigning to notice this or that person.

Mr. Clamarin, understanding that she had no wish to further examine the murder, told her of his estate in Yorkshire. It was rather remote, but then the remoteness added to the charm of the place. It was nearby a tidy village and his tenants were hardworking. He carried on as his father before, never taking for granted the men and women who made the estate run.

Prudence was rather charmed to hear that the servants got two days off a week. She'd never heard of anybody arranging things in that manner.

Though, as Mr. Clamarin said, "When the people who worked for one were valued and felt they got fair treatment, the work that needed to be done never took half as long."

It was something she would keep in mind when she ran her own household.

At that thought, the reason for her coming to London washed over her again. She was here to marry. She was here to establish her own household.

"Do you attend many entertainments during the season, Mr. Clamarin?" she asked. She would not at all mind if he were to put his name down at a ball.

"I am afraid I do not," he said. "I am a rather retiring sort of person. I'd much rather be at home with a book. I enjoy the quiet, though it does not sound particularly exciting."

"There is a peace to quiet though," Prudence said. "That cannot be undervalued."

"Just so," Mr. Clamarin said, nodding his agreement.

Lady Featherstone came blowing back to the table. "My theory that it was indeed Mr. Farthey and that his sister lied on his behalf is being taken up everywhere," she said, delighted.

Prudence pressed her lips together to stop a smile. That particular idea had been Mr. Clamarin's.

Mr. Clamarin only said, "Well done, Lady Featherstone."

It was generous of him, Prudence thought. So often, a man felt compelled to claim credit for a success. It was very fine of Mr. Clamarin to allow Lady Featherstone her happy delusions.

THE LAST OF the society's members had departed the house and Ambrose had gone up. He poured himself a brandy from the decanter in his dressing room.

What he *should* be doing right now was debriefing his staff. Had anybody noted somebody with particular eyes for Lady

Prudence?

What he *was* doing though, was morosely considering the lady's views. She had not liked it. She had not liked it at all and wished to be far away from his society meeting.

He'd even got the feeling that she'd like to be away from him personally.

Why? He was not repulsive, he did not think. At least, according to all the fan-waving ladies who'd endlessly flirted with him over the seasons he was not. Though, he was a marquess and that made it hard to tell. There were some who would marry a troll in order to find themselves a marchioness.

Perhaps he *was* repulsive and had just got used to himself in the looking glass.

No, that could not be it. Depsford would have pointed out any repulsiveness in unpleasant detail.

What was it, then?

She certainly seemed to prefer others over him. She'd seemed to have had plenty to say to Mr. Clamarin. She'd smiled at him more than once. Clamarin, so soft-spoken and mild.

Was that it? Did she prefer that sort of gentleman? Did she look for a wet rag of a man? Why would she?

More importantly, why was he thinking about it so much? Why was he thinking about her so much? All the time, really.

Good God, he could not have fallen into the state of...love. Could he?

It could not be so. It would be too ridiculous.

It was impossible. For one, he did not believe the lady favored him. For another, he had no room in his life for that sort of venture.

Depsford threw the door to his bedchamber open. He glanced at the glass in Ambrose's hand. "Drinking, are we? I can't say I'm surprised. How Clamarin ever got the inside track I'll never know."

"What on earth are you rattling on about?" Ambrose asked, though he thought he knew.

"Lady Prudence. She seemed to take a shine to him, though I don't see what he's got going for him except for that estate of his. He's a marshmallow, to my mind."

"He's good at keeping records, which is why we have him do so," Ambrose said.

"Maybe she prefers a marshmallow, some women do. They latch on to a man they can browbeat."

"Latch on? Browbeat?" Ambrose said. "An earl's daughter does not latch on and browbeat."

Depsford took the drink from his hand and helped him out of his coat. "Meanwhile, none of us saw anybody keeping a special eye on Lady Prudence so we're no farther than we were in identifying who is associated with Lucknell."

Ambrose stayed silent as his neckcloth and then his shirt were removed.

He glanced into the looking glass. He seemed to be well-formed. Broad shoulders, he'd not gone to fat. He was all but certain that he could not be entirely repulsive.

"Hah!" Depsford said, laughing to himself. "Maybe it's Clamarin right under our noses. Maybe the marshmallow isn't as soft as he seems."

"Don't be ridiculous."

⇶⇇

MR. CLAMARIN RETURNED to his apartments. He was satisfied with the evening, though less satisfied with his houseguest. His associate would be lounging around in nightclothes he'd borrowed and drinking port that he'd never get back. Lucknell had been forced to abandon all his belongings at the inn in Swanley after being spotted by Lord Ryland.

That circumstance was fraught with danger. Ryland was now connected to Lady Prudence and, somehow, the boy who'd been left behind at Morris House was one of the party. As well, Paxton was out there somewhere, having nightmares and shouting things in his sleep.

All along, he'd involved himself in that ridiculous criminal society because he knew Ryland was after the diamond too. The man had different reasons for it, of course. He wished to discover who had murdered his parents for it, as he was convinced that those parties would have found the diamond by now. Find the jewel, find the murderers.

Unfortunately, and unbeknownst to Lord Ryland, the murderers had not found it yet. Nevertheless, if Ryland should come upon clues to the jewel's current location it would be convenient to be nearby to hear what they were.

As for those murderers, well, one of them had been standing right in front of him all along. Ryland, fortunately, was not as clever as he thought he was.

He was clever enough though. If one made a mistake in his vicinity, he'd catch it.

So far, he did not believe Ryland had got any closer to the diamond than he had himself.

That was all he'd known going into the evening. Now he knew more. The earl had come to London too. Lucknell had spotted Lady Prudence that day at the inn, but he'd not seen her father.

As he'd expected, Mr. Clamarin found Lucknell in his library with one of his books and a glass of his port, dressed in his own favorite banyan.

"Well?" Lucknell said.

"The earl has come and resides at Lady Featherstone's along with his daughter. Copeland Hall is ripe for picking over. If the diamond is in there, this is our chance. It may be, or they may have brought it with them for safekeeping, or it may be hidden in some unlikely place. It is impossible to know."

"Will you go to Kent, then?" Lucknell asked.

"No, *you* will go to Kent. I am needed here and my absence would be noted. Eventually, the earl will likely discover that somebody has been in his house, particularly if we find the jewel. My time away would correspond with the theft. Nobody knows where you are these days."

Lucknell looked rather petulant over the idea, but shrugged and said, "Very well. And Lady Prudence? Did she come to Ryland's affair? Was she as skittish as ever?"

"She came and she was, though that is to my advantage, I believe. She is naturally a cautious person and your bumbling wooing, if that's what you would call that assault on Copeland Hall, has made her even more cautious. She will trust me over time and if she knows about the diamond and where it is, I will find it out."

Mr. Clamarin paused, then he said, "Though how to get time with the lady is another matter. I dare not go to Lady Featherstone's house, Thomas is there and would recognize me from York."

"That little scoundrel. I'd like to know how he managed to attach himself to them."

"Lady Prudence does not enjoy the society's doings," Mr. Clamarin went on, ignoring Lucknell's commentary, "so I cannot know if she will come next week to please Lady Featherstone, or whether she will invent an illness to get out of it."

"I know *I* would. It sounds dreary."

He ignored that comment too. Rather, he said, "I do not get the sort of invitations that would bring me together with her. I have always put it about that I am a retiring sort of person, so as not to draw too many eyes on my supposed estate in Yorkshire."

"What will you do, then?"

"She did say she enjoys riding and that Lady Featherstone has arranged a horse for her. I will rent my own horse and get proper riding clothes. I'll haunt the park until I see her and get an idea of the schedule they have arranged for that activity so that I might encounter her regularly. It is an outlay of money, but I believe it will be worth the investment."

"Get *me* some clothes while you're at it," Lucknell said, glancing down at the banyan he wore. "Your clothes are not the right size—they are too small and bind me in the shoulders."

Mr. Clamarin did not respond. After all, if he listened to Lucknell's complaining, it would be all he'd have time for in a day.

"Just get to Kent, will you?" he said.

⟫⟫⟩⟨⟨⟨

THE MORNING HAD dawned bright and Prudence had got up early. It felt as if she'd turned a corner now that the criminal society meeting was done with. Done for this week, anyway.

Now, there were only pleasant things to regard. The duchess hosted a ball this evening, which was far better suited to Prudence than considering a murder.

The modiste had brought a dress she had rushed to finish for the occasion, and it was a lovely pale blue silk with an overlay of cream tulle. Prudence already owned slippers that would complement it and Lady Featherstone had lent her a satin cloak in a darker shade of blue.

Lady Featherstone was in fine fettle in general, feeling herself victorious the night before, thanks to Mr. Clamarin's generosity.

Prudence found her father in the drawing room, with Thomas standing at the ready by his side.

Thomas, for reasons known only to himself, reported on what the earl had consumed for breakfast. Apparently, toast and jam were the highlight.

"I *said*," Thomas whispered in Prudence's direction, "that he ought to have some eggs. He wouldn't hear of it, though."

"You *say* far too much," the earl answered. "Not every thought must be spoken."

"Interesting point," Thomas said, nodding.

Though Thomas pretended to find the point interesting, Prudence doubted he'd take on the advice. He was proving himself to be a rather unrepentant chatterer.

Not long after the breakfast report, Danforth brought in a letter for the earl. Thomas raced forward before the butler had got halfway into the room. "I'll take that, my good man."

"I am not your man," the butler answered.

Thomas ignored the sentiment and snatched the letter off the silver salver it lay on. He raced across the room with it as if it were a missive to a king from a general on the field of battle.

The butler left, looking disgusted.

The earl took it from his page and said, "It is from Lady Barlow."

"Lady Barlow?" Prudence asked, rather surprised that Lord Gresham's mother would write to her father.

"Indeed yes, we agreed to correspond. We have many common interests, you know."

Prudence was not so certain she did know. Though, she had noted them walking the gardens at Barlow Hall.

The earl perused the letter and then laid it down.

"Very interesting. Lady Barlow has consulted with Nurse Maddington, who has made inquiries with some nurses in her circle and the lady has sent me the result. She advises lemon water twice daily and keeping to a two-glass limit of white wine, but no ale, red wine, or port whatsoever. I should also avoid coffee, bacon, venison and trout. Well! Cakes and biscuits have not been banned at least, so I suppose I must try her remedy."

"I suppose you must," Prudence said. The earl's own doctor had advised something similar to no effect whatsoever. Perhaps the message had not come by the right messenger.

Thomas ran to the drawing room doors, opened them, and shouted, "Lemon water for the Earl of Copeland!"

"Stop shouting, you little heathen," the earl said to his page.

He turned back to Prudence and said, "She ends with a description of a dessert she was recently served at dinner. It was a ginger cake and she says it was very good. She's included the recipe. I ought to pass it on to Lady Featherstone's cook."

Prudence could not help but smile. The poor cook, receiving recipes from Barlow Hall, though she'd certainly not asked for them.

The earl rose. "I will go to find pen and paper. I would not like Lady Barlow to wait long for a reply."

"I can go, my lord," Thomas said, poised to race out of the room and harass Danforth for writing instruments.

"I will go," the earl said. "Lady Barlow says I must not be afraid of walking, as she's found it has a good effect."

"Can I come with you, then?" Thomas asked.

"I supposed you'd better," the earl said. "I can't very well leave you behind to annoy my daughter."

As the two left together, Prudence noticed that her father's cane had been quite forgotten, as it lay against his chair.

Lady Barlow seemed to energize her father somehow. She hoped the lady would continue sending letters with instructions.

CHAPTER THIRTEEN

The day had passed pleasantly—a final fitting had been done for Prudence's new riding habit and then she'd taken Lady Featherstone's advice in having a long nap in anticipation of the duchess's ball. Meggy, seeming to be acquainted with this operation, had brought her a tea tray in the early evening.

Now they were on their way and, much to her delight, Prudence's father had consented to come. Lord Featherstone had lured him with a few pleasant ideas—the duke's card room was well-appointed, the duke's wine cellar was unsurpassed, the duke employed a French pastry cook, and the carriage could take him home early if he tired.

While everyone else was delighted that he would come, it seemed Thomas was less so. He'd lamented over the idea that there would be no tea and a story, as it seemed the earl read to him at night before they retired.

It ought to have been the other way round, but Thomas could not read. Her father was giving him some instruction in it, though Thomas swore that one missed night of tutoring would likely cause him to forget everything he'd learned.

The earl had finally cut off the boy's complaints with strict instructions not to irritate Danforth while he was out.

Prudence thought that rather wishful thinking, and it appeared that Danforth thought the same, though Thomas had nodded vigorously.

The duke and duchess resided in Hanover Square and there was quite the line of carriages making their way to a fine brick house.

Finally, they were helped out and entered the doors.

The duchess was in a full regalia of yards of brocade embroidered with silver thread, ostrich feathers gamely waving over her head.

"Anne," the duchess said. "Lady Prudence, Lord Featherstone. And what is this? Lord Copeland, I wonder if you remember that we were once acquainted. I seem to recall you were often in Town back in the 1790's."

The earl bowed. "Of course I remember, Your Grace. You were just to be married at that time and the belle of the season."

"Oh, nonsense, belle indeed. And let us not have formality between us, you must call me Duchess. Now," she said, glancing at Prudence, "it seems you have brought your own belle of the season. Is that not right, Duke?"

The duke was then introduced and proved himself to be an amiable gentleman. Prudence got the idea that he generally would agree with his wife, unless there was a dire reason not to. They moved on to deposit their coats and collect Prudence's card.

A card. A real ball. Oh, she had been to balls in her own neighborhood, but they were always very small and the rules mostly ignored for the sake of rationality. If there were only four gentlemen available to dance, then it would be likely that a lady would dance with one of them more than once, with nothing meant by it.

Mostly, there were no cards at all and guests just carried on as they liked. The larger assemblies were a bit more regulated. But this—a ball in a duke's house—would be everything her old dancing master had tried to pound into her head.

They had just entered the ballroom and Prudence marveled at the crowd of people. This certainly was no neighborhood affair.

Next to her, Lord Featherstone and her father had already put their heads together and Lord Featherstone was pointing out the direction of the card room.

"My dear," the earl said to her, "you will be quite all right?"

Prudence laughed and said, "Indeed, go and find a comfortable chair and a hand of cards, Papa."

"Excellent, yes," Lord Copeland said. "Lord Featherstone says if we get there before it is crowded, we can get a table nearby one of the buffets. He says there is a French pastry cook on the premises."

Prudence nodded, amused at her father's determination to get to the pastry. The earl hurriedly followed Lord Featherstone out of the ballroom.

"Lord Ryland!" Lady Featherstone said, all enthusiasm.

Prudence glanced up and curtsied. "Lord Ryland," she said quietly.

"Lady Prudence, Lady Featherstone," he said.

He was looking rather glorious in his dress clothes. His coat was a very dark blue and fitted with gold buttons, his cream-colored breeches were no less fitted. His neckcloth was fine linen and intricately tied.

Prudence suddenly imagined him walking into one of their little balls at home. He would dwarf the other gentlemen, both in size and confidence.

The injured lamb from Swanley had entirely disappeared and the lion had returned.

"If I may, Lady Prudence," he asked, holding out his hand for her card.

Her card. Goodness, she'd nearly forgotten she had one.

She handed it over, not particularly sure if she wished to. But then, she did not know many gentlemen yet and would feel like dying were she to sit out for lack of partners. It would not only be a personal embarrassment, but an embarrassment for Lady Featherstone and her friends too. And then, he was bound to be a skilled partner.

Yet, he was also the outsized Lord Ryland.

He handed back her card and said, "I have taken the liberty of putting myself down for supper. As this is your first outing, I believe that is sensible. While all of the duchess's guests will be respectable, there will of course be those who are not suitable."

"Lady Featherstone, Lady Prudence."

Mr. Vance had approached.

Lord Ryland glanced at him as if he were not particularly happy to see him. "Vance," he said, "I did not expect to see you here."

Mr. Vance seemed to find that exceedingly amusing and said, "I suppose you did not. However, the duchess tolerates me when she has use of me. She has directed me to escort Miss Rightstone to supper, as I am known to do a favor when I can."

He'd reached for Prudence's card, which she gladly handed over. Mr. Vance was rather more jolly than might suit her temperament, but she liked him.

"I see Ryland has swooped in for supper, though I shall not be down about it since I am promised to Miss Rightstone," Mr. Vance said. "In any case, Lord Ryland, you cannot be everywhere all the time and have helpfully left the first open."

Lord Ryland bowed and moved off, looking distinctly annoyed.

Mr. Vance put down his name and then bowed. "Lady Featherstone, Lady Prudence," he said, before moving off himself.

"What is the favor Mr. Vance does for the duchess by taking a lady into supper?" Prudence asked Lady Featherstone.

"Well, you see, the duchess is friends with Miss Rightstone's mother, Viscountess Rembly. Miss Rightstone is here for her fourth season, unfortunately. You see, she is rather…"

Lady Featherstone had trailed off.

Prudence said, "You do not make comment on her looks?"

"Goodness, no. She's comely enough. It's just that she's…well, if you must know, she's as dumb as a post and has a terrible temper."

That was indeed an unfortunate combination. Though certainly, something might be done about the temper.

"Mr. Vance has been conscripted to step forward for supper as…perhaps nobody else might," Lady Featherstone said.

More gentlemen approached and Prudence was both thrilled and nervous to be introduced and have their names put down. It seemed her card would be filled, which would be a relief. However, she was also cognizant that any one of those gentlemen might prove himself a suitor.

Or the ghastly idea that nobody would.

She supposed every lady coming to Town must feel this odd mix of enthusiasm and dread. What if a gentleman decided to pursue her? What if no gentleman decided to pursue her? It seemed either direction was equally fraught.

When they had a moment between approaches, Prudence said, "Lady Featherstone, how did you manage your nerves when you came for your season?"

The lady whipped out her fan and said behind it, "Strong wine when I could get it and deep breaths when I could not."

Prudence took a few deep breaths.

⋙⋘

THOUGH AMBROSE LIKED Vance well enough, at least usually, he really had not expected the fellow to turn up at the duchess's ball. The duchess held a dim view of anybody coming from trade so recently. He suspected she would only be satisfied with that sort of history if it originated in the 1600's.

However, she had made an exception because Miss Rightstone would indeed need pawning off on *somebody*. He had, himself, been cornered into taking her into supper at a ball during her first season.

Never again. She was all but illiterate. When he'd corrected her on her assumption that Shakespeare was yet living, she'd rapped his knuckles with her fan and announced that she did not care for his tone. She was a fool.

Despite her hefty dowry, there had so far been no takers. Ambrose very much doubted Vance would fall for it.

The viscountess and the duchess had really better focus their efforts on somebody like Lymington. He was to be a duke, but his lack of understanding was equal to Miss Rightstone's. If the lady could be satisfied to listen to a man tell the same endless stories about his horses, Lymington was her man.

In any case, Vance seemed far too interested in Lady Prudence to be drawn in by the likes of Miss Rightstone. What did that fellow mean, taking the lady's first? For that matter, what did they all mean, those men lining up to be introduced?

He would very much like to chase them off, if it could be done with any sort of dignity. Which, it could not.

Still, he had secured supper. *He* had secured the most sought-after place on the lady's card.

He had, over a long night of thinking and drinking, finally admitted that he had quite fallen for the lady.

There were so many problems with it! He had not meant to develop feelings for anybody, he had too much to accomplish. Even if he had wished such a thing, she was not the least attracted to him and might even find him repulsive.

Then, he had no place for a lady in his house. How was somebody like Lady Prudence to descend each day to find all sorts of rough people coming and going? How was she to entertain her friends while he had his operation going in his dining room?

None of it made any sense whatsoever. And yet…

He knew what he wanted, but what was it that Lady Prudence wanted? Depsford thought she wished for somebody docile that she could manage.

Well, he'd never thought of himself as docile so he could only hope his valet was wrong.

He was not even certain how to go about such a thing.

PRUDENCE FOUND HER nerves beginning to settle once the dancing commenced. It was often the case, she thought, that when one felt nerves in considering a thing, the nerves faded away once a person was actually doing the thing.

Mr. Vance was of course helpful in that regard. He was unflagging in his cheerfulness and kept the conversation going on mostly neutral topics. He was also a wit, which proved entertaining.

Her next partners were genial too, though she found Lord Lymington a little bit of work. He had somehow managed to tell her the same story about a horse named Macbeth three times in three different ways. He did not seem to notice that he did so, ending each tale with a vigorous nod and then a solemn, "Horses, you know."

She did find her nerves picking up again as her dance with Lord Ryland grew near. Prudence reminded herself that it was only a dance. And then supper. Where he'd probably wish to talk about a murder.

But maybe he would not talk about murder. That was something to hope for anyway.

As she waited for Lord Ryland to collect her, Lord Lymington had escorted her to the edge of the ballroom.

Prudence blushed as she spotted Lady Featherstone and her friends eyeing the situation with interest.

The duchess was smiling, Lady Easton was nodding, Lady Redfield looked very encouraging, and Lady Featherstone had gone so far as to apply an opera glass to her eye. All that was missing from the scene was Lady Mendleton and her remarkably destructive grandbaby.

"Anyway," Lord Lymington said with a sigh, "horses, you know."

Prudence nodded dutifully, though this horse of his sounded

like an awful lot of aggravation.

Lord Ryland was crossing the ballroom floor and looked very determined about it.

"Lady Prudence," he said, holding out his arm.

"Oh, say, Ryland," Lord Lymington said, "did I hear right that you bought Rendiver's stallion?"

"No," Lord Ryland said, leading her off.

Behind her, Lord Lymington said, "Now, I was sure that I did hear that."

As they took their place, Prudence said. "Lord Lymington seemed disappointed to be misinformed."

"He is not misinformed. Not about the horse anyway," Lord Ryland said. "I just did not care to engage in a conversation that went round and round." He paused, then said, "Horses, you know."

Prudence laughed despite herself. Poor Lord Lymington. "I rather think I do know, now that we have danced. Though, he seems a gentle sort of soul."

This recommendation seemed to strike Lord Ryland in some particular way, as his expression grew serious. "Is that a temperament you would prefer?" he asked.

The question caught her off guard and she did not know precisely how to answer it. She did prefer a gentle soul, just not Lord Lymington's gentle soul.

Fortunately, the music struck up and their attention was turned to the steps.

As she had suspected, Lord Ryland was a graceful partner and led her expertly. Though he was so tall and broad-shouldered, she did not feel overwhelmed by him. He actually had a very light touch and guided her gently.

She had not expected that.

Nor had she expected any feelings to arise from their close proximity.

And yet, they did arise. She could not exactly name them. Dancing with him felt somehow more intimate than it had with the other gentlemen. Or any gentleman before. He was a larger-than-life figure in both stature and confidence, and yet close to him it did not seem so.

There was something more contained about him on a dance floor. She had mostly viewed him talking about murder or chasing down Lucknell.

That first night at Copeland Hall, he'd practically burst in, then strode out in pursuit of the man. Then in Swanley, he'd chased him through the wood and come out of it with a banged head. And of course, the society meeting all about crime.

This showed a more civilized side to him. It seemed a more manageable side.

She liked this side very much.

IF AMBROSE HAD learned anything at all from his years managing the criminal society, it was to see a pattern emerging. He was beginning to notice a pattern now.

Lady Prudence was so graceful, so feminine, and also so cautious. She was not at all like a typical London lady, which seemed to come in two general varieties.

There was the brash and teasing lady who liked to think she skated the line of propriety though she did not. And then there was the fan-waving type who looked as if she had just been born into the world and was shocked at what she'd found.

There was no pretense to Lady Prudence. She was not attempting to present herself a certain way. She was just herself and Ambrose began to think her rather complicated.

He also began to think she did indeed have a preference for a docile man. Not for the reason his valet had speculated on. She did not wish to manage anybody. But for the reason that a very mild man was not threatening.

She had seemed to favor Mr. Clamarin the evening before,

and this evening she had named Lymington a gentle soul.

And why did she have that preference? Ambrose could not be certain, but he had an inkling that Lucknell had something to do with it.

She had been through a war, and like so many men who had been through an actual battle, she had not come out the other side the same as she had been.

He had seen such things before in women who had been subjected to a crime—their friends and family would remark on how they'd changed or how they were always fearful though the danger had long passed.

Though Lucknell had never got anywhere with his plans, perhaps the situation had terrorized Lady Prudence to such a degree that she could not put it aside.

It was a theory, anyway, and he was determined to discover if he were right.

The dance had ended and he took her into the supper. The duke's table was already crowded.

Ambrose scanned it as he slipped a coin to a footman to ensure the proper attention, then he led Lady Prudence to the ideal location.

It was across from Lord Marchstone and Lady Felicia. They had just become engaged a week prior and would have eyes only for each other. The less intrusion from other people the better.

The footman, having been tipped, had filled their wine glasses as soon as they'd sat down.

"I should have asked," Lord Ryland said, "do you take wine? At my society meeting, you had only tea."

"I do take wine, just not then," Lady Prudence said.

Ambrose allowed a silence to develop. He'd found that simple strategy to be invaluable in encouraging another person to talk and had often used it in an interrogation. In general, people had the instinct to fill a void.

Lady Prudence sipped her wine. Then she said, "I must admit, Lord Ryland, that I was not entirely comfortable that evening. I thought wine might make me even more…"

"Even more…?"

"Feeling as if I would like to run from the room," she said.

"I am sorry to hear it," Ambrose said. "I would not wish anyone to experience unpleasantness within my walls."

"Mr. Clamarin says it is because I was thinking of the real people involved, while to others it is more of a game."

Was that what Mr. Clamarin said? It seemed the fellow had been quite solicitous.

"It is not a game to me," Ambrose said. "It is *because* these victims are real that I involve myself in this work. Criminals are like a rising tide and the criminal society is the dam that at least holds some of them back. It is true that some attend the meetings for amusement, but they are helpful in the effort despite themselves."

Lady Prudence looked thoughtful. "I had not considered it in that light," she said.

"In any case, Lady Featherstone will not press you to attend when she understands your feelings."

"Oh no, I will not tell her. She has been so kind to me and my father, and she is so enthusiastic about the evenings. I am certain I will get used to it."

Ambrose was both pleased that she would come, and not certain if she ought to.

He said, "Aside from Mr. Clamarin's ideas, are you perhaps more struck than another person due to your recent upheavals at the hands of Lucknell? I only ask because it has been my observation that a person who has found themselves a victim can carry unseen injuries. Injuries to the heart and mind that make them more sensitive or fearful than they once were."

Lady Prudence did not immediately answer, but rather took another sip of wine. A much larger sip than she had done.

Ambrose motioned for the footman to refill her glass.

She said, "I do not know if I have grown more sensitive. I am not certain I would have ever been much good at solving crimes. If Lucknell has left any lasting impression upon me, it was that he would not listen, he would not accept no. It was as if I might shout my opinions from the rooftops and they would just vanish into the air as if they had never been said. I felt run over and do not wish to ever feel so again."

And now they'd got to it. That was why she seemed to favor a mild man. Lucknell had made the lady feel powerless.

Women *were* powerless in so many ways, but it was a gentleman's duty to afford them every consideration so that they did not feel it unnecessarily. It was one of society's unspoken agreements—the accommodation of a lady must always be gracious and liberal.

A decent man understood that responsibility. A woman must have a voice and some power of her own, even if that power was given her by her protectors rather than the courts.

Ambrose was certain that while the duke had paid for the ball, it had been the duchess who'd made all the decisions, as it should be. That lady probably made most of the decisions between them outside of investments and managing the estate, also as it should be.

Lucknell had broken the societal agreement and Lady Prudence had felt herself powerless against it.

"He did not act as a gentleman," Ambrose said. "A gentleman must always be guided by a lady's opinion. If he is not wanted, he may lament it in private. To force oneself is criminal."

"Yes, but he did," Lady Prudence said. "That helped me to understand that there were such men. Lucknell is not alone in the temperament, I am sure, and he has opened my eyes to it."

Ambrose nodded. "I only hope, Lady Prudence, that you do not confuse a weak man for a safe harbor. That sort may not give you trouble, but he will not be very competent at protecting you either."

He noted a faint blush on her lovely cheeks and felt he'd made a point that struck home.

He certainly hoped so. He could do many things with the right effort and discipline, but he could not turn himself into a Clamarin or a Lymington.

CHAPTER FOURTEEN

PRUDENCE HAD NOT got much sleep. For one, they did not get home until three, though her father had left hours before. For another, once she was in her bed she could not help but think of her conversation with Lord Ryland over supper.

How had he got her to reveal so much of her private thoughts? She told him things she had only said to her father.

It was something in his manner. When he was not chasing down a man or talking about a murder, he was very easy to talk to. Comforting even.

His opinions of the female lot were to be admired. Though, she did of course wonder whether he would always practice what he preached.

Lord Ryland did seem the sort of man who was used to gaining his point and getting his way. Might not his future wife, whoever she may be, find herself going along very pleasantly…until she was overruled?

But then, he'd made a valid point that she had not considered. A very gentle gentleman might not have the strength to protect her if there were a need.

She had really not considered that.

But she was not certain that was enough to amend her decision about the sort of gentleman she sought. Yes, there had been danger with Lucknell and she had been grateful for Lord Ryland's strength, but surely that had passed and another danger lurking was highly unlikely.

There was something very unsettling about Lord Ryland. She was both attracted to him, and sure she should not be.

She ought to rule all her decisions with her head and leave her flighty feelings out of it. Feelings were not to be trusted, as they did have the habit of changing so often. Considered judgments were far more reliable.

Now, she turned her thoughts from such considerations. Her riding habit had been finished, a horse had been secured, and she was on her way to the park. A ride would no doubt clear her head.

As they made their way toward the park, she, Lady Featherstone, and her father rode in an open carriage while a groom rode Spirit behind. Prudence had got a look at the mare before they set off and she seemed very spirited indeed.

"Papa," Prudence said, "I am so pleased that you agreed to come out with us."

The earl nodded and said, "Lady Barlow has advised as much fresh air as I can bear. She says she herself was once averse to it, but she has become quite accustomed and it does seem to have a good effect. I think she may be right."

"I think she is right too."

"Ah yes," Lady Featherstone said, "Lady Barlow was once a very sickly creature. Lady Heathway hired a nurse and between her and Sir Henry's ministrations they chased her out of bed. The lady discovered she was not dying after all and is in much better health."

"She does say those early days of treatment were very trying," the earl said, "but she carried on despite it. I must attempt to do the same."

Prudence found herself delighted with Lady Barlow. It seemed the lady had been through her own trials of ill health and was now determined to pass on her knowledge gained. Further, she was listened to, which made her better than any doctor her father had yet seen.

They'd gone through the gates of the park and made their way to a mounting block. A footman opened the carriage door and Prudence climbed out.

"Do be careful, my dear," the earl said. "Taking the air is one thing but falling off a horse is another."

"Do not fret, Papa," she said, "I have not fallen from a horse in ages." As she said it, she glanced at Spirit. The groom was leading the mare to the block and she did a little dance as she went.

Prudence had no intention of falling off, though she thought Spirit would require two very spirited hands on the reins.

MR. CLAMARIN HAD very sensibly set a watch on Lady Featherstone's house. The moment Lady Prudence was seen departing in a riding habit, he was to be informed.

The boy he'd hired had come not an hour ago to tell him that while she'd set off in a carriage, she wore a habit and a groom rode a mare behind.

Certainly she was on her way to the park.

He had hurriedly dressed and made his way to the stables where his hired horse was currently housed.

He knew how to ride a horse, naturally. Though, it was not his preferred mode of transportation. He much more favored the comforts of a carriage and allowing somebody else to manage the beasts involved in the operation.

Nevertheless, today he must ride and look like he enjoyed it.

He'd ordered the groom to hurry in saddling the horse and set off through the crowded streets. He had been clever in selecting a stable nearby the park and lucky in finding a stall open for renting.

He'd also been clever in choosing his horse—Muddy was a large but plodding sort of animal who did not appear to get excited by what he saw around him. Or excited about anything at all, really.

Mr. Clamarin was through the gates and now he must just find Lady Prudence. Hopefully, she would not be surrounded by gentlemen wishing to have her attention.

He made his way to the carriage road. He was certain that was the route they would have taken as Lady Featherstone and the earl would wish to stay close by Lady Prudence.

And there she was. She rode a fine mare alongside Lady Featherstone's barouche.

He pushed Muddy to speed up, though the horse did not seem inclined to do anything at all energetic. He eventually convinced him to go at a rather lackluster trot.

"Lady Prudence," he called from behind.

Though this calling out was not meant to alarm anybody, and had likely not alarmed Lady Prudence, her horse seemed to take exception to it. The mare danced sideways and the lady had to duck under tree branches to avoid getting knocked out of the saddle.

A groom leapt off the carriage and hurried toward the horse. Lady Prudence maneuvered it away from the tree and said, "It's quite all right, she was only startled. Hello, Mr. Clamarin."

The horse calmed and Lady Prudence adjusted her hat and brushed the marks from the branches that had swept across her coat around the arms and shoulders.

"Oh my dear," Lady Featherstone said, "a leaf in your hair. Just there."

Lady Prudence removed the offending greenery and patted her horse's neck.

Mr. Clamarin said, "I do apologize, Lady Prudence. Lady Featherstone, how do you do?"

"Very well and no harm done," Lady Featherstone said. "Earl, may I present Mr. Clamarin? He is a key member of Lord Ryland's society. We collaborate together often, as our minds tend to race along at high speed, always along the same lines. Mr.

Clamarin, this is the Earl of Copeland."

"Lord Copeland," Mr. Clamarin said, bowing from the saddle.

"Ah, the society," the earl said, "I did not attend the evening."

"Were you planning to attend in future?" Mr. Clamarin asked, by way of making conversation.

"No, I do not think so. Unless Lady Barlow recommends it."

Who on earth was Lady Barlow?

The carriage set off again at a walk and Lady Prudence steered her horse back on the path.

"Do come along with us if you like, Mr. Clamarin," Lady Featherstone said.

"Delighted," he answered.

As they went along, Lady Featherstone chattered on about the society, often asking Lady Prudence for her own impressions. That lady's impressions appeared suitably vague, though he knew she had not enjoyed the evening.

How was he to have a private conversation with Lady Prudence with her father and Lady Featherstone so engaged in conversation with her? He had hoped that whoever was in the carriage would occupy themselves.

"My locket!" Lady Prudence suddenly cried. "It's come off somewhere!"

The coachman stopped the carriage. The groom began looking around on the ground.

"When were you last certain you wore it, my dear?" the earl asked.

"I do not know," Lady Prudence said. "Oh, Papa! Mama's locket!"

"It's bound to be here somewhere," Lady Featherstone said, "I'll search the carriage."

Mr. Clamarin had a better idea of which somewhere the locket was likely located. He was certain it would have come off in that scuffle with her horse. A tree branch would have caught it.

At least, he hoped so. Otherwise, the chain had simply broken of its own accord and the locket could be anywhere.

"I will go back and search under the tree," he said to Lady Prudence. To the groom, he said, "Begin here and slowly make your way back to me."

The groom nodded and Mr. Clamarin set off, pushing Muddy as fast as that layabout was inclined to go. If he could find her locket, it would be a feather in his cap.

He reached the tree and there it was, glinting gold among the blades of grass. Never had a feather gone into his cap so effortlessly.

He dismounted and snatched it up. The chain had broken, no doubt becoming snagged on a branch as he had suspected. He held it over his head for Lady Prudence to see.

The relief on her features was profound. Perhaps finding the locket was more than just a single feather in his cap.

As he thought with pleasure of her gratefulness in getting her locket back, two things slowly dawned on him. One, the locket had no hinge. Two, it was far heavier than he would have expected.

It was no ordinary locket.

⟫⟫⟫✦⟪⟪⟪

AMBROSE SAT IN his library with Depsford, waiting for Parker to join them.

"Will you send her flowers?" Depsford asked.

"Send who flowers?" Ambrose asked, though he knew full well who.

"Lady Prudence," Depsford said. "Clamarin won't think of it and you'll have beat him to the punch."

"Are you suggesting that I am in some sort of competition with Mr. Clamarin? I am a marquess," he said haughtily. Though, he did not actually feel very haughty. Was it possible he *was* in competition with Mr. Clamarin? The notion seemed absurd.

"Even so," Depsford said.

"I see," Ambrose said. "And if Mr. Clamarin *did* have the idea to send flowers, what sort would he send?"

Depsford rubbed his chin. "Hard to say. Flowers got all sorts of meanings, and yet I don't know one that says, 'I am Mr. Clamarin, a very dull and quiet person.'"

"I believe flowers are meant to express feelings, not personalities."

"Does Mr. Clamarin have feelings? I hadn't noticed."

Ambrose had in fact thought of sending flowers. He had not decided on it though. For one, such a gesture might frighten the lady off. For another, there was no flower that said, 'I am a mild man.' Or what he really should say if he were going with the truth, 'I may not be an overly mild man, but I am not Lucknell.'

Parker opened the door and strode through it, closing it behind him. His butler carried a rolled-up piece of paper and said, "This just arrived. It was left in the dry box at the Seven Dials."

Ambrose looked up with interest. There were locked boxes set strategically across the town. Anybody who wished to give them information about a crime could leave an anonymous note.

The boxes were reinforced iron, with a complicated locking system and they were securely set in stone. They were located in places a person could pass by but not be observed if they put something in the box. Alleyways going from one place to another with no overlooking windows were preferred.

It was surprising how often something would turn up. Ambrose was certain that most of the notes had come from wives who wished to see the back of a no-good husband.

Regularly beat your wife and then come home with bloodied clothes one night and admit to a murder? That fellow might just find himself the subject of a note. He had not failed to notice how often a wife wept at a hanging, seemingly inconsolable and yet surprisingly dry-eyed.

Those not being able to write a note themselves took advantage of certain scribes who asked no questions and met their customers in what amounted to a Catholic confessional with a curtain between them.

There were secrets all over London, and on occasion some-body had their own reasons that compelled them to tell one of them.

"I believe it's about your father," Parker said.

"What!" Ambrose shouted, leaping up from his chair. "Give it here."

He hastily unrolled the paper.

About the old marquess, the mistake was a confusion in the order of his name.

"That could not be more vague," Depsford said.

"The order of my father's name?" Ambrose said. "Our sur-name is Thorpe. What could be mistaken about the order? Does this reference my father's given name, perhaps? Martin?"

Ambrose paced the room, then stopped. "Maybe they'd been after another Thorpe. It's certainly not an uncommon name. Maybe they had really meant to look for a man named Thorpe Martin."

"I'll set some men on the search for a man with that name," Parker said.

"And let's not rule out an anagram. That would be about the order too," Depsford ventured.

Ambrose had not thought of that, which was one of the rea-sons he kept Depsford around despite his daily effronteries.

"Work on it, Depsford. And have Clamarin work on it too. He's good with puzzles of that nature."

Somebody out there knew something. He'd always known it, of course. There had been three men attacking his father's carriage that night, so at least three knew about it.

It would not be so unusual for men of that kind to have a falling out. It would not be unusual for one or all of them to tell someone what they'd done, usually a woman and usually in a drunken moment.

But why would somebody go to the trouble to tell *him*? It

could not be a feud between the villains, as if one was caught it was inevitable that they'd all be caught. They would know that.

This was likely a person, possibly a wife, who wished somebody in her life to be captured. Though, it was atypically vague. A woman wishing to get rid of a criminal husband typically wrote down his name. This was more of a game.

Who had written it?

"Speaking of Mr. Clamarin," Parker said, "Robbie has just come back from his watch over Lady Prudence. Apparently, they were riding in the park together."

"Were they?" Ambrose said, attempting to keep the irritation out of his voice. What business did Clamarin have, riding in the park with the lady?

"They did not go together. Rather, Clamarin spotted her and hightailed it in her direction. At least, as fast as he *could* go on what Robbie says was an old and heavy-looking horse. Then, there was a whole palaver of Lady Prudence losing a necklace and Clamarin finding it for her and looking the right hero."

A hero? Clamarin?

"What time was this?" Ambrose asked.

"Around about four," Parker answered.

"I see," Ambrose said. Though, he really did not see at all. What was Clamarin doing, chasing after Lady Prudence and finding things for her?

As for himself, he very well might ride to the park at four on the morrow. He also very well might send flowers.

In fact, he would. He would send daffodils. They would signal regard without pinpointing any violent feelings. He did not wish to frighten her.

Though, he *was* feeling a little violent at the moment.

MR. CLAMARIN HURRIED back to his house. He had arrived at Lord

Ryland's house past six, after his jaunt in the park with Lady Prudence. He'd been giddy over the success of the outing and only went there to briefly show his face. At least, he had been giddy when he'd arrived. Not exactly giddy by the time he'd left, though.

Parker had shown him the note left in a dry box nearby the Seven Dials.

About the old marquess, the mistake was a confusion in the order of his name.

The only people who knew that were himself, Lucknell, and…Paxton.

Until recently, he'd never worried about either Lucknell or Paxton turning on him. If one went down, they all did—they were in too deep together.

That though, assumed all three of them were rational. Paxton had not been rational in Kent. He'd been having nightmares and had begun to seem unhinged. Then he was gone to nobody knew where.

An unhinged man was highly dangerous. Rational thoughts, the prediction of actions and reactions, and a care for one's neck, might all be gone out the window.

As Parker had stood there explaining what they suspected, he'd felt as if the room were collapsing in on him. He'd used all his self-control to keep his expression neutral. Once the butler had finished, Clamarin had claimed he must hurry off to an engagement, though he did not know if that had been believed. He was not exactly known for a robust social life.

He'd made a copy of the note and assured Parker that he would work on it later in the evening. He must pretend to work on it, and preferably come up with a plausible solution that was not the actual solution.

It might be possible. So far, Parker, Depsford, and Ryland were all focused on Ryland's surname. Thorpe.

The only bit of luck in this calamity was that Paxton had

worded things not quite correct. There had never been a confusion of the order of the name, there had been a confusion about the order of the name of the title. Ryland.

He found Lucknell once more lounging in his banyan and drinking his port. Mr. Clamarin began to suspect he'd never get that item of clothing back.

He'd wished Lucknell to be off to Kent this day, but his associate had claimed that the morrow would be soon enough. He was waiting for some clothes from the tailor to replace what he'd lost at Swanley.

Mr. Clamarin had been irritated by the delay, but he now saw it as fortuitous. There was no longer a reason to go to Kent and risk a break-in.

"I need a drink," he said, crossing the room and pouring himself a large brandy.

"As do I," Lucknell said. "I am bored out of my skull hiding out here all day long."

"Prepare to throw over your boredom, then."

Lucknell sat up. "Why? What has happened?"

Clamarin took a long draught to steady himself. "First, I believe I know where the diamond is. It is round Lady Prudence's neck, enclosed in gold and meant to look like a locket."

"How do you know? Did she tell you?"

"She lost it in the park and I found it for her. I cannot tell if she knows its value or not. I do not believe so. She was distressed when it was missing because of its sentimental value. But, neither she nor her father had been positively panicked, as they would have been if they'd thought they'd lost the Lisbon Diamond."

"Why do you think the diamond is in the locket, though?"

"One, it is a locket with no hinge. Two, it is far heavier than it should be. So, it is either the diamond, or it is solid gold. My instincts tell me it is the diamond."

"You had it in your hands! Why did you give it back?"

"Because I was in full view of the lady, her father, and Lady Featherstone. Had I known, I would have ground it into the dirt and pretended it could not be found and then retrieved it later. I did not guess at it until I picked it up."

"Ah well, we must just find a way to get it from her. Perhaps you could offer to take it to a jeweler to make the clasp more secure?"

"That is no more subtle than just running away with it in the park."

"We could have another made and fill it with lead! She'd never know!"

Clamarin considered the idea, which was not bad at all. Though, how to retrieve the locket was not their only problem.

"There's more," he said. He pulled out a copy of the note from the dry box. "This was left in the Seven Dials box."

As Lucknell read it, his face went white. "Paxton."

"Yes, Paxton. What are we going to do about it?"

"I don't know. He's slippery. He might not even be in London still. It would be like him to leave the note on his way out."

"Indeed," he said.

"But what is wrong with him? If we hang, he goes with us. Why is he suddenly wracked with guilt?" Lucknell asked plaintively.

"I am not certain it is suddenly. He may simply have reached a breaking point. Do you not recall the night things went...so very wrong? It was he that fired the shot and we had to pour a pint of gin down his throat to calm him down. Perhaps that panic never really went away and now he's lost his faculties."

"Idiot," Lucknell said.

"In the meantime," Mr. Clamarin said, "Ryland's people are looking at his surname, not the name of his title. We'll need a solution that both fits and leads away from the truth."

"I'm no good at puzzles of that sort," Lucknell said.

"No, you are not," Mr. Clamarin said.

CHAPTER FIFTEEN

PRUDENCE CAME DOWN the stairs the following afternoon in high spirits, ready to go to the park. They'd had a night at home the evening before and it had been very pleasant indeed!

Her father and Lord Featherstone got on so well and occupied themselves with categorizing Lord Featherstone's various collections of bath salts.

The lord had been keeping them in brown paper packets but had now purchased elegant glass jars. Her father had purchased a cabinet with a glass front to store them in.

The selection was to be located in a nook at the end of the upper hall and the bath boy would bring any that were requested. They had gone so far as to make a printed menu for a would-be bather, outlining which salts should be taken for which condition.

She could not say Thomas had been any particular help in the effort, though he did appear impressed with the two lords' handiwork, which tickled them both. He'd also wrangled a promise from those two gentlemen that he might take a bath with salts on the morrow, which would be his first in both salts and actual hot water.

Prudence and Lady Featherstone had done some talking, some reading, and some sewing. They'd had tea, and then a cherry cordial before going up. She'd really felt at home, as if she did not need to stand on ceremony. She guessed Lady Featherstone might feel the same, as she'd taken to calling her Pru—just

177

as Prudence's father did.

Now, they would go to the park in the barouche and Prudence would ride Spirit.

Her father had bowed out this time as he'd just received a letter from Lady Barlow and was far more interested in reading it and then writing a reply.

Seemingly in place of Lord Copeland, Lady Featherstone's dog Tulip was to accompany them. According to the lady, though Tulip was generally against walking, she held a very favorable opinion of riding in a carriage.

This evening, they would attend Lady Easton's musicale evening. Lady Featherstone was quite looking forward to it, though she was rather concerned that they should arrive on time. She'd mentioned it several times the night before, as apparently Lady Easton was a stickler about the clock.

Prudence entered the drawing room and Lady Featherstone said, "There you are, Pru. Well, will you guess what's turned up? Flowers!"

Just then, Danforth brought in a vase of daffodils. They were quite lovely and cheerful.

"Who has sent you flowers, Lady Featherstone?" Prudence asked, touched by the lady's enthusiasm over the gesture.

"Me? Nobody! They are for you. From Lord Ryland."

"For me? From Lord Ryland. But I do not see why he should—"

"Here is the note," Lady Featherstone said, handing it to her. "I have been a proper chaperone by reading it. I hope you do not mind."

"Of course I do not mind," Prudence said hurriedly. "There can be nothing at all private communicated between us."

"At least not yet," Lady Featherstone said cheerfully.

Prudence glanced down at the note.

Lady Prudence—

I thank you for allowing me to escort you into supper and show-

ing yourself such a thoughtful and genial partner.

Ambrose Thorpe

There was nothing particularly wrong with the note. In truth, it was in some way touching. But it was unnecessary. It was too much.

"Daffodils, too," Lady Featherstone went on enthusiastically. "They speak of regard. It is just the right tone, I think."

"Well, it was very kind, though not at all called for," Prudence said, laying the note next to the vase. "I suppose we really should be off now?"

THEY HAD ARRIVED at the park in good time and Prudence had mounted Spirit. The horse was still very lively, however, she seemed more composed upon being ridden by a person she had already become acquainted with the day before.

Prudence had worried that Tulip's presence might disturb the horse, as the little dog did take to yapping and growling for no apparent reason, but it seemed Spirit had seen her fair share of yappy dogs and was neither concerned nor impressed.

They passed by single gentlemen who tipped their hats and young couples riding out together. It seemed that absolutely everybody knew Lady Featherstone. Tulip was no less of a celebrity, as there were those who called out to her, while she returned an enthusiastic bark.

Very suddenly, Mr. Clamarin appeared beside Prudence atop his rather stodgy horse.

"Lady Prudence, Lady Featherstone," he said. "I spotted you a good distance away, but I dared not shout out as that did startle your horse yesterday."

"Hello, Mr. Clamarin," Lady Featherstone said. "Very good thinking on your part."

"We must be on the same schedule," Prudence said. "Is this your regular time for coming to the park?"

"It is a recent schedule, though I do find this time of day

pleasant. It is not yet so crowded as it will be. About yesterday, though, I did feel terrible about the damage to your necklace," Mr. Clamarin said.

"I do not know why you should," Prudence said. "There was no real harm done."

"No harm done?" Mr. Clamarin asked in evident surprise. "Your necklace was lost and had it not been found…"

"But it was found," Prudence said.

"You must permit me to make amends," Mr. Clamarin said. "Please allow me to take it to a jeweler to repair the chain."

Tulip stared at Mr. Clamarin and growled ferociously.

"Never mind Tulip, she is always so naughty. That is a very kind offer, Mr. Clamarin," Lady Featherstone said, "but I have beat you to it. It's gone to Mr. Gray this morning."

"Mr. Gray?" Mr. Clamarin said.

"Indeed, yes, everybody uses him. He's quite good."

They had come to a turning and a quieter area of the park, away from the Serpentine.

Old trees dotted the landscape and it seemed almost incredible to Prudence that this scene was to be viewed in London. Just beyond the park's borders, there would be thousands of people going about their business.

But, for one blessed moment at least, they had this lovely expanse to themselves. Prudence supposed by the next hour there would be far more people milling about.

"I do not believe I know Mr. Gray," Mr. Clamarin said. "Where is his shop? You must at least allow me to pay for the repairs."

Before Mr. Gray could be discussed further, a horde of young boys, all eleven or twelve years old, came around a turn just ahead of them. Before Prudence could fathom what they were doing, they'd surrounded Lady Featherstone's carriage.

"Give us coins, your ladyship," the supposed leader said to Lady Featherstone.

"Give 'em over, princess, and we'll be on our way," another

said.

A young groom had driven the carriage, as Lady Featherstone's coachman had been given leave to go to a wedding. The boy stood up and raised his whip. "Off with you," he shouted.

The other groom pushed away a boy who had grabbed at Lady Featherstone's sleeve. That groom was instantly set upon by three of the rogues who tackled him to the ground. The groom acting as coachman brought his whip down, striking one of the boys.

Mr. Clamarin called, "Now, that is enough, you scoundrels. Move on."

Nobody seemed to pay any attention to him. The groom at the head of the carriage was knocked off the box and his whip taken from him. Another of the boys was attempting to get hold of Tulip as Lady Featherstone screamed.

Prudence steered Spirit, who was very close to rearing, around to the boy and beat him with her crop. He retreated, but she feared not for long.

"Mr. Clamarin," she called, "I'll take this side, you take that side."

Prudence was certain that with she and Mr. Clamarin wielding their crops and most of the boys currently occupied with wrestling the grooms who were putting up a very good fight, they could protect Lady Featherstone until somebody came along to help.

If only Mr. Clamarin did not seem frozen in his spot.

Behind her, Prudence heard hoofbeats pounding. Somebody *was* coming, and just in time. She turned her head and saw Lord Ryland atop a seventeen-hand black stallion.

Lord Ryland. Thank heavens.

The lord reined in and set upon the boys, beating them with his crop. They, seeming to understand that reinforcements had arrived and they were reinforcements that would not be overcome, began to scatter.

As the last of them turned to run, Lord Ryland leaned down

and grabbed the back of his threadbare coat, lifting him off his feet.

One of the boys running away shouted, "Don't dare talk!"

"He will talk when I am done with him," Lord Ryland said. "Ladies, have you been hurt?"

Lady Featherstone hugged Tulip, who for all her prior yapping and growling just now buried her head under Lady Featherstone's arms in a less than courageous fashion. "Tulip and I are unharmed. Pru?"

"Perfectly fine," Prudence said, though she did feel a bit shaken.

"Thank goodness you came along, Lord Ryland," Lady Featherstone said.

"Indeed," Mr. Clamarin said, seeming to have woken from his frozen state. "We attempted to drive them off, but they were putting up a fight."

Prudence blushed for Mr. Clamarin. The *we* he referred to consisted of her and the grooms.

Lord Ryland dismounted, still holding the struggling boy. The grooms had both got to their feet, dusty and no doubt bruised but seeming not terribly hurt by the encounter.

"What do you have in the box to tie this creature up?" Lord Ryland asked.

"I don't need tyin' up," the boy said. "I'll go quietly."

"You will go quietly and you'll go tied," Lord Ryland said.

The grooms lifted the top of the coachman's seat and rummaged around. "Will a spare pair of reins do, my lord?"

"Excellent, yes."

The boy was tied up in the next minutes.

"Mr. Clamarin, take this scoundrel to Sir Robert on St. Michael's Street. He is the nearest magistrate. You can manage it, yes?"

Prudence was not so certain Mr. Clamarin *could* manage it, though he said, "Yes, of course, Lord Ryland."

"I will escort the ladies home and then repair there to interrogate the boy. I will have the names and addresses of every single one of them."

Lord Ryland had tied the boy's hands in front of him, leaving a long lead coming out of the knot. He handed it up to Mr. Clamarin.

Mr. Clamarin, seeming to have located his bravery, yanked on the lead and said sternly, "No more nonsense from you!" He then turned his horse and lumbered off in the direction of St. Michael's Street.

"You two," Lord Ryland said to the grooms, "are you fit to carry on?"

In unison, they said, "Yes, my lord!"

"Then let us proceed."

One groom climbed onto the coachman's box and swept up the reins while the other hopped on the bar at the back of the carriage and it rumbled forward.

"You have had a shock, Lady Featherstone," Lord Ryland said. "I suggest you and Lady Prudence seek out quiet when you return home to better recover yourselves."

"It was quite the adventure," Lady Featherstone said. "I never thought to be set upon in broad daylight!"

"These gangs of boys are becoming more common," Lord Ryland said. "They look for opportunity and when they saw you with a very young coachman and nobody about, they took their chance."

"I am surprised they did not hesitate in seeing we had Mr. Clamarin with us," Lady Featherstone said.

Lord Ryland pressed his lips together to stop himself from smiling. "Yes, well, some gentlemen do not appear very threatening. I suspect those little criminals were given a far harder time by your grooms and Lady Prudence."

The groom on the back of the coach beamed. Prudence could not see the driver's expression, though his head was nodding vigorously.

Prudence found her own head in a whirl. Mr. Clamarin might

not have been there at all for the amount of good he did. She had heard of men freezing at the onset of a battle. The fear overtook them and they could not move. But, she had not imagined a man would freeze in the face of children, violent though they may have been.

Of course, if that were what had happened to him, she could not condemn him. She could only sympathize with his plight. And yet, she did feel a little bit condemning.

Her utter relief at seeing Lord Ryland had told the tale, she supposed. She had, in that moment, experienced the utmost confidence that he would rescue them.

Lord Ryland had pointed out, when they'd dined together at the ball, that a mild gentleman might not be relied upon to protect. She had understood the validity of the point, but now she had experienced it firsthand.

It caused so much confusion! She had been resolved to marry a mild man, but did that mean she would only have herself to count on should another dangerous situation cross her path?

But if she were to wed a man like Lord Ryland…then she might always feel protected though likely lose herself and her opinions in the union. Would herself and her judgments be worth trading for physical safety?

She did not know.

Would she not resent a man like Mr. Clamarin should something like this happen again? She very well might, as she felt a bit resentful now.

But then, would she not resent a man like Lord Ryland when there was no such danger about and she was quietly at home, having been overrun?

How was it possible that there was no easy way to turn?

Lord Ryland interrupted her musings. He'd wheeled his horse alongside her and said, "Are you certain you are unhurt, Lady Prudence?"

"Only a little bruised, I think," she said. In truth, her arm was quite sore. She had hit it hard against the carriage door in the midst of the melee.

"My advice is, rest when you get home, decide on the precautions you will take when you enter the park, and then think no more about it. It is not helpful to dwell on a danger that is passed."

Prudence nodded. She wondered if he meant more than what had occurred today. Perhaps he referenced Lucknell too.

They had come to a gate and entered a busy thoroughfare, headed in the direction of Russell Square.

"Do not let us take you out of your way, Lord Ryland," Lady Featherstone said. "We will be quite safe from here."

"It is no inconvenience," the lord said. "I will see you both safely inside your house."

"Then you must come in for tea," Lady Featherstone said.

"Thank you, but I will decline. I have a young rogue to interview. Assuming Mr. Clamarin has managed to get him to the magistrate."

"Poor Mr. Clamarin," Lady Featherstone said. "He is not suited for that sort of encounter."

"No, I do not think he is," Lord Ryland said.

"Goodness!" Lady Featherstone cried. "Prudence, in all the furor, we've completely forgotten about the daffodils."

Prudence felt her cheeks go hot. She *had* forgotten. "I am sorry, Lord Ryland, my manners were somehow lost in the excitement. I thank you for sending the flowers. They are lovely, though it really was not necessary."

"I thank you for accepting them," Lord Ryland said.

Accepting them? Was there something in that? Had there been some option of not accepting them to send a message of disinterest?

She did not know. She'd not heard of anything like that.

Would she have rejected the flowers, though? In truth, she was not so certain of that either. She might have been a deal more certain this morning, but now her thoughts would not settle on one side or the other.

It seemed she was becoming the most indecisive person on earth. She did not find it an attractive quality.

"Do you attend Lady Easton's musicale evening this night, Lady Prudence?" Lord Ryland asked.

"Indeed, we are meant to go. Though, perhaps Lady Featherstone will not feel up to it after what has happened."

"Nonsense," the indomitable lady said. "Tea and biscuits will set me right as rain. In any case, Lady Easton *does not* favor last-minute cancellations. Or last-minute anything, if the truth were told."

They had reached the square, and Danforth and a footman came out to greet them and help Lady Featherstone from the carriage.

"Ladies," Lord Ryland said, tipping his hat, "good day to you and I look forward to this evening, when we will all meet again."

He turned and trotted down the street.

Much to Prudence's surprise, she looked forward to it too.

MR. CLAMARIN WAS well aware of what he was. His strengths did not lie in his physical person but were located in his mind. This had, in general, served him well.

But today! What he would have given to be one of those gentlemen who boldly rushed into a fray.

He had not been, though. The attack had been so unexpected, and he'd not known what to do about it other than tell those scoundrels to move off.

Which, they had not paid the slightest mind to. He might have been a fly buzzing round their ears for all they feared him.

As if that were not bad enough, Lady Prudence had seemed to have no hesitation at all throwing herself into the fight.

And then the final nail in the coffin. Ryland had turned up. Why could it not have been anybody else? But no, it had been

Ryland. He'd somehow divined Lady Prudence's plan to ride in the park and turned up too. It was no accident that he'd been there.

He would not be surprised if Ryland had set a watch on the house and discovered the plan just as he had himself.

Oh yes, Ryland was a man's man. Tall, muscular, all physicality and willing to risk his person. Everything he was not. Ryland must strike Lady Prudence as very impressive.

He had been all but certain that Lucknell had colored Lady Prudence's preferences. He'd been sure she would turn away from that sort of man and instead gravitate to mildness and a gentle manner.

Now, though…she had seen those two temperaments in action. It might have affected her thinking. It might have affected his own ability to charm her and get close to her.

Where did she go this evening? Would Ryland be there? Would the lord take his chance at cementing his victory and earning the lady's gratitude?

Was Ryland intent on pursuing her? If something were to come of it, it would be too ironic to have the ghosts of his dead parents and the diamond they were murdered for all living quietly in the same house unbeknownst to one another.

And where was this Mr. Gray located? Did he dare attempt a break-in to retrieve the necklace?

Mr. Clamarin sighed as he put his key in the door. Mr. Gray, wherever he was located, was a jeweler. He would have his place guarded very well indeed.

He would have to bide his time and wait for another opportunity. Things had not gone all his way on this particular day, but he must take heart. At least he knew the location of the diamond. That was far more than he knew a week ago.

CHAPTER SIXTEEN

AMBROSE HAD BEEN to the magistrate and despite the young rogue's friends warning him not to talk, Tom Janks had talked within an hour. Names and addresses were recorded and the lot of them would be rounded up.

He'd had a conference with Sir Robert and the magistrate had agreed to Ambrose's plan. The boys' parents, if they could be found, would be given the option of signing them into a school of reform located in the countryside. Otherwise, they were off to the Old Bailey to await trial.

Ambrose had founded and funded the school himself after realizing that most young criminals were only doing what they knew how to do to put food in their mouths.

The school was located in a lonely area, ensuring there was nowhere to run. It was founded on self-discipline and grounded with education. There was a working farm that served to provide physical exercise, and classrooms for attaining an education. There was another school five miles down the road that catered to girls.

Breaking the rules at either of the schools meant removing privileges, not a beating, as violence would only beget violence.

The boys were taught a trade that would allow them, after so many years of employment, to support a household. On occasion, it might be that a boy would show a real aptitude for farming and Ambrose would buy him a plot. Or it might be that a particularly clever boy might go on to become a teacher.

The girls were taught those things that might honorably bring in money. Training them as seamstresses, housemaids, and for a gifted student even perhaps as a governess or a teacher for a girls' school had found the most success.

Both boys and girls were taught manners and had their accents worked on so they might travel into spheres that had been closed before. Ambrose had no trouble at all inventing a false history for these children, so they might reenter the world washed clean.

He did not manage to save every young person coming through his doors. Of that, he was well aware. Some would go back to precisely what they had been doing once they were released. Of those that succeeded, presenting them as having come from the merchant class, born of parents suddenly taken by illness, was found a serviceable story.

What he offered was a chance and what he provided to society was to take these ruffians off the streets for at least a few years.

He presumed all of the boys involved in the attack in the park would opt for the school. As invincible as they no doubt imagined themselves, their bravery would waver when they considered the Old Bailey.

Their bravery might waver, but Lady Prudence's had not. Who had been braver than she in the face of that crowd of boys? Ambrose had suspected she was a complicated person, and that certainly was the case. She'd not hesitated to attempt to defend Lady Featherstone from the onslaught.

She was everything feminine, but there was will of iron there too.

He was sorry he could not say the same for Mr. Clamarin.

No, that was not right, he was not particularly sorry. Lady Prudence had got this idea that she required a mild and inoffensive man. Well, all of Mr. Clamarin's mildness had been on stark display and he had been no more effectual than a kitten.

Ambrose hoped viewing that particular debacle had influenced her views. He would do his best to add his own influence this night at Lady Easton's musicale evening.

THE HOUSE HAD been all commotion as the tale of the encounter in the park was told. Lord Copeland had been found in the garden walking, just as he'd promised Lady Barlow he would do in his last letter. Lord Featherstone was fetched from his club.

Both gentlemen were extremely solicitous, which Lady Featherstone seemed to enjoy very much.

In fact, the lady seemed rather invigorated by the attack and its aftermath. She insisted the physician be called in to examine them all, including the grooms.

Those poor boys had not known if they were to be welcomed as heroes or condemned for letting the thing get so far, but they were quickly relieved of their fears. Their mistress gave them a day off on the morrow and an extra pint of ale for this evening's supper.

Lady Featherstone and Prudence revived themselves with a suitable number of biscuits, and though Lord Copeland did not require reviving he was just as enthusiastic in the effort.

Lord Ryland was praised to the skies, first by Lady Featherstone and then by each person who heard of the encounter. "Thank heavens for Lord Ryland," became a near-constant refrain in the Featherstone drawing room.

The physician that had been summoned turned out to be the eminent Sir Henry Halford and Prudence felt rather foolish. That particular gentleman was called in regularly by the palace. How ridiculous that he'd been asked to examine a collection of bruises.

Sir Henry was obviously fond of Lady Featherstone and he'd been very kind about looking at Prudence's arm. He advised a warm vinegar bath and Meggy had arranged it.

Prudence could not say whether it had any effect or not. It

seemed the bruising was developing as bruising always did—growing darker by the hour. Its soreness would peak on the morrow and then it would begin to fade.

Their leaving the house to set off to Lady Easton's had been far more exciting than it should have been. The carriage had been called for twenty minutes to eight, giving them ample time to make their way there for a prompt eight o'clock arrival.

Lady Featherstone and Prudence had come down by seven-thirty. Everybody had been thoroughly briefed on Lady Easton's abhorrence of tardiness and that she could never be fooled due to the abundance of clocks in every corner of her house.

As the time grew near, Lady Featherstone began to pace the great hall, awaiting Lord Featherstone and Lord Copeland.

At seven thirty-five, mere minutes before they were to set off, Lord Featherstone's valet called from the top of the stairs. Lord Featherstone was just getting out of the bath and would be down in a half-hour or so.

Lady Featherstone had staggered at the announcement and Prudence had caught her by the arm to hold her upright.

Then, Lord Featherstone and Lord Copeland appeared at the top of the stairs, fully dressed and laughing.

It had been a joke and both gentlemen thought it riotously funny.

That was, until they were in the carriage and Lady Featherstone explained to her lord that he must make it up to her for giving her such a fright and she'd only recently seen a very charming diamond necklace in Mr. Gray's shop. The lord was a bit less amused, and the lady was a deal more sanguine, by the time they turned down Lady Easton's avenue.

If Portland Place had anything to recommend it over other neighborhoods, it was the astonishingly wide avenue.

Prudence had made comment on it and Lady Featherstone said, "Clara quite adores it, she often says so. Though, she doesn't have a convenient square, so I am never certain why she's so wild about it. I've not the nerve to ask her."

"Let us never inquire," Lord Featherstone said. "Do not poke a bees' nest!"

With that cheering advice, they entered the house and were greeted by Lord and Lady Easton. Prudence had of course already been introduced to Lady Easton, but not to her lord. That gentleman seemed rather more jolly than she would have imagined, as Lady Easton was rather stern.

They moved down the receiving line and Prudence was introduced to Lord and Lady Bertridge. She was very interested in them, as she had a good notion of their history from Lady Featherstone. He was Lady Easton's nephew and she was Lady Easton's sponsored lady.

Apparently, it had been a great shock to Lady Easton to discover they would wed.

Lady Featherstone, who seemed on intimate terms with them both, said, "So how is the great buttoning up and buttoning down coming along?"

Prudence had no notion of what Lady Featherstone meant and her confusion must have been evident.

Lord Bertridge sighed and said, "I fear Lady Prudence is the only person in London who has not heard of the idea. Heaven forbid we allow that to continue."

Lady Bertridge laughed merrily and said, "You see, Lady Prudence, Bertie is a bit of a stick and I am not enough of a stick, so we determined to meet in the middle. We shall be as a willow branch—both strong and flexible. Lady Featherstone, you are to know the effort goes swimmingly."

Lord Bertridge smiled indulgently at his wife. "Among other things, my wife has taught me that being a few minutes late is not worse than death."

"Yes it is!" Lady Easton said from his other side.

How extraordinary that they should have such an exchange. More interesting, the couple *both* had expectations of the other one making changes to better suit one another. Prudence had not thought that a possibility. At least, not for a man. She had presumed the woman must do all the changing.

Of course, her father had been willing to move heaven and earth to please her mother, but that was his choice, not a requirement. Or so she had assumed.

They moved off to the music room and Prudence found quite a number of new people and some she had already met, or if not met them then at least knew who they were. Lord Ryland caught her eye. Once she'd seen him, he did almost seem to be the only person in the room somehow. Prudence felt as if a light and cold finger ran down her back.

The duchess suddenly came into her view as she approached with two ladies in tow.

Lady Featherstone, pretending she did not see them coming, drifted in another direction. Lord Featherstone and her father had already made their way to the buffet, leaving Prudence quite on her own.

"Lady Prudence," the duchess said, "allow me to introduce you to Viscountess Rembly and her daughter, Miss Rightstone."

Prudence curtsied. These were two people in the category of "had not met but knew who they were." Lady Featherstone had described Miss Rightstone as dumb as a post and having a terrible temper. Prudence hoped, for the lady's sake, that had only been a fanciful exaggeration.

"Lady Prudence," both ladies said in unison. Their expressions were in unison too, and those expressions were rather stone-faced.

Though, those expressions were instantly transformed at the approach of Lord Ryland. It was as if the dawn broke bright and chased away a gloomy dark.

After the greetings were exchanged, Lord Ryland said, "Lady Prudence, how does your arm fare? I trust a physician was able to treat it?"

"It is only a bruising," Prudence said.

"I wonder if it is wise to exercise it by playing," the lord said.

"*I* had a bruise on my arm," Miss Rightstone said. "Just last week. *I'm* going to play."

"Excellent," Lord Ryland said, though his tone hinted at how not particularly excellent he found the information.

He turned back to Prudence. "I am certain Lady Easton will not mind if you do not find yourself up to it."

"I am sure it will be all right," Prudence said.

"Guess what I am going to play, Lord Ryland?" Miss Rightstone said.

"I haven't the faintest idea," the lord said.

"I said guess," Miss Rightstone repeated, her tone descending into something threatening. She smacked Lord Ryland's arm with her closed fan, hard by the sound of it, and said, "Go on, guess."

"No," Lord Ryland said.

Prudence bit her lip. He was an irascible creature. If he had any sense at all, he'd have named a piece and allowed Miss Rightstone to inform him of his mistake and of what she would really play.

However, just as he'd done with the delightful Mrs. Geleder, mistress of the ramshackle farmhouse, he was determined to cross swords when there was no hope of coming out of it in any sensible fashion.

"Oh Mr. Vance, there you are," the duchess suddenly called. "Come and take Lady Rembly and Miss Rightstone to get a glass of punch."

Mr. Vance had just entered the room and he appeared both good-humored and resigned to be called to duty. Prudence supposed Miss Rightstone had been the cause of Mr. Vance receiving an invitation.

"Lady Prudence," Mr. Vance said, before leading his charges away, "I look forward to hearing you play."

"And me," Miss Rightstone said.

"Yes, of course," Mr. Vance said dutifully.

"Guess what I will play, go on, guess."

"Robin Adair, I am sure of it," Mr. Vance said.

"You are wrong!"

The duchess followed them with a look of despair.

When they were out of earshot, Lord Ryland said, "She is a confounded creature. Now both our arms are bruised. Fans ought to be left at the door, along with pistols."

Prudence could not help but laugh. "It is your own fault. You insisted on being uncooperative."

"Yes, I suppose so. It was ill-advised not to guess and be done with it."

"Well, your arm has paid the price with a bruise, so you must be absolved."

Lord Ryland suddenly appeared thoughtful. "I wonder if the attack today has left the sort of bruises that are unseen," Lord Ryland said. "They are often far slower to heal. Are your thoughts unsettled over it?"

"No, I do not believe so. I am determined to subscribe to Lady Featherstone's attitude—she's found the whole matter an adventure. In any case, it is not at all like Lucknell, our villains today were young and very unwise boys."

"They will all very shortly be shipped off to a reform school I fund. Let us hope they come out of it a deal more sensible than they go in. But, Lady Prudence, about Lucknell—you have indicated that his treatment of you has encouraged you to look for mildness in a gentleman—"

"And you said a mild gentleman would not do very well at protecting me," Prudence said. "I believe you mean to draw my attention to Mr. Clamarin's less than competent mastery of the situation in the park."

"I do, and I hope it does not offend you."

"It does not, though you need not have imagined I did not notice it and must be told. It has given me reason to think, though I cannot say where my thoughts will land on the matter."

"I only say, one need not be mild to be measured and reasonable. It is not black or white and good or bad."

"Ah, as you were measured and reasonable just now to Miss Rightstone?"

"Very well, that was idiotic, as she provokes me. But I am exceedingly reasonable and measured. In fact, I am downright indulgent. To people I like."

Prudence colored. She was not precisely certain what he was saying. Or if he were saying anything at all.

Blessedly, she was not required to respond. Lady Featherstone tapped her on the arm and said, "Lady Easton has come in and is ready to begin the entertainments. We dare not delay her timetable."

Prudence was led away and found herself seated between Lady Featherstone and her father.

There was a great shuffling in the row of chairs ahead of them, led by the redoubtable Miss Rightstone. Somehow, and Prudence could not fathom how she'd done it, Miss Rightstone ended seated between Lord Ryland and Mr. Vance.

However she'd done it, the lady's mother looked upon the scene approvingly. Prudence did not dare imagine Lord Ryland's expression, though perhaps he would take his own advice and be measured and reasonable. Perhaps.

Lady Easton was welcoming her guests and outlining who was to play when. Prudence was third, and so had time to allow her mind to drift.

And time for her eyes to drift too, apparently. They kept drifting toward Lord Ryland's back.

He did tower so over other people. It was not that he was that much taller and broader, though he was both those things. He was just somehow more substantial, as if he took up more space than was natural, though he did not actually do so.

How odd their conversation had been. They'd seemed to fall very naturally into a rather intimate discussion of temperament. *His* temperament. Her own opinions about temperament.

And then what had he meant by telling her about his indulgence of people he liked? Did he mean she was one of them? Did he mean to say that he held her in particular regard?

She thought so. As well, she was not such a ninny as to pretend it had no effect on her. Just now, Miss Rightstone was leaning persistently toward him, whispering in his ear. Prudence had a great urge to take her own fan and nudge the lady with it.

She could not deny that she was attracted to him physically. Powerfully so, as it happened. And that she did not like Miss Rightstone's appropriation of his person.

But if she were to allow…or to encourage…and then something came of it. What would the years bring? Would she not grow to despise him as he forced his will upon her and told her what to think and how to be in the world? How could he not—he was that sort of man, despite his claims of indulgence.

Would she not chafe as he applied his standards, as if her opinions were meaningless? As if she did not have any opinions at all? She did not think he would even mean to do it or be aware that he did it. Men had rights and power that they hardly noticed.

Would she not feel as a trapped rabbit, just as she'd felt when Lucknell had haunted her neighborhood? Was all that not too much to trade for a passing attraction? Ought she not carefully consider the future and what would be best?

Mr. Clamarin might not curl her toes, or for that matter have been a hero in the park, but a future with that gentleman would be comfortably predictable.

Or if not him, somebody like him.

She was certain Mr. Clamarin held an interest. He did not arrive at the park to encounter her by happenstance. He'd taken a chance that she would come at the same time she had the day before. He'd sought her out. He'd wished to pay for the repair of her necklace and taken the fault of the mishap onto his shoulders, though all he'd done was call out to her.

Spirit had been the real culprit, after all.

She thought Mr. Clamarin's actions around that event gave her an idea of how he would carry on in future. Kind, calm, and solicitous. And really, it was not as if one was in danger of being harassed by a gang of boys as a regular thing.

Her heart would not beat fast at the sight of him. But then, her heart would likely not beat fast at all over anything, and perhaps that was best.

Prudence's thoughts drifted back and forth, tugged and pulled, up and down. Sensible and insensible battled for preeminence. The unknown on one end and predictability on the other. Agitation or calm. Risk or certainty. Jittery or placid. She knew perfectly well what she *should* do but she was beginning to know what she *wanted* to do, and these two things were polar opposites.

CHAPTER SEVENTEEN

AMBROSE STOOD WHILE Depsford removed his coat. It had been a long evening, very long indeed.

"How was Lady Easton's musicale evening?" Depsford said. "Regulated to within an inch of its life, I suppose."

"Had it been, the alarming Miss Rightstone would not have been permitted to use her fan as a bayonet for most of it."

"Oh dear, that lady does have a way of provoking you, and now she's taken to poking you."

"That lady preys on my temper," Ambrose said.

"You ought to tell her once and for all," Depsford said, laughing. "Madam, please board the nearest conveyance to the Far East, as I really cannot have you too far from me."

Ambrose did not answer, though he would not mind saying something similar. In general, he worked very hard to always be courteous, but it was no use with that woman! He had subtly relayed his disinterest a dozen times over the seasons, but it was all water off a duck's back. All he'd ever got for his trouble was getting hit with her fan, or worse, her ham-handed hints that she ought to be a marchioness and as he was a marquess…

He'd used all of his self-control this night. He'd had to—Lady Prudence would not care for it if he did otherwise. Why would she? He'd claimed he was measured, reasonable, and indulgent.

He *was* those things. Just not those things when it came to Miss Rightstone.

"And Lady Prudence?" Depsford asked. "I suppose she was there?"

"She was."

"And? Did she play like an angel? Did she provide a sharp contrast to the dreadful Miss Rightstone?"

"I am certain that is not your affair," Ambrose said.

He had no intention of informing his valet of his correct guesses. Lady Prudence *had* played like an angel—modest, competent, and with no fanfare. And naturally, she could not have provided a sharper contrast to Miss Rightstone.

More importantly, he'd said what he wished to say to her. He'd reiterated his views. She'd said she was thinking over her ideas about a mild man and he could only hope that her decision fell his way.

"We've not been able to locate a Thorpe Martin or make anything of an anagram," Depsford said, "so we are still at zero in unraveling the meaning of the note left in the dry box. Unless you have had any more ideas on what a confusion of the name could mean."

"Not presently," Ambrose said. "Perhaps another note will come."

"Perhaps," Depsford said. "Should we put a watch on that particular box, in case somebody turns up?"

Ambrose had thought of that idea and dismissed it. Were it to be known that the boxes were watched, they'd never get another piece of information through those means. He could not jeopardize the entire operation.

There were other murderers out there and other families who yearned for justice.

"No," he said. "The boxes are anonymous and must stay so or we will shred our credibility. We must keep working on the clue in the note. Perhaps we are wrong in assuming the confusion was in my father's name—Martin Thorpe. Perhaps the confusion was in some other name? My mother's perhaps? Marianna Thorpe? Her maiden name was Westcott. See what you can do with that."

Depsford nodded and helped him into his banyan. Then he handed him his brandy.

"I'll set Clamarin on it in the morning," Depsford said. "Though, we'll see how much he puts into it now that he's haunting the park after Lady Prudence. But maybe he'll give that up since he's embarrassed himself."

"Perhaps," Ambrose said. Though what he might have said, if he were to be direct, was Clamarin could take all his mildness and jump into the Thames with it.

<hr>

A LETTER FROM Lady Heathway, who still attended her nephew at Barlow Hall, had set a series of events in motion. It seemed word had reached her that Lady Mendleton had fallen into the habit of bringing her grandbaby on her calls.

This had caused Lady Featherstone to send out urgent missives to the other ladies and by two o'clock they had gathered in the drawing room.

Prudence had moved to excuse herself on account of her taking her father to the park, but Lady Featherstone had said, "Now my dear Pru, you do not go for over an hour. Do stay and refresh yourself, it will do you good."

She'd reluctantly sat down, not certain she wished to know more about Lady Mendleton's faux pas.

Lady Redfield was the last to arrive and Lady Easton looked meaningfully at the clock on the mantle to indicate that she had noticed the time.

"Anne," Lady Redfield said, sitting and shaking out her skirts, "I have just heard the most alarming report. Mrs. Frederick, who is great friends with Lady Montrose, who is married to a magistrate, says you were attacked by ruffians in the park yesterday!"

Lady Featherstone looked enormously pleased to hear it. "It

is very true, we were set upon. However, Lady Prudence was quite heroic and then Lord Ryland came to save us all."

There were the usual exclamations that can be expected from matrons who had been reminded that there were those who would dare disrespect their person.

"Lady Prudence," the duchess said, "you must have been quite frightened."

"Yes, as it was happening, I was. Especially when one of them tried to get hold of Tulip."

"Tulip!" Lady Redfield cried.

"But it was soon over," Prudence hurried on, "and they were boys, after all."

"Pru was very levelheaded about the whole circumstance. Poor Tulip though," Lady Featherstone said, looking indulgently at her fat spaniel asleep on the sofa, "she was rather shaken."

"There is something ignoble about a person's dog being set upon," the duchess pronounced.

"And do you say you go back to the park this afternoon, Lady Prudence?" Lady Redfield asked, looking as frightened as if she'd been there herself.

"Have no fears on that score," Lady Featherstone said. "My coachman and two grooms will accompany Prudence and her father. You see, Lord Ryland explained that those ruffians took their chance because I did not have my coachman. One of the grooms drove us."

"Yes, well, it sounds safe enough. Now Anne? May we get on?" Lady Easton said. "I do not like to be late for my next appointment."

Lady Featherstone pulled a letter from the pocket of her dress. "This came today from Penelope, as she remains at Barlow Hall. I will read you what she wrote about this particu-lar…matter."

Lady Carnarden writes me that Louisa drags that grandbaby into every house in town. She says the little thing is a one-girl Navy leaving a swath of destruction in her wake.

Lady Canarden knows of at least four other ladies who have lost good pieces of porcelain at that baby's hands and Lady Marie has lost a prized crystal paperweight.

She says that a joke has begun making the rounds—when Lady Mendleton is announced, the beleaguered hostess whispers, 'God save me, did Bwandbaba bring the baby?'

I say, is nobody to have a full set of china anymore? Are we all to be set upon by a staggering toddler? Is there no nursery in Louisa's household? Are we all to allow children to run rampant through our drawing rooms?

You must do something about this. Louisa is making herself a laughingstock, and by association, us too. Rest assured, though I remain ensconced at Barlow Hall and eagerly await what I am certain will be a girl because the fates would not cross me in this matter, there will be no baby calling me Bwandbaba and making calls!

Prudence lifted her teacup to her lips and pretended to drink, though she did not. She had her lips pressed tightly together to stop from laughing and used the cup as a further cover.

Lady Featherstone laid down the letter. "I had no idea things had gone so far."

"Dear Louisa," Lady Redfield said, "she is quite besotted with that baby. We cannot blame her too much, I do not think. After all, perhaps we will act just the same if our own time comes."

"Do not be ridiculous, Cecilia," Lady Easton said. "This nonsense must stop at once."

"I agree," the duchess said. "We must intervene on behalf of the *ton* before any more teacups or crystal crash to the floor."

"An intervention of sorts, very good notion," Lady Featherstone said. "We will invite her to a tea."

"For…here?" Lady Featherstone said reluctantly.

"It certainly cannot be at my house," Lady Easton said. "Bramley would expire from apoplexy if the baby were to break something. He's still thinking about the ruined platter my lord knocked off a sideboard in 1801, I know he is. As am I."

"I'm afraid…well, that is," Lady Redfield said, "you know I've just so recently redecorated!"

"My things are far too valuable," the duchess said. "And in any case, Anne, the girl has already broken one of your cups. She's ruined the set, so what is the loss of one more?"

"Very well," Lady Featherstone said, looking resigned to it.

"*Bwandbaba* is about to be set straight," the duchess said.

⊷⊶

MR. CLAMARIN HAD not had any intention of riding out in the park. It had seemed to him that it might be best to allow the fullness of time to dull any recollections of his less than heroic performance of the day before.

However, Lucknell had pointed out that something must immediately be done about Lord Ryland. A wedge must be driven between him and Lady Prudence. If Ryland were allowed to proceed with his pursuit of the lady, and it *was* looking like a pursuit, things might move speedily.

Ryland's valet, Depsford, had made all sorts of snide comments about his and Ryland's supposed competition for the heart of the lady. The last had been—"I don't know, Mr. Clamarin, this is like watching a badly matched horse race. Lord Ryland seems to be surging ahead."

If Ryland were to move quickly and find success, he would go for a special license and the couple could marry in the next days. If that were to happen, he and Lucknell might discover the diamond out of their reach forever.

Or worse, Ryland might discover that the necklace weighed more than it should. He might investigate. He might find the diamond himself. From there, he would likely unravel the meaning of the note that Paxton had left in the dry box at the Seven Dials—the confusion of the name had not been a name, it had been a title. Then it would be all up for them.

Mr. Clamarin did not *think* things would progress so quickly. Lady Prudence must still have her doubts about a man like Ryland. He must just keep it that way. If they were to marry, he would have little opportunity to get close to her again. He had to somehow find a chance of getting that necklace off her neck.

Lucknell had thought up the wedge that was required, and Mr. Clamarin would wield it this very day if he had the good luck to encounter Lady Prudence in the park.

He must just hope two things: that she did not stay at home, too frightened of what had occurred the day before, and that if she *was* there, Ryland was not also.

As Lady Featherstone had explained to the ladies, Prudence and her father were well guarded in the park. A burly and armed coachman drove the carriage.

They had left the house with Thomas on the steps waving a sad goodbye. Prudence was certain he was angling to come along and her father told her she was right. However, fond as he had become of the rascal, it was pleasant to have a break from his company now and again. The boy could talk, and then talk and talk more.

Prudence was on Spirit and had entertained the earl with the story of Lady Mendleton's grandbaby, the broken porcelain laying in heaps across London, and the ladies' plan to inform her of her missteps.

"Poor Lady Mendleton," the earl said. "She would not be the first to be blinded by motherly affection. I say, is that Mr. Clamarin coming toward us? He seems very determined to catch your eye."

Ahead of them and coming in the opposite direction, Prudence saw Mr. Clamarin approaching. She was surprised to see him, she had not thought he would venture into the park so soon after yesterday's misadventure. In truth, she did not know if she welcomed it. She could not deny that she harbored the smallest amount of disdain for his lack of effort to protect Lady Featherstone yesterday.

Perhaps he did not realize the effect of his actions? Or lack of actions, as the case was. And perhaps she ought to consider that if she felt a mild contempt now, what would she feel over a lifetime?

She forced herself to smile.

Mr. Clamarin reached them and then did a wide circle to guide his horse in their direction. It was an awkward performance and Prudence could not be certain if it were the horse's fault, or the rider's fault, or both.

"Lady Prudence," Mr. Clamarin said, tipping his hat.

"Mr. Clamarin," Prudence said.

"Lord Copeland," Mr. Clamarin said. "A pleasure, my lord."

"Mr. Clamarin was with us in the park yesterday," Prudence said. Of course, her father would be well aware that Mr. Clamarin had been present the day before when they were set upon, but she had not told the earl of his lack of bravery. All he'd heard from Lady Featherstone was that Mr. Clamarin had been *quite shaken.*

It was just as well. She could not say how her father would have received the gentleman if he understood the specifics.

"Mr. Clamarin," the earl said, "I have heard of the unpleasantness of yesterday. I am only grateful you and Lord Ryland were on the scene."

Mr. Clamarin flushed up to his ears. "It was nothing," he said hurriedly.

This almost caused Prudence to laugh. It actually was nothing.

"Might I accompany you?" Mr. Clamarin said.

"I have no objection," the earl said, glancing at Prudence.

She nodded, though she was feeling as if she'd rather not have

Mr. Clamarin's company just now. Still, what was she to do?

It did remind her that courtesy rather boxed in a lady. Lord Ryland might wield his masculine power more obviously, but even Mr. Clamarin could have his way simply by asking a question that was difficult to decline.

"I feel I must come straight to the point," Mr. Clamarin said.

Goodness, was he really going to reference the events of the day before and apologize for his lack of assistance? Prudence hoped not. It seemed to her that it would be far better to leave the matter silent.

She was beyond surprised when he spoke of no such thing.

"Naturally," he said, "through my work with Lord Ryland and the society, I have built up a network of informants. Many of those are servants—it is quite surprising what is said in their presence as if they do not have ears."

Prudence glanced at the grooms, who were studiously looking in the other direction.

"It pains me to bring this to your attention, Lady Prudence, but I would not forgive myself if I did not."

"Bring what to my attention?" Prudence asked, beginning to be alarmed.

"What do you speak of, Mr. Clamarin?" the earl said. "Explain yourself at once."

"One of my informants serves in a gentlemen's club. Last evening, he overheard a conversation. There was talk of Lucknell, though the speaker called him Lord Luckstone. And there was talk of Lord Ryland too."

"What sort of talk?" the earl said, signaling the coachman to halt the carriage.

Mr. Clamarin cleared his throat as if the words were stuck inside. "It was said that Lady Prudence had thrown over her engagement with Lord Luckstone and she might very well be poised to do the same with Lord Ryland. It was suggested that Lady Prudence was a jilter."

"What!" her father cried.

Prudence could hardly believe it. Certainly, Lucknell had managed to somehow put the story about. But why? For revenge? What could he hope to gain by it? Why was Lord Ryland mentioned at all? They were not engaged! They were not…anything!

"I am very sorry to be the bearer of this news, I know it is distressing."

"Distressing?" the earl said. "It is more than that. It is cause to call this teller of tales to the green."

"Father, no," Prudence said.

"Was it a member of White's who repeated this tale to you?" the earl asked.

"I cannot reveal any of my sources, but I will confirm it did not take place at White's."

"Brooks's I imagine," the earl growled. "I must know the man."

"Lord Copeland, if I might suggest—it would be far more beneficial to squash this ridiculous report than spread it further with open accusations. Through their valets and butlers, I can put it out to the gentlemen who were present that the speaker of this tale is a reprobate who has been paid by Lord Luckstone to invent the story."

Mr. Clamarin paused and then shrugged. "For all we know, it may be true. The gentleman who regaled them all with the idea does not have much clout and is in debt. Those attending will wish to divorce themselves from him. That would clear Lady Prudence's name, stop the talk, and punish the rogue."

The earl considered it. "I do not like it. I do not like all this creeping about behind the scenes."

"But it is sensible, Papa," Prudence said, her mind still reeling from the shock of it. It seemed Lucknell would follow her wherever she went.

Further, though Lord Ryland was prepared to pound Lucknell if he could be caught, that had not proved successful. Lord Ryland claimed that Mr. Clamarin could not protect her, and physically he could not. But he seemed to have an idea of how to end this difficulty at least.

The earl had reluctantly nodded his acquiescence. "You must do as you think best, Mr. Clamarin," he said.

"Excellent. Now, I would also advise putting some distance between Lady Prudence and Lord Ryland. It would be best that there is no circumstance that appears to align with the story."

Prudence blushed furiously. "There is no circumstance," she said.

"Then, the appearance of one," Mr. Clamarin said gravely. "I would also advise not informing Lord Ryland of this matter as he is likely to…well, he would surely do something intemperate that would only bring attention to the situation."

Intemperate. Yes, he probably would do something intemperate. Prudence could hardly think. She could barely understand her own ideas. Was she against his acting intemperate in this matter? Or would she approve of it?

Her head said she would counsel against it. Her heart said she would thoroughly condone it.

In this matter, though, her head must rule. If they were to trust Mr. Clamarin to manage this situation, they must follow his advice.

Prudence slowly nodded.

"I do not understand what you are asking my daughter to do," the earl asked. "She will encounter Lord Ryland at various entertainments. Are you saying she should cut him?"

"No, not at all, that would be the worst thing," Mr. Clamarin said hurriedly. "It might spark talk of a jilt. Perhaps it would be best if Lady Prudence simply avoided him where she could, and where she could not…perhaps express interest in somebody else."

Prudence would almost think he was hinting at himself as the somebody else, but Mr. Clamarin did not attend society parties.

"Mr. Vance, perhaps? Or Lord Lymington?" Mr. Clamarin suggested.

"There is a criminal society meeting this night," the earl said to Prudence. "I suggest you do not attend. Then, we will have time to think."

"What shall I tell Lady Featherstone?" Prudence asked.

"That you are ill," the earl said. "Then we will have a quiet evening in together. We have not had many of those recently."

Prudence nodded.

Mr. Clamarin tipped his hat. "I will leave you now and set the plan in motion."

As she watched Mr. Clamarin awkwardly trot away on his lumbering horse, her father said, "Do not be dispirited, my girl. Gentlemen talking nonsense is hardly a new or rare occurrence and some other tidbit will capture their imaginations quick enough."

"Do you think so, Papa?"

"Oh yes," the earl said, smiling. "It is usual that we name the female sex as the gossipers, but the truth is a gentlemen's club rivals any henhouse. My reintroduction to White's has caused me to remember this—I have heard all sorts of nonsense."

"What sort of nonsense? What do the gentlemen talk about?"

"Goodness, let's see," the earl said, rubbing his chin. "Only yesterday I heard two ridiculous reports. One, Lady Langley, she is the mother of Lady Mendleton's remarkable grandbaby, once saved her husband from footpads. Can you imagine? Two, Lady Bertridge and the duchess went swimming in the ocean in the middle of a violent storm last summer, just for fun. That cannot be true, can it? So you see, even if a tale about you and Lord Luckstone were to travel, most would take it as nonsense."

That did cheer Prudence a bit. Further, she would not at all mind a quiet evening with her father. She'd had mixed feelings about this evening anyway. She felt herself drawn to seeing Lord Ryland again, but she did not look forward to hearing about a murder.

She would go back to Lady Featherstone's house and claim a headache. Perhaps she would actually have one.

CHAPTER EIGHTEEN

AMBROSE HAD BEEN surprised to see Lady Featherstone come into the society meeting on her own. Where was Lady Prudence? Had her arm been more injured than had at first been thought? Or perhaps she had strained it by playing at Lady Easton's musicale evening.

He was swiftly disabused of those ideas. Lady Prudence had a headache.

The time-honored illness that stood in for preferring not to go somewhere.

He'd been aware that she was not as enthusiastic as Lady Featherstone and some others about his society meetings. However, she had said that she planned to humor Lady Featherstone and continue her attendance. He'd thought she would come.

Perhaps she avoided him.

No, he did not think so. She might not be decided about her ideas of what sort of man she might prefer, but he did not think she would actively avoid him.

It was the meetings. It was the work itself. That did not bode well.

Even if she decided that her ideas had been wrong, that she required a not-so-very-mild man, she would not wish to involve herself in the sort of life he lived.

He would not, he could not, give up the hunt for his father's murderers. However, if he wished to win Lady Prudence, adjustments would have to be made to how he did business. The society must become more separate from him, starting with this house.

The society must move to its own location and this house must become what a lady would expect. How could she possibly contemplate living in it if he kept it as it was? He had thought of that problem before, but he'd been thinking of a natural progression—secure the lady and *then* deal with the living situation. That had been all wrong.

His mind drifted to how it could be done as Lady Featherstone chattered to Mr. Clamarin about her theories regarding the case that had been presented to the society. The poor lady was as wide of the mark as ever, the wife had not a thing to do with the murder of her husband. It had been a rival, disguised as a fast messenger.

"Lady Featherstone," Mr. Clamarin said, "I am intrigued. Do you say, then, that Mrs. Rayburn disguised herself as a man?"

"Precisely, Mr. Clamarin," Lady Featherstone said. "Do not you see? The witness reports the villain that went to the door was bearded. The Rayburns had a dog. She snips off some of the dog's hair and glues it to her face!"

"But then," Mr. Clamarin said, "how does she get the beard off so quickly?"

"Turpentine, Mr. Clamarin. Turpentine!" Lady Featherstone said victoriously.

Ambrose glanced at Lady Featherstone. He would never understand how the lady's mind worked. A dog hair beard and turpentine, indeed.

PRUDENCE AND HER father had played piquet in the drawing room after a quiet dinner. The card game was less quiet than the dinner, as Thomas chattered on about card games he knew from the streets of York, which had nothing to do with piquet. The earl finally sent the boy to bed.

Lady Featherstone had been solicitous upon hearing Prudence had a headache, feeling very sorry that she would miss one of Lord Ryland's meetings.

Prudence herself was not at all sorry to miss the account of a terrible crime, though she could not deny that she had some sort of quiet longing to see Lord Ryland.

In the distance, Prudence heard the door knocker. A minute later, Danforth entered the room. "My Lord," he said, carrying a pretty vase of zinnias, "this has just arrived for Lady Prudence."

Danforth set the flowers on a side table and held the note, looking expectantly at the earl to be directed what to do with it.

"You may give it to Lady Prudence directly, Danforth," the earl said.

Prudence took the note. After Danforth had departed and closed the doors behind him, she unfolded it.

Lady Prudence—

I was most aggrieved to understand you suffer from a headache. May you recover swiftly.

Ambrose Thorpe

Prudence felt a thrill go through her. Lord Ryland had sent flowers. Again. And just because she did not attend his house this night.

It must have been very hard to arrange at this hour. His society meeting had not even yet concluded and every florist would have been long closed.

She handed her father the note.

The earl read it and nodded. "I see," he said, smiling. "And zinnias, no less. Lord Ryland thinks of absent friends. Well, one would usually expect the absence to be of some weeks or months, not one evening. Lord Ryland does not allow the grass to grow under his feet. Is there anything I should know?"

"No! At least… I do not know, really," Prudence admitted. "He is not what I was looking for…he is rather…"

"Oh dear," the earl said. "I had thought that notion of finding the mild gentleman was just a fleeting idea. Lack of a backbone does come with its own difficulties."

"Lack of a backbone? I had not been thinking of it in that particular way," Prudence said. "I was thinking of it more as mild and gentle and perhaps a little retiring."

"And you do not think Lord Ryland is any of those things."

"I do not."

"Nor do I," the earl said. "At least, he is not mild and retiring, though I think him a fine gentleman."

"And yet," Prudence said, "he is…well I do not even know what I mean."

"You have been greatly affected by Lucknell, my dear. But you might remember that it has been recent. The upset and all the feelings it has brought on will fade. And then what will you be left with? Some marshmallow of a gentleman? You might as well marry a fellow like Mr. Clamarin and begin your misery at once." The earl laughed heartily. "Though, you'd have to slow your horse down to keep pace with his."

Prudence blushed deeply. Little did her father know that she had contemplated Mr. Clamarin. Was he right, though?

"It will be up to you to choose, of course. Assuming you do not bring me someone who cannot support you in a way that is proper. But I will tell you this—whoever he is, you must be able to respect him. I do not mean obey, I mean mutual respect. If you do not have that, your marriage will turn bitter indeed."

Prudence nodded. She had thought something along those lines when she'd seen Mr. Clamarin approaching in the park. How could she respect him?

She did respect Lord Ryland, of course. He was an honorable man. He had not flinched at the danger in the park. He had not hesitated to pursue Lucknell.

"Furthermore," the earl said, "while I know you have a fear of being overpowered, I do not believe a woman is particularly powerless in a marriage. I am sure your mother did not think so."

"But Papa, that is because you afforded her every consideration."

"And if I had not?" the earl said, laughing. "Any gentleman failing to afford consideration will find himself very uncomfortable in his own house. Oh, some do it, of course. They spend a good deal of their lives at their club. But you see, what have they won? The lady has won the house and they have only won rooms which must be paid for. I do not believe Ryland to be so stupid, nor do I think it is in his nature to act domineering to a wife."

Prudence glanced at the zinnias. Perhaps she ought to be less concerned with a gentleman's bravery or lack thereof and more concerned with her own. Perhaps she ought not make any decision born of fear.

Where was her *own* backbone?

A WEEK HAD passed and Ambrose thought all that could be said for it was that nothing could be said for it. They had got nowhere attempting to make anything of the note communicating that his father's murder had occurred because of a confusion of names. No new communication had been received.

Worse, Lady Prudence had all but disappeared. He'd gone to Lady Murkell's card party, certain she would attend. But again, Lady Featherstone had come on her own. Again, Lady Prudence did poorly.

Then, he'd called at the house, only to find everybody he was *not* looking for. Instead of Lady Prudence, Lady Featherstone and her cabal of matrons had received him in the drawing room.

And what a reception it had been.

Lady Mendleton clutched a squirming toddler as if it were on the verge of being kidnapped, a footman was sweeping up a broken cup, and as he walked in he'd overheard the duchess say, "Listen here, *Bwandbaba*, this nonsense must stop instantly!"

He was announced and the room had fallen to silence, but for the occasional shout from the wriggling toddler.

"Ladies," he said, bowing, "I just called in to see how Lady Prudence was recovering."

Lady Mendleton stared at her friends, appearing to be unaware that he'd said anything at all.

"Anne, Clara, Louisa, Theodosia," she said, "I will be off. Daisy and I are going to the park."

She stormed out of the room with the child clasped tightly to her bosom.

He'd wished to follow the lady and get out of whatever it was that he'd walked into, but that was not to be.

Rather, he was subjected to a long explanation regarding Lady Mendleton's baby-fever and all the broken porcelain associated with it.

He'd listened patiently and was finally able to ask again about Lady Prudence.

"Oh, she is quite recovered today, Lord Ryland," Lady Featherstone said. "I urged her to go to the park since we were planning on having this…discussion with Lady Mendleton."

He rose and said, "I will not impose upon you longer. Please give Lady Prudence my regards. I do hope, Lady Featherstone, that Lady Prudence is well enough to attend my ball this evening."

"Heavens yes," Lady Featherstone said. "We are all looking forward to it."

Then he'd bowed and quick-walked out as fast as he could go.

Ambrose had mounted his horse and made his way to the park, but he did not find her there either. He felt like a letter attempting to catch up with a recipient always on the move.

It was said that absence made the heart grow fonder. As far as he could see, absence made the gentleman go madder.

At least she would attend his ball. He hoped she would understand the compliment that he'd arranged. She did not like to think of murder, and so there would be no murder to be thought of.

Now, Depsford fussed with his neckcloth. "Are we to never be told why we've thrown out the mystery we'd planned and are now going with riddles?"

"Too many of my guests do not enjoy it," Ambrose said. "Most of them have nothing to do with the society and do not wish to hear about a murder."

"I see. And are we really going to decamp the whole operation somewhere else?"

"Yes."

"Well, I hope we do not move far," Depsford said. "I'll be going back and forth, back and forth."

Ambrose did not answer.

"What does Lady Prudence think of all these changes?"

"Why should she think of them?"

"Certainly, these changes are all for a lady and what other lady could it be unless you've finally succumbed to Miss Rightstone? I suppose you've pulled ahead of poor Clamarin in Lady Prudence's estimation. He does not go to the park anymore."

"Does he not?"

"Not as far as I can see. Though I did see him atop his horse last week, he does not cut a very fine figure. He appeared more a farmer uncomfortably wearing somebody else's clothes."

"Does he call on Lady Featherstone?" Ambrose asked, wondering if Clamarin had decided the safety of a house might show him to more advantage. There would not be gangs of ruffians in the drawing room.

"He has not. Though, one of the boys reported that Lymington had been there with a pot of ivy in hand. He did not gain admittance long, so I believe Lady Prudence heard it was him and hid behind a sofa until he left."

"Lymington," Ambrose said, practically spitting out the name. Certainly, that fellow could not have a chance with Lady Prudence. He was mild enough and would be a duke someday. Though, if there were any justice, he'd be a *stable hand* someday. Lady Prudence might prefer mild, but she did not seek out a buffoon.

"There," Depsford said, stepping back to admire his handiwork. "You'd best make your way down while I put the finishing touches on these delightful riddles. Lady Easton has the uncomfortable habit of turning up precisely on time—I can almost hear the clip-clop of her carriage barreling toward us."

PRUDENCE FELT JITTERS leaping around her insides. She had followed Mr. Clamarin's advice and avoided Lord Ryland for over a week. She'd even gone so far as to direct the carriage be turned round and exit the nearest gate when she'd spotted him in the distance in the park.

That had perhaps clarified her feelings more than anything else. She'd felt a real pang at doing it. She'd much rather have stayed and talked to him.

Now tonight, she *would* talk to him. Certainly, she need not be so careful anymore—a full week had gone by and she thought Mr. Clamarin must have tamped down any talk. And, as her father said, any tale regarding her would blend in with all the other nonsense nobody took seriously.

Now she might just be a lady going to a ball and meeting with whom she would. Nothing more than that.

Meggy had dressed her before going to Lady Featherstone and she might have waited patiently in her room but her jitters would not allow it. She'd gone downstairs to wait for the lady and found her father and Thomas in the drawing room. They had a book open between them and the earl was listening as Thomas slowly read from it.

The earl had begged off going to Lord Ryland's ball, claiming his gout had flared. Prudence did not quite believe it. Her father had been dutiful in following all of Lady Barlow's suggestions and seemed to leave his cane behind more than he took it. His gout seemed much improved, not flared.

"Ah, my dear," the earl said. "What a dress!"

Prudence glanced down. She had to admit, it was rather smashing. The palest lilac silk draped elegantly, with gauze cap sleeves and a lace bodice.

"Me own ma never wore such," Thomas said admiringly.

"Your mother was a washerwoman," the earl said sternly. "What on earth would she have done with such clothes?"

"Washed 'em, I reckon," Thomas said cheekily.

"That is enough from you. Back to reading if you please."

Thomas did as he was told and was very good at pretending he did not eavesdrop, though Prudence was certain that he did. He made quite a pretense of silently sounding out words.

"I doubt you will enjoy Lord Ryland's mystery very much," the earl said, "but do try to enjoy the ball. Shake off your worries and be as any other young lady going out."

Prudence nodded. Of course, he was right. She had searched her heart for bravery and thought she had found just a little of it.

Lady Featherstone swept into the room. She wore a dark green silk decorated with her beloved emerald brooch, and she carried the walking stick she'd won at the last of Lord Ryland's balls. "Pru, you look lovely."

"As do you, Lady Featherstone," Prudence said.

"Nonsense, I am a matron swathing myself in silks. Well, at least I am not the duchess—I am certain she'll be carrying ten pounds of brocade on her shoulders."

Thomas snorted and the earl rapped him on the head.

Prudence said nothing. The last thing on her mind at this moment was what the duchess would wear.

She kissed her father and gave Thomas a stern warning not to be naughty, which he seemed to take great offense to, and they were off.

THOUGH MR. CLAMARIN kept a very low profile amongst the *ton* and did not vie for invitations to society parties, Ryland's mystery ball was one he did attend. He did not spend much time in the ballroom, but rather provided assistance leading up to the supper.

He had been informed by a smirking Depsford that Lady Prudence would attend Lord Ryland's ball. He supposed that was meant as a jab at his prospects. Instead, it had given him information.

Mr. Clamarin had not known that Lady Prudence would attend. He'd thought she'd follow his advice to the letter and steer clear of Ryland for the foreseeable future.

Lucknell, being apprised of the circumstance, was certain it could be used to advantage. He'd pressed him to attempt to retrieve the necklace this very night, though his associate could not explain how he was to do it.

Then the idea of claiming a dance had come up. He'd resisted at first. For one, he did not really know the steps.

Lucknell had brushed off that difficulty. He'd learned them himself when he'd taken on the persona of Lord Luckstone. It was the easiest thing in the world, he would teach him how to do it.

He'd caught on to it fast enough, he supposed. But what then? Was he to rip the necklace from her as they moved through Le Pantalon?

He'd explained to Lucknell backwards and forwards that he would not allow himself to be seen taking the necklace. He would not forevermore be a fugitive, always hunted. The jewel must be gained by stealth.

And, though Lucknell did not know this particular part of his thinking, once the jewel was sold, he'd take his share and buy some property in Yorkshire. He would become the gentleman he'd all along been pretending to be.

There was no plan of action for this evening other than cementing his usefulness to Lady Prudence and continuing to turn her away from Lord Ryland.

However, he would keep his eyes open. Sometimes an opportunity fell into one's lap. Such a thing was impossible to predict. The only thing that could be predicted was that one must be on one's toes lest the chance slip by untaken.

⇾⇾⇾⇽⇽⇽

LORD RYLAND STOOD at the door looking as prepossessing as ever. Prudence had noticed that some gentlemen's clothes hung too loose, as if they did not have a very good tailor. On the other hand, some gentlemen's clothes were entirely too tight, as if they felt they needed fabric to hold themselves together.

Lord Ryland always seemed to strike just the right note—his coat was fitted and outlined his broad frame without looking as if it were ready to burst at the seams.

"Lady Prudence. Lady Featherstone," he said, greeting them.

"Lord Ryland," Prudence said.

"My lord," Lady Featherstone said, "we have been looking forward to your annual ball all week."

Lord Ryland nodded. "Lady Prudence, though you do not yet have your card, might I request supper? I would follow you in, but as I am a bachelor I would leave nobody here to greet my guests."

"Yes," Prudence said, faerie's wings brushing her insides.

"Lady Featherstone can sign for me if she does not mind it," Lord Ryland said.

"No, no, she does not mind at all," Lady Featherstone said.

They proceeded into the house and Lady Featherstone leaned

close. Quietly, she said, "He does pay you marked attention, my dear."

Prudence did not answer. She knew the truth of Lady Featherstone's words, he *did* pay her marked attention. She just was not certain what to do with it. Not yet.

His attention was thrilling. That was enough for now.

They retrieved her card and Lady Featherstone happily wrote in for Lord Ryland. Then, the two ladies advanced to the ballroom.

The room was exceedingly large and was already beginning to fill. Among the sea of faces, Prudence noted Lady Featherstone's armada sailing across the floor in their direction.

The duchess led, her yards of brocade acting as the sails that kept the armada afloat. Lady Easton and Lady Redfield were her seconds-in-command. And then, most surprisingly, Lady Mendleton brought up the rear. That lady was currently unaccompanied by the toddler she'd been bringing everywhere.

"Anne, dear," the duchess said. "Lady Prudence, you look positively enchanting."

Prudence curtsied and said, "Thank you, ma'am."

The ladies had fanned out in a semicircle around them. "Louisa," Lady Featherstone said, "how wonderful to see you at one of these entertainments and without…"

Lady Featherstone had trailed off, perhaps not certain the missing toddler ought to be mentioned.

"It is all right, Anne," Lady Mendleton said. "Lady Redfield was kind enough to come to me this afternoon and point out two things I had not thought of myself. One, little Daisy is more enthusiastic to see me after I have been absent. Two, it will be a blink of an eye before she will be ready to be introduced to the *ton*. If I am to assist, and I *am*, then I must not retreat from society."

"From now on," the duchess said, "Louisa's new and sensible habits must be our guide. If we ourselves find granddaughters and grandnieces among us and struggle with the proper way to go on,

Louisa is to be consulted."

Lady Mendleton appeared rather thrilled with this new responsibility. "I have been through the wars, I can tell you," she said breathlessly.

"Ladies, duchess," a man's voice said.

The ladies turned. The duchess said, "Mr. Vance."

That was what she *said*, but it sounded as if her meaning was closer to "Why are you here?"

The duchess glanced around the ballroom and said, "Where is Miss Rightstone, pray?"

Mr. Vance smiled and said, "I cannot be certain, though wherever she is I imagine she is beating a gentleman with her fan. Lady Prudence? May I?"

Prudence bit her lip to stop from laughing. The duchess looked as if she might hit Mr. Vance with her own fan.

She'd handed over her card and he'd filled in his name for the first. It would be a pleasant way to start the ball—Mr. Vance was all amusement.

The gentleman moved away, and the duchess muttered, "We will never get Miss Rightstone married. I told her mother to confiscate that fan!"

❧

CHAPTER NINETEEN

AMBROSE HAD, BETWEEN carriages arriving to his door, had a look in the ballroom. He did not know why he did it, as it only served to irritate.

Lady Prudence was quite predictably surrounded by gentlemen angling to get on her card. Mr. Vance had dived into the circle of Lady Featherstone's friends like a hawk on the hunt. He was jolly enough; did that make him mild in Lady Prudence's eyes?

Lymington was his usual bumbling self, pushing his way in. Was he mild enough? Ambrose did not know, only that he was stupid enough.

There were others, of course. But then had come the real surprise. Clamarin.

What was the man doing? He never danced at the ball. He never danced at *any* ball.

There was no particular reason why he should not, he was an invited gentleman after all. But he never did. He always spent his time assisting Depsford and Parker in ensuring that all was ready for the supper. Could he even dance? Nobody knew.

Depsford had continually hinted that Mr. Clamarin was pursuing Lady Prudence. The lady herself had said she sought a mild man and there certainly was nobody milder. For all that, though, he'd not really believed Clamarin being up to pursuing anybody, much less a lady like her.

Did Clamarin really think he had a chance?

Blast it, *did* he have a chance?

How could he, after his pathetic performance in the park?

Finally, it had grown late enough that Ambrose could leave the door only attended by two footmen for latecomers.

He would go into the ballroom and observe. He'd not put his name on anybody's card but for Lady Prudence. He would be forced, naturally, to step in if he noted a lady sitting out and looking forlorn about it. A host would be unconscionably rude to fail to do so.

He hoped that would not be the case and he would be at his leisure to examine Lady Prudence's partners. Or, if it *were* necessary to step in, then please God do not allow it to be Miss Rightstone. She'd already smacked him with her fan on her way in.

Ambrose very much wished he could have left Miss Rightstone off the invitation list. However, that would be a cut to her viscountess mother. If everybody in society began leaving off those they did not like, the *ton* would collapse.

He pushed that lady out of his thoughts. Lady Prudence was being led out to the first dance by Mr. Vance.

He would keep an eye on Vance.

⟫⟫⟩⟨⟨⟨

Prudence thought that, so far, the ball had been one of amusements both shared and private.

Mr. Vance was such a wit that he kept her laughing nearly all the way through the first.

Lord Lymington kept her laughing too, though silently, as he told her a very roundabout story regarding a horse who would only eat oats. As he'd droned on, all she could think of was Lord Ryland's mimic of him at duchess's ball. "Horses, you know."

As for Mr. Clamarin, she had at first been a little shocked that he'd applied to put his name on her card. He'd always claimed he did not go in for entertainments.

Her surprise had slowly given way to irritation. No matter what she did, she could not forget his less-than-courageous behavior in the park.

However, it seemed he *had* forgotten it. She would have thought it would be an embarrassment he would nurse for weeks, but he'd seemed to have shaken it off. There was something unchivalrous about it.

It was very irritating.

Then, though, the moment had come and she'd danced with him. She had never seen anything like it in her life—he was entirely absurd. She could not fathom what his dancing master had been thinking. It was less dancing than it was…well she supposed she would call it some sort of…scampering.

The steps were almost what they should have been, and yet had such a bizarre styling to them, and his sense of the tempo was so entirely missing… All of this was capped off by his expression, which seemed to indicate supreme confidence and condescension.

Her irritation had flown away in the face of this merriment. All she could think of was that it was a shame her father was not here to view it. He did so find amusement in the ludicrous.

Mr. Clamarin's carrying on did not go by unnoticed. There were wide eyes and frowns and mouths covered to hide laughter. He went on entirely oblivious to it.

Prudence supposed another lady might be humiliated to be a part of this ridiculous scene. She, however, was far too busy attempting to control her laughter.

It felt rather wonderful, as if she had spent too many weeks taking everything far too seriously.

Mr. Clamarin had deeply bowed and bore a grave expression as the dance ended. It appeared that he viewed the thing as having gone rather well.

Prudence curtsied and hurried away, swallowing a very unladylike snort. Her eyes were watering at the hilarity of the situation.

She had just got to the edge of the floor when Lord Ryland strode up to her. "Lady Prudence," he said quietly. "I must apologize. Had I known…what was the man thinking? To engage you in such buffoonery!"

Prudence could hold back her laughter no longer. As she worked to catch her breath, she said, "Goodness, you must think me quite the anxious lamb if you fear I am undone over it. I have never been so entertained in my life."

Lord Ryland certainly did look perplexed.

"Oh dear," she said, "I am afraid that is it. I *have* been a rather nervous creature these past weeks. However, I believe Mr. Clamarin may have cured me of it."

"If you are certain you have not been harmed by that display," Lord Ryland said. "I am fully prepared to throw him out. I can do so discreetly."

"Please do not, my lord," Prudence said, taking in deep breaths to regain her equanimity. "He would not even understand the cause. I fear poor Mr. Clamarin thought it went exceedingly well."

"Then he is deranged," Lord Ryland said.

"Quite possibly," Prudence said, another peal of laughter escaping her.

Lord Ryland's features relaxed as he seemed more convinced that she had not felt herself humiliated on the ballroom floor. He put his arm out and said, "I will do my best to lead you creditably."

Prudence happily followed and did not harbor the least fear of *that*. Though, the idea of Lord Ryland performing such a tangle of leapings and slidings that Mr. Clamarin had just accomplished nearly sent her into fits of laughter again.

MR. CLAMARIN STRODE confidently into the dining room to check on the arrangements. Lucknell had been right, dancing was no high fence to jump.

Lady Prudence had appeared delighted with him. He'd never seen her smile so much. He was glad he'd overcome his reluctance to take to the ballroom floor. It seemed she'd entirely thrown over whatever hesitations might have arisen from their encounter with ruffians in the park.

It appeared that it had been fortuitous to have the opportunity of showing Lady Prudence a new side to him. It would give her pause regarding Lord Ryland and that was all he was seeking at this moment—a slowdown and a pause.

Footmen scurried this way and that while Parker examined each table with a ruler. Depsford passed him by and said, "Well, Mr. Clamarin, that was *quite* the performance."

Mr. Clamarin nodded in acknowledgement. "I thank you, good sir."

AMBROSE WAS ONCE again reminded of how difficult it could be to predict a lady's reaction to something. He had watched in horror as Clamarin had bounded round his ballroom floor. At first, he thought it must be a joke. But no, the fellow was clearly in earnest.

His first instinct had been to grab the man by the collar and drag him away. He made a scene and involved Lady Prudence as he did it. But then, he'd realized that interjecting himself would only cause more of a scene.

If he were to throw the man out of his ballroom it would be the talk of every drawing room for weeks. As it stood, he could hope that Mr. Clamarin's performance would only be the talk of every drawing room for days. The odd gentleman from Yorkshire who danced like a lunatic.

Fortunately, the next dance with Lady Prudence was his own to claim. He must turn his attention to supporting her through this hideous circumstance. And for it to occur in his own house!

He'd not known quite what to do when he found her laughing.

It *was* rather funny, he'd just not imagined she would think so. She'd claimed she had been an anxious lamb and been cured. This confirmed his idea that she had been psychologically damaged by Lucknell. That Lucknell had caused her to believe she must engage herself to a mild man.

He was hoping she'd thrown over all her ideas in that direction. In any case, he did not believe he need worry about Clamarin as a suitor any longer. The fellow might be mild all day long, but the lady would never be able to erase from her mind what she had witnessed this night.

Ambrose was very careful throughout the dance. He would not tolerate a single missed step from himself. Lady Prudence deserved to be led expertly, and furthermore, there were eyes upon them.

It was as if all who had witnessed Mr. Clamarin's debacle wished to assure themselves that Lady Prudence was not doomed to be partnered with buffoons forevermore.

As the dance ended, Lady Prudence was still in a gay frame of mind. She said, "I shall count on the merriment of the ballroom to carry me through whatever mysterious murder will be described to us at supper."

"There is to be no description of a murder," he said.

"Why ever not, Lord Ryland? I thought that was the idea of the evening."

"It was, but you do not like it."

The lady's face went a shade deeper than it had been. He could not have said things more clearly. He'd changed how he did things to please her and flat-out told her so. If there had been any other way to declare his suit before a formal proposal that could be more pointed, he did not know what it was.

"That was most considerate! But Lady Featherstone…she was so looking forward…I would not wish to be the cause of her disappointment…"

"You will not be," he said. "I have something special planned for Lady Featherstone. Shall we proceed to the dining room?"

PRUDENCE WALKED INTO the dining room on Lord Ryland's arm, though her body felt like a far-off thing. Lord Ryland had just informed her that he'd changed the evening on her account.

He'd declared his suit. He did not say it in those words, in fact he had not used words. He'd used action. How like him to use action to speak for him.

She'd already understood he'd taken an interest. He'd sent her flowers and, well, she would have known anyway. Women generally did know, though nothing had been said.

But to say it, to make it a real said thing…that felt different.

Hours ago, she would have questioned whether she was brave enough for it. She would have hemmed and hawed and gone back and forth. Mr. Clamarin really had cured her of her fear and indecisiveness. His ballroom antics had thrown the curtains open to let in the sunshine. Her mind was suddenly awake to the absurdities of life, the light side.

Her mind was also very cognizant of the idea that she'd been fearing what *might* have happened to her regarding Lucknell, not what actually *had* happened. She was well, her father was much improved, she was surrounded by new friends, and Lady Featherstone had become like a dear aunt. Her life was going exceedingly well.

She need not fear the future or attempt to build something so safe that she could never be hurt. She'd been afraid of being overpowered and subsumed, but that would not happen if she did not allow it.

If Lord Ryland were to take his suit to a proposal, she would say yes. She would also inform him that she had no intention of being bossed about.

Prudence was beginning to think he'd take it rather well.

Lord Ryland led her to a table that already hosted Lady Featherstone and the Duke of Stanbury, the duchess's husband. Then he excused himself to consult with his butler.

Lady Featherstone whispered across the table. "My dear, you are holding up rather well. Poor Mr. Clamarin, he really ought to stick to sitting down."

Prudence felt the familiar laughter bubbling up. "I am holding up very well, Lady Featherstone. I have not laughed so much in a long time."

"Now that's the way," the duke said. "Too often these young people look ready to expire at the drop of a hat. In our day, we carried on. I am glad to see some of that old spirit, Lady Prudence."

Lady Featherstone nodded along with the duke. "Excellent, now that's out of the way, I could not help but notice—you seemed to enjoy yourself exceedingly in your dance with Lord Ryland."

"Indeed, I did," Prudence said. "He is very skilled, and perhaps never looked so skilled as tonight. He was an expert counterpoint to my earlier dance."

"Yes, but did he say anything?" Lady Featherstone said, keeping her tone low. "Did he hint at anything?"

The duke leaned forward to hear her answer. Prudence smiled and said, "Well, perhaps a hint, but who can say?"

Lady Featherstone clapped her hands. "I knew it!"

The dinging of a glass quieted the room and Lady Featherstone sat back looking enormously pleased with herself.

"My friends," Lord Ryland said, standing at the top of the room, "I have brought you all here under rather false pretenses. Year after year we gather in this room to hear of a murder and guess at the culprit. But not tonight. This evening we engage in lighter fare by way of three riddles. Lest you be disappointed in the change, I will assuage your gloom by informing you that there will be *three* prizes. Carry on!"

Lady Featherstone was the first at table to snatch her paper from underneath her plate, all the while muttering, "So unusual. I wonder why Lord Ryland did not inform the society? Well, there will be three prizes so that is something."

Lord Ryland returned to their table and said, "I pray you are not too disappointed, Lady Featherstone."

"No, certainly not," Lady Featherstone said, barely attending to him. She had applied her lorgnette and was reading furiously.

Lord Ryland smiled at Prudence, as if to say, "See, she is perfectly content."

"What shall you do to occupy yourself, Lord Ryland?" Prudence asked.

She really had no idea what a host of such an entertainment might do. She only knew what Mrs. Rowley from her own neighborhood did, as that lady was known for hosting evenings with riddles she composed.

Though, Prudence was fairly sure he would not go round the tables scolding people and dropping heavy hints as Mrs. Rowley liked to do.

"I will see if I get anywhere with them," he said. "I have only seen one, the other two were composed by my valet and butler, so who knows what is in store for us."

Prudence unfolded her own paper and read the first of the three riddles.

My first floats effortlessly upon the air,

to attain heaviness it would never dare.

My second won't float and is hard on the toes.

My whole is esteemed wherever she goes.

Prudence could not make heads nor tails of it. Though, she thought the primary entertainment of the evening would be what

Lady Featherstone made of them.

As footmen came round and poured the wine, Lady Featherstone talked her way through the first riddle.

"In the air, that is a bird of course, and then won't float…lead. Bird lead? No, bird boots? Bird rocks? Bird boulders? Perhaps it is not bird after all. Cloud! Yes of course. Cloud boots? Cloud lead? But oh dear, it is a she—the moon! Do not poets always call the moon a she? Moon boots, moon lead, moon stone. Wait, that's it!"

Lady Featherstone leapt up and caught the butler's eye. She held up the paper victorious and cried, "Moonstone!"

The crowd began clapping and then slowly petered out as the butler sadly shook his head no.

Lady Bertridge stood up at the next table and said, "I believe I have it. Feather and stone, esteemed wherever she goes? It must be Lady Featherstone!"

"Yes, yes, it must be. What else could it be?" came calls from various parts of the room.

The butler nodded in the affirmative.

There was clapping all round and Lady Featherstone almost appeared as if she'd solved it herself. She graciously nodded at the onlookers.

Lord Ryland rose and met his footman, who carried a round object—it appeared as a large wheel with a smaller wheel sitting on top of it.

"Lady Bertridge is now the proud owner of an Alberti Cipher," Lord Ryland said. "Should she wish to send a message in code, she is now equipped. Should she not, it is a collector's piece."

Lady Bertridge shook her head. "Oh no, Lord Ryland," she said. She rested her hand on her husband's shoulder. "I already have my own cipher. I insist it go to the subject of the riddle, Lady Featherstone."

The guests were rather wild in their approval of this idea. Lady Featherstone demurred as long as she could, but she was finally overcome.

Prudence was delighted for her, though she had not the first idea what the lady would do with such an object.

"How wonderful, Lady Featherstone," she said.

"Goodness, it seems I've won without winning," Lady Featherstone said.

They went on very merrily after that. Lady Mary guessed the second riddle:

My first is a no, though said very long past.

My second is voiced from first to last.

My whole is confounded and causes some trouble,

but lacking it could lead to problems that double.

The answer was naysayer and Lady Featherstone whispered, "Thank goodness Lady Heathway is out of town—her nickname is Lady Naysay, you know."

Prudence could very well believe it.

Dinner had come round while the guests considered the third riddle. At their own table, she, Lord Ryland, and the duke spoke on a variety of subjects. Only Lady Featherstone could not be persuaded to join in. She was far too busy considering the last riddle, and then occasionally distracted by her Alberti Cipher and murmuring what she would do with it.

Then came the last solution and Prudence felt almost frozen in her seat. Lord Croydon called out, "Is it measured prudence?"

The butler had nodded and there was a polite round of applause, though most people had turned their full attention to their dinner.

Upon hearing her name included in the solution, Prudence read through the riddle again. Surely not?

My first requires it, particularly in baking.

My second ensures wisdom is soon in the making.

My whole is a virtue that may cause a halt.

Though, failing the first, may be safe to a fault.

She glanced at Lord Ryland. He stared down his valet and butler, one of whom winked.

"Well look at that," Lady Featherstone said. "Both of our names have been included in the festivities."

Yes, indeed. Look at that.

✦

CHAPTER TWENTY

T HE GUESTS HAD long departed, and Ambrose sat in his library with his butler and valet before him.

"Well?" he said.

"I did not approve that riddle," Parker said, narrowing his eyes at Depsford. "The one that was supposed to be there had the solution of snowflake."

"Well, now," Depsford said, "I have to amuse myself some way. In any case, Lady Prudence would not have understood the reference."

"She could, and I am certain she did," Ambrose said.

"Then, I've done you a favor. Don't you think? Get it all out in the open—"

"If you ever attempt to do me another *favor*, I will pound you from here to Cornwall."

Depsford held up his hands. "Fair enough," he said. "But you really did need a boost after Mr. Clamarin seduced the lady with his twirling and leaps on your ballroom floor."

Despite himself, Ambrose burst into laughter. Even Parker almost smiled.

"What in blazes was he thinking?" Ambrose asked.

"I am not certain," Depsford said. "But it sets my antennae up like an ant wondering what's approaching. There is something strange in it. Stranger than the idea that he's courting Lady Prudence. Though, I cannot put my finger on it."

Ambrose didn't think there was much in it but a man who was not particularly self-aware. There were those gentlemen who thought themselves a wit when they were not, or a dandy though they were not, or possessing a towering intellect when they did not. Why shouldn't there be a gentleman who thought he could dance when he could not?

In any case, despite Depsford's meddling with the riddles for his own amusement, the evening had gone precisely as planned. The only thing that could have made it more perfect was if he'd proposed to Lady Prudence.

He'd not, though; it would have been too much of a rush. He'd thought he would begin, now that his aim had been made clear to her, with making a call to the house. Then more flowers. Perhaps a ride in the park. More calls. Then when the time seemed right…

He'd been fooling himself, though. He was not prepared to drag the whole thing out while gentlemen circled her.

No, he would do it on the morrow at the Tredwells' masque. This evening was too soon after he'd made his intentions known, but he could not wait longer than that. She understood his purpose and had a night to think about it.

If he could not convince her…well, he just must convince her.

"What is this step called, anyway?" Depsford said, staggering across the floor in imitation of Mr. Clamarin.

"Prepare my clothes. I am going to bed, you reprobate," Ambrose said, laughing.

PRUDENCE HAD HARDLY slept. How could she? Lord Ryland had made himself as clear as possible, short of a proposal. And he would propose, she was sure of it. He had rearranged his entire evening, an evening that had a tradition, to suit her. And then, had not the last riddle been a message?

My first requires it, particularly in baking.
My second ensures wisdom is soon in the making.
My whole is a virtue that may cause a halt.
Though failing the first, may be safe to a fault.

Measured Prudence. It was meant to make her understand that being prudent was all well and good, but being *too* careful was not. It was meant to turn her from her ideas of wedding a mild man. An ineffectual man, actually.

She smiled to herself. She had already come to that conclusion.

What a compliment it had all been. He'd taken her supper, he'd offered to throw Mr. Clamarin from the house on account of his bizarre performance on the ballroom floor, he'd entirely changed his plans from murder to merriment, he'd taken Lady Featherstone's feelings into consideration. And then finally, a gentle hint to avoid being too careful.

She spent the entire afternoon wandering round the house, here and there, out to the garden and back again. She could settle on nothing.

Flowers came. Heaps of them, all from Lord Ryland. Pansies and forget-me-nots—fidelity.

As she walked along the vases that had been fetched to accommodate them and now lined the windowsills, her father came into the drawing room.

"My word," the earl said, taking in the scene. "Now I think you must have something to tell me."

He settled himself in a chair and said, "Thomas, you are to go out to the garden for a constitutional. A young boy must take the air every day."

"But I—"

"Now, if you please," the earl said sternly.

Thomas trudged out of the room and closed the door behind

him. Prudence was well aware that the boy was not opposed to strolling round the garden. He was just opposed to missing what would be said.

Prudence went to her father and knelt beside him. "I do not have anything certain yet to say, Papa."

The earl looked at the flowers filling the room and said, "But may I presume that these are all from Lord Ryland?"

"Yes, they are."

"Then certainly he means to propose," the earl said. "A gentleman does not signal fidelity a dozen times over unless he means something by it. Not a gentleman like Ryland anyway."

"I think so too," Prudence said. "Oh Papa, I am at once thrilled and terrified, delighted and wishing to run the other direction."

"Will you run though?" the earl said, gazing at her affectionately.

"No," she said softly. "No, I will not. I have taken in what you said about marriage. I do respect Lord Ryland, as well as having…other feelings. And, I am resolved to make him understand that I shan't be run over."

The earl smiled. "Spoken as the true daughter of Jóia," he said.

Prudence lightly touched her mother's necklace. "She will be with me in spirit tonight."

"I am certain of it. And I will be there in the flesh."

⇶✕⇷

MR. CLAMARIN ADMITTED to himself that he'd not accomplished much at Ryland's ball, other than conquering the quadrille. That had gone surprisingly well, but what had it got him?

Now, though, he *was* poised to accomplish something and that something had been their goal for above twenty-two years.

They'd first heard of the diamond when they were all but

sixteen and just getting their feet wet robbing people. They were always led to pursue the diamond, as it seemed it must be theirs someday. It would be the thing that set them up for life. Finally, that someday had actually come.

He pored over the drawing they'd put together of the Tredwells' house. This was it, tonight was the night.

He was a little surprised the idea had not come to them before. How else could they snatch the diamond from around her neck without anybody ever discovering it had been them?

He would present himself at Ryland's house and pretend to work for a while. After Ryland had departed for the ball and Depsford and Parker wandered off, he'd slip out himself. He and Lucknell would don dominos and slip into Lady Tredwell's masque via a balcony window.

He would be disguised and, in any case, nobody would be able to put him at the scene. He'd been at Lord Ryland's house, working.

They must just fly like the wind out of the house once they had the diamond in hand. The alarm would be raised quickly and there would be no end of gentlemen wishing to be the hero of the hour. Not the least of them, Ryland.

He and Lucknell would separate, confusing any pursuers on which way they should go, and they'd already mapped out their routes away from the house.

It set up a better mystery than any that had been presented at one of Ryland's balls. Nobody would understand why they had been intent on stealing Lady Prudence's gold locket.

It was also necessary; they could delay no longer—the meaning of the last riddle, *measured prudence,* had not been lost on him. Ryland was moving quickly and might propose at any time.

The diamond was so close! He'd been within arm's reach of it, he'd held it in his hands before he knew what he held. He could not allow it to slip away forever.

FOR THOMAS, RULES and orders were something to consider and then follow when it seemed best. The earl had taken him in and he would not disappoint the old fellow for the world, but sometimes he decided to act not exactly as he'd been told.

Earlier in the day, he'd been sent to the garden so that Lady Prudence could have a private word with the earl.

He'd not gone to the garden. Seeing Danforth and the footmen were nowhere in sight, he'd stayed just by the door to hear what was said.

He was always a little bit afraid that somebody would notice that the earl did not actually need him. Might Lady Prudence think to say, "Papa, is it really necessary to have a page, now that you grow stronger?"

He'd tried to prove himself clever and worked hard to impress the earl. His reading had gone along pretty well and he knew the entire alphabet and could sound out words. What once had been so mysterious had begun to make sense.

To challenge him, the earl had given him some anagrams to work out. They were like little puzzles—the letters rearranged said something else altogether. He'd worked on them fiendishly until he solved them.

He even went so far as to design one of his own and just the other day he'd handed it to the earl. The earl's own surname—Landry. What else did it spell? Ryland! The lovers were meant to be!

He'd thought it enormously clever and he was certain the earl did too, though he'd boxed him in the ears.

Was it enough, though? Was he needed enough? If they began to think he was not, then it would be all up with him. He'd be back on the streets where he'd started.

So, he'd eavesdropped to be certain he was not on the verge of a sacking. But lo! What he'd actually heard!

Lord Ryland would propose to Lady Prudence and the earl was all for it.

Now, they were leaving for the ball and Thomas stood by the door looking suitably aggrieved to see his master go.

The carriage pulled away and Danforth said, "Cook will have put a light repast on the table. You may partake of it, but see that you do not eat it all. Like you did last time."

"Excellent, my good man," Thomas said cheerfully. "I'll be down in a tick. The earl asked me to collect some of his things from the drawing room and take them up."

"I am not your man," Danforth said, huffing away toward the stairs that led to the servants' quarters. The footmen followed their butler and Thomas was left alone.

After the door had closed behind them, he made straight for the front door. Slipping out, he set off at a run to Berkeley Square. Lord Ryland was paying him two shillings a week to keep an eye on Featherstone House and its occupants. So far, the only thing he'd reported was that Lymington had dropped off a pot of ivy.

Now, he would arrive with the biggest news of all—Lady Prudence would say yes, and the earl would approve the match.

He probably ought to ask for a raise.

MR. CLAMARIN HAD seated himself at his usual table in the dining room of Lord Ryland's house. Everything had been put back in order from the festivities of last evening and all his papers were precisely as he'd left them. The room was not crowded this night, just a few people here and there. It did not matter—he only required a few to see him and remember he was there.

The doors to the great hall were left open and he heard Lord Ryland coming down them with his usual heavy and quick steps.

Ryland paused in the hall and Mr. Clamarin stopped his paper shuffling and leaned forward to listen.

"You're setting off so early, my lord?" Parker said. "I was going to send up a brandy."

"He needs to get there early, you unromantic creature," Depsford said. "He must be on the lady's card for supper so he can ask the momentous question."

"Depsford," Lord Ryland said in a terrifyingly growly voice, "stop yourself from talking. Permanently, if you do not mind."

"Sorry, my lord," Depsford said, "I'm lips buttoned and fingers crossed."

"Parker, why did you order this costume?" Lord Ryland asked. "I am sure I requested a domino."

"I didn't order it! Depsford did," Parker said in the outraged tone Mr. Clamarin had heard so often.

"Well now, the cat's out of the bag on that one," Depsford said.

"You told me Parker ordered it when I was being dressed."

"I did say that. But you know me, I shift blame when I can and you were looking very irritated," Depsford said. "You'll thank me later, though. I was able to fish around a bit and discover what Lady Prudence would wear. *You* go as Poseidon and *she* goes as Amphitrite."

"I see. I was hoping to leave the trident at home."

"But then you would not look like Poseidon," Depsford said.

"I am going now."

Lord Ryland left the house and Depsford and Parker drifted away. He and Lucknell had been right to assume they must move quickly. Ryland was going to propose this very night.

Poseidon and Amphitrite, indeed. These society people were tedious.

He would stay another hour, enough time for the ball to be in full swing. Then, he would make his move.

Then, the Greek god and his goddess would be down one spectacular diamond.

With any luck at all, they'd never know what they'd lost.

PRUDENCE HAD BEEN made aware that it was rather a tradition that a sponsoring lady choose her girl's dress for Lady Tredwell's masque and keep it a secret until the last moment.

Had she not had so much else on her mind, or really *someone* on her mind, she might have spent all day wondering about it.

She did not, though, and it almost took her by surprise when Lady Featherstone came hurrying into her room with the costume.

What a lovely surprise it had been. She was to go as Amphitrite, Goddess of the Sea.

The dress was in the Greek style with a straight skirt, though gently flaring at the bottom as a fish's tail might be. It was sewn with hundreds, perhaps even thousands, of tiny sequins in both silver and blue. The blues ranged from the lightest aqua to the darkest navy. The different colored sequins were all interspersed, giving it an almost mirage effect and representing all the different tones and moods of the ocean.

There was a lovely crown of abalone and a mask to match, the shells' blue and green iridescence matching the dress perfectly.

The mask was securely attached to the abalone crown, which was very clever. Prudence would not find it slipping all evening, as masks were wont to do.

She tucked her mother's necklace under the neckline, as the gold did not complement the silvers and blues of the dress. She ought to leave it behind, as it did leave a bit of a lump under the dress, but not tonight. This night, of all nights, she wished her mother close by.

Lady Featherstone would go as Veturia, courageous mother of Coriolanus, and wore a very simple white muslin in the Roman style. What it lacked in complexity, it had gained in volume, as the folds were quite lovely. She said she'd wished to go as Veturia for several years, but Lady Heathway had put her off it when she'd long ago said, "So now you're the savior of Rome, are you?"

Since Lady Heathway was safely away at Barlow Hall, Lady Featherstone had felt daring enough to go forward with it. Or as she said, "I *do* have a mind to save Rome, as it happens."

The earl could not be persuaded to don anything more exotic than a domino, though that was quite satisfactory to Prudence. The important thing was, he would come.

When it was their time to depart the carriage and step into Lady Tredwell's house, Prudence felt her nerves at a fever pitch. What would happen this night?

Something would happen this night.

How would it happen?

Her father had leaned over and whispered. "Clear your mind, my dear. Do not preoccupy yourself with how or when or what you should prepare yourself for. The gentleman must take the lead in this matter. Therefore, prepare for nothing at all and allow events to unfold as they may."

Prudence had taken a deep breath, realizing she'd been hardly breathing at all. Her father was a wise, wise man.

Along with Lady Tredwell and her lord at the door to greet them, Lord Ryland stood just beyond them.

There he was. Right there.

As he saw them come in, he shoved the trident he held into the hands of a very surprised passing gentleman and approached their party.

"Lord Ryland," Lady Featherstone said. "What luck! You have come as Poseidon and Lady Prudence comes as Amphitrite!"

Prudence's father looked most amused. "Yes, it is a most remarkable coincidence," he said.

Was it a coincidence? Prudence could not say. She would not put it at all past Lady Featherstone to have engineered the thing. It would be very endearing if she had.

"Lady Prudence," Lord Ryland said. "May I put myself down

for supper?"

"Yes," Prudence said.

He had waited at the door for her to ensure that nobody else beat him to it. That was lovely.

"Perhaps my daughter ought to retrieve her card first, Lord Ryland," the earl said goodhumoredly.

"Yes, of course. This way, Lady Prudence," Lord Ryland said, holding out his arm.

Prudence breathed deep. She would keep her mind clear, anticipate nothing, and allow events to unfold as they would.

So far, they were going rather swimmingly.

CHAPTER TWENTY-ONE

THOMAS HAD REACHED Berkeley Square and jogged along looking at the house numbers until he reached the right one. Lord Ryland had told him to enter through the door on the mews. He was to knock with two sharp raps, a pause, then another sharp rap. Once he was in, he was to ask for Parker or Depsford, or if all else failed, Clamarin.

The only other time he'd been there he'd found Depsford, who was a rather jolly fellow. Hopefully, he could find him again and be taken to Lord Ryland to deliver the good news.

The poor lord was probably ready to collapse with nerves, thinking of what he must do to get Lady Prudence to hitch her wagon to him.

Thomas couldn't imagine ever doing such a thing himself, his ma had not exactly been a recommendation for the state, but Lord Ryland was set on it. The fellow had sent so many flowers to the house that the scent could bring on a headache if he were prone to such.

He knocked in the right sequence and the same young boy who'd opened the door last time peeked out.

"There you are, my good man," Thomas said, "let us in, will ya?"

Unlike Lady Featherstone's butler, the boy *did* appreciate being called "my good man," and swung the door open.

The room was not nearly as crowded as it had been last time.

Thomas said, "Where can I find Depsford?"

"He's probably in the library upstairs," the boy said. "Him and Mr. Parker go up there and drink the lord's brandy when he goes out."

Lord Ryland was gone already!

That was a shame. Well, if he could not tell Lord Ryland, Thomas could at least tell his valet and butler. He was sure they'd be very relieved to hear it, and anyway, he had to earn his money.

He was set to jog across the room, through the doors, and up the stairs when he stopped in his tracks.

A man had just leapt up from one of the tables. A man he recognized very well.

It was Mr. C.

It was Lucknell's associate from York.

The man had been momentarily frozen. Thomas was frozen too. What was Mr. C doing *here*?

The man came at Thomas at a run.

"Out of the way, my good man," Thomas said, pushing the boy aside and bolting out the door.

Behind him, he heard the boy say, "Mr. Clamarin, ought I have stopped him?"

Mr. Clamarin was Mr. C? He was one of those who was supposed to take a message from Thomas. He was one of those who was trusted.

Lord Ryland had a traitor in his house all along.

Thomas ran as fast as he could across the square and down streets, making turns and backtracks. He'd eluded enough men chasing him in York, trying their best to get back a loaf of bread, or a handkerchief, or a watch slipped out of a pocket.

He found a narrow mews and followed it, slipping into its dark and empty stables. He grabbed a shovel and climbed up to the hayloft. It was a snug little hidey-hole.

Mr. C would not find him there. Or if he did, he'd get a nice bump on the head for his trouble.

But what to do now?

The boy had said that Lord Ryland had already left. Thomas would go to him, but he did not know where they all were. They'd gone to a Lady Tred-something's house, but where was it?

He'd no time to go back to Lady Featherstone's house to find out from Danforth, even if Danforth would tell him. It was too far.

He had to get back into Lord Ryland's house and find Depsford or Parker.

They would know what to do about Mr. Clamarin, who he now knew was also Mr. C.

❧

LORD RYLAND HAD put himself down for supper and then glared at Prudence's card. "I suppose I'll have to leave the rest open," he said.

"Indeed you will," the earl said.

If Lord Ryland had not been slow to claim his dance, Mr. Vance was not far behind. He had come as a fox, with pointed ears and a fox fur cape. "Lady Prudence," he said, bowing. "Ryland."

"Vance," Lord Ryland said.

"Father, this is Mr. Vance. Mr. Vance, the Earl of Copeland."

"My lord," Mr. Vance said, holding out his hand for Prudence's card. He quickly wrote himself down for the second. "Now, I must move off quickly. There is a certain duchess and a certain lady with a fan who are hunting me no less determinedly than if I really were a fox in a hunter's sights."

He hurried off, looking rather furtive as he glanced right and left.

"What a strange man," the earl said.

"I believe he has his reasons, Papa," Prudence said laughing.

They proceeded to the ballroom, and it was not yet overcrowded. It *was* delightfully odd, though. All sorts of costumes presented themselves—bishops, milkmaids, judges, gods and goddesses, kings and queens, and of course a large smattering of simple dominos.

Though, there was nothing simple about what approached them now.

A lady dressed as Queen Elizabeth I wore a high red wig collapsing under a heavy gold crown and her face was powdered very white. The dress was a thick mustard satin embroidered in gold, with a cinched bodice and oversized puffed sleeves running down to her wrists. The costume was topped with an enormous ruff collar and she was dripping in paste jewelry.

Whoever she was, it was a very good disguise. If not particularly flattering.

Prudence did not wait long to discover the lady's identity.

"Lord Ryland," a familiar voice said from under layers of white makeup.

It was Miss Rightstone.

She whipped out her bejeweled fan, smacked him on the arm, waved her card, and said, "Well?"

Prudence could practically feel the irritation coming from Lord Ryland. She glanced at him and caught his eye.

He let out a long breath and said quietly, "Very well."

He penciled his name in more slowly than a boy just learning to write.

Miss Rightstone snatched it back and examined it. "The second? When my first and supper are open? Well!"

Fortunately, whatever Miss Rightstone would say further on the matter was interrupted by the duchess.

The lady was dressed as an Egyptian, though somehow she'd managed to turn what should have been a simple kalasiris into something more elaborate by having it done in a purple brocade.

"Miss Rightstone, is that you?" the duchess said peremptorily. "Your mother told me you were determined to appear as a Tudor queen, though I cannot imagine why. Where is Mr. Vance?"

If Miss Rightstone afforded the duchess any more courtesy than she was in the habit of, it was only that she did not smack the lady with her fan.

"He's a fox," she said. "I saw him a minute ago, somewhere over there," she said, pointing. "But he's gone down a foxhole as far as I can tell. Also, why is he always laughing?"

"I am sure I do not know," the duchess said. "Why are you never laughing? Temperament, I suppose. Now, let us find him."

With that, the duchess marched her queen off in search of a fox.

Other gentlemen approached and put their names down on Prudence's card, all under the glare of Lord Ryland and the amusement of her father.

Even Lord Lymington, generally so oblivious, appeared to notice and backed away as if Lord Ryland were a horse not yet tamed.

It seemed Lord Ryland had staked a claim and had no intention of moving off.

She was glad of it.

❯❯❯◄◄◄

MR. CLAMARIN HAD run up and down streets and peered into dark mews. He could find no sign of Thomas.

The brat had seen him!

Why had he come to the house, anyway?

He supposed it did not matter. He sank down on a park bench as the enormity of what had happened washed over him.

He was exposed. It would only be a matter of hours before Ryland was told of it.

Mr. Clamarin shuddered to think about the lord's reaction to understanding that all along he'd had a viper in his midst. He might not even have the good luck to get as far as a magistrate's chains before Ryland was done with him.

When the lord was told, he would not yet know that the viper was also one of his father's murderers, but how long would it be before he put it together? He'd untangle Paxton's note. He'd start thinking through why Clamarin had inserted himself in the house and why Lucknell had pursued Lady Prudence.

He'd understand the confusion of the names.

Mr. Clamarin had felt they were under a time pressure simply because Lady Prudence was on the verge of becoming Lady Ryland. He'd toyed with the idea of allowing that to happen and then stealing the necklace once she'd moved into the house, but decided against it because of Thomas.

How often would the earl visit, bringing his page along with him? How long could he be avoided?

And, even if he did manage to get the necklace, he'd have to run because Thomas would eventually turn up. Then his story of being a gentleman from Yorkshire would fall apart. They'd know it had been him.

Now Thomas had made the time pressure tenfold. He and Lucknell had to get the diamond and then head for the coast and board a ship. There was no anonymity left. They would have to run fast and run far.

They'd better have the diamond in their possession when they did so, or they'd have little to live on. This pursuit of untold riches had taken years and taken almost everything they had.

Mr. Clamarin leapt up. He must go to meet Lucknell, tell him what happened, don his domino and get that jewel.

PRUDENCE'S DANCE WITH Lord Ryland fast approached. The evening had, so far, gone by in almost a dream. Everything was lovely, everybody was lovely. She even found herself indulgent of Lord Lymington's endless horse stories.

She was rather glad he said the same thing over and over. It left her attention free to wander.

Lord Ryland, excepting the dance he'd been pressganged into by Miss Rightstone, did not squire any other lady.

Prudence was certain Lady Tredwell was frowning over it. There was little a hostess liked less than a single gentleman standing around and failing to do his duty.

Her Poseidon did not seem to care about the disapproval surely coming his way—he stood at the edges of the floor catching Prudence's eye when he could.

It was all a beautiful, floaty dream and they would have supper and he would ask and she would say yes.

Prudence smiled as Lord Lymington concluded the third round of the same story as he always did. "Horses, you know."

"Indeed, Lord Lymington, I believe I *do* know."

Lord Lymington appeared enormously cheered by the sentiment. "Did I say how he kicked at the stall door? Did I put that part in?"

"You did not."

"Blast," Lord Lymington said. "Let me start over."

"As you wish, Lord Lymington."

THOMAS HAD CIRCLED back to the house, careful around corners lest Clamarin be in wait.

It seemed the fellow was long gone, and Thomas was not at all worried that he'd return to the house. Mr. C had been caught out and would never go back to that house again.

He boldly jogged up the front steps and banged on the door knocker.

A boy near his own age answered it, dressed in a swanky footman's uniform. "Who are you?" he said.

"Thomas. Who are you?"

"Robbie. What'd you want?"

"Parker and Depsford," Thomas said. "You won't understand a lick of this, but Mr. Clamarin is the same Mr. C what I seen at York and they got to be informed of it—"

Robbie grabbed his coat collar and yanked him into the house, slamming the door behind him.

"*Clamarin* is Mr. C? God save us, follow me."

Much to Thomas' surprise, Robbie seemed to know all about it. He jogged up the stairs behind the boy.

Robbie threw open a door to Depsford and Parker lounging with glasses of brandy. "Clamarin is Mr. C from York. Or so says this one," the footman said, hooking a thumb in Thomas' direction.

Both men leapt up and shouted, "Clamarin!"

"Settle your feathers," Thomas said, quite enjoying the circumstance of knowing more than others did. "I knew him as Mr. C in York when he visited Lucknell and now I seen him when I turned up to give Lord Ryland the good news. He gave chase but I lost him handily."

"Wait, what good news?" Parker asked.

Thomas folded his arms. "I happen to know that the lord will ask Lady Prudence for her hand, and I happen to know she'll say yes, and I happen to know that the earl is all for it."

The three household staff looked enormously pleased with the news.

"Now," Thomas said, "I only hope he goes through with it. *Tonight.* I wouldn't like to see the lady dejected on account of the gentleman getting icy toes."

Depsford grabbed him by the collar. "Icy toes? A marquess does not experience icy anything."

"All right," Thomas said, wriggling out of Depsford's grip.

"Let us return to the problem, if you please," Parker said. "Why was Mr. Clamarin ingratiating himself into this household and becoming a valued member of the society if he is also an associate of Lucknell? What would bring those two criminals into the sphere of both Lord Ryland and Lady Prudence? What's the connection?"

As the three fellows before him rubbed chins and stared off into the distance, Thomas ventured the only similarity he'd ever noticed between Lord Ryland and Lady Prudence Landry—the anagram he'd presented to the earl.

"Maybe," he said, "Lucknell and Clamarin got some kind of attraction to the letters."

"What letters?" Parker asked.

"The letters in the names," Thomas said, feeling very pleased with himself. "They're the same if you mix 'em round. Ryland and Landry. Get it? Same letters, different order. The earl says it's called an anagram. It's when—"

"We know what an anagram is," Depsford said. "Parker, are you thinking what I'm thinking?"

"The confusion of the names," Parker said. "It was never the lord's surname, it was his title. Clamarin was tasked with working it out, and he knew we were off track all along."

"How stupid we've been," Depsford said, "But then, if the lord's father was murdered for the Lisbon Diamond, which he never had because there was a confusion of the names…"

"That means however they found out about it, it came as some sort of anagram to be worked out and they'd thought they'd done it when they spelled out Ryland. But all along, it was Landry, not Ryland," Parker said.

"Somehow they figured that out," Depsford said, "and that's what brought Lucknell to Lady Prudence Landry's door."

Parker leaned over Thomas and said, "Have you seen a large diamond of very good clarity in Lady Prudence's possession? Have you ever heard mention of a diamond?"

"No," Thomas said. "Lady Prudence don't go in for drippin' in sparkles. She only ever wears a gold locket she got from her ma."

"From her mother!" Depsford said, "Her mother was Portuguese! Could it be hidden in the locket? If so, does Lady Prudence know it or did her mother expire before telling her?"

"All of that is speculation," Parker said. "The only thing we can be certain about is that the connection between Lord Ryland and Lady Prudence is that their names are an anagram and there was a confusion in the name in the hunt for the Lisbon Diamond."

"We can also be certain that Mr. Clamarin just now finds himself in desperate circumstances," Depsford said. "He's been unmasked and so whatever he planned, now he must come up with another more immediate plan."

"First Lucknell was attempting a courtship to get to Lady Prudence. Since then, Clamarin has bumbled along trying to make something of it," Parker said, "which makes me think—"

"That *he* thinks Lady Prudence has got it," Depsford finished for him. "I bet he thinks it might be in the locket."

"I know what I'd do if I were him," Thomas said. "Tonight, they all went to some kind of lunatic party in costumes at Lady Tred-something's. Perfect cover. I'd throw on my own costume and slip in unnoticed. Then I'd do the old sprint and grab, easy as you like."

"The old sprint and grab?" Robbie asked. "What would you know about thievery, exactly?"

"Oh, me personally?" Thomas asked. "Nothing. I've only heard about it."

"We'd better get to Lady Tredwell's masque," Parker said.

LUCKNELL HAD BEEN quite shaken to hear that Thomas had spotted Mr. Clamarin and that they were well and truly unmasked. The fellow had wished to set off running immediately until Mr. Clamarin calmed him by slapping him and reminding him that they'd have very little to live on.

Once Lucknell had got himself back under control, they donned their dominos and raised their hoods.

It was no great matter to slip into the house. As usual, all the household staff were either running and fetching for guests or stationed at the front doors. The *ton* never thought anybody would have the audacity to interfere with one of their parties.

Usually, they were right.

They had arrived just when they'd planned to. Mr. Clamarin peeked into the dining room and noted the hive of activity there. Dishes were rushed to sideboards and wine was decanted. It would soon be time for supper.

It was Mr. Clamarin's understanding that ladies generally visited what was called a retiring room but was actually a toilet to relieve themselves before proceeding into supper.

That would be their moment. She would be in the company of other ladies and without a gentleman escort.

The ballroom was crowded but Mr. Clamarin had no trouble locating Lord Ryland. He towered over the other fellows just now gamboling round the floor. He danced with Lady Prudence. Of course he did.

Mr. Clamarin pushed off the wistful wish that it might have been him. Since he'd been bold enough to take the floor himself, he'd replayed the glory of it often in his mind.

"She hasn't got it!" Lucknell whispered furiously.

It seemed impossible that she would not have it. She'd made such a fuss about it when she could not find it in the park, as if she never took it off.

Mr. Clamarin, who was a deal shorter than Lucknell, stood on his toes. It was true that the necklace was not visible, but as she turned in profile he noted a telltale lump under the neckline of her dress.

Blast. That made it ten times harder to get.

"She's got it, but it's under the dress."

"Why? Why would she do that?" Lucknell said in a panicked whisper.

"How should I know?" Mr. Clamarin said.

As he said it, a vision appeared across the ballroom floor that froze his bones and made his heart jump.

Parker, Depsford, Robbie, and Thomas had just pushed their way into the ballroom with Lord Tredwell running after them.

That little rogue Thomas had circled back to the house and spilled what he knew. It was all up.

Mr. Clamarin grabbed Lucknell's arm and turned him toward the sight.

Lucknell let out a high-pitched squeal.

He watched the men push through the dancers toward Lord Ryland.

"Run!" he whispered to Lucknell. "We meet in Portsmouth. We have just enough money to get to America and get something going there."

"Oh God, America," Lucknell cried before racing toward the balcony windows.

CHAPTER TWENTY-TWO

LORD RYLAND HAD been leading Prudence round the floor and telling her all sorts of lovely nonsense. Apparently, her hair, her eyes, her lips, and her dress were all unparalleled.

She smiled at him, knowing he'd really gone too far to turn back. He would ask for her hand, and he would ask soon.

Suddenly, she'd been surrounded by two men and her father's page, Thomas. One of the men whispered furiously to Lord Ryland and before she could really comprehend what was happening, she was hustled off the ballroom floor.

Lord Ryland had her by the arm and guided her into a library.

A sudden idea came to her. It was the only idea that made any sense. "My father!" she cried. "What's happened to him?"

"No, it's nothing to do with your father," Lord Ryland said. To the men he said, "I'll keep Lady Prudence in here. See if you can find them before they escape. Thomas, find the earl and bring him here."

As they went to do Lord Ryland's bidding, Prudence said, "Who do you speak of? Who is trying to escape?"

"Lucknell and Clamarin. It seems Mr. Clamarin has been all along associated with the villain. He is the Mr. C from York that Thomas told us of."

"Mr. Clamarin? With Lucknell?" Prudence asked, her thoughts spinning. "That seems impossible. But if it is true, what do they want from me? Why does Lucknell never go away?"

"I believe they want the necklace round your neck. I believe that gold locket is not actually a locket but a clever cover for a jewel called the Lisbon Diamond. My father was murdered for it, and tonight you may have been too."

Prudence touched the lump under her dress. "Your father? Murdered?"

"They were mistaken, of course. He did not have it, it was only a confusion."

"Why should I have it though?" Prudence said, her voice dropping to a near whisper. "This necklace was my mother's. Why would she have it? It was a parting gift from the Queen of Portugal when my mother left for England."

"It may be that she did not know what she had. I believe she was from a family named Távora. That would explain the queen's involvement as she and her mother were instrumental in getting some of the wives and children away when the Távoras were rounded up and accused of an attempt on the king's life. I suspect Maria Francisca kept the diamond for safekeeping and then returned it to the last Távora left."

Prudence pulled the necklace from under her dress. My mother claimed her surname was Ratavo."

"An anagram for Távora," Lord Ryland said. "She would have been instructed to hide her identity for safety."

Though the tale seemed incredible, it also had the ring of truth. Her mother had been vague about so much of her life in Portugal. Prudence had never really understood how she'd had no relatives and was a poor orphan raised in a convent, yet the queen had taken an interest in her.

"I suspect the necklace is heavier than it ought to be," Lord Ryland said, brushing her hand as he reached for it.

"Yes, my mother had speculated that it was solid gold."

The enormity of what she'd been told began to sink in. Lord Ryland's father had been murdered in search of…what she had round her neck.

"But oh no, your father was murdered…and it was my

fault…now you can never…" Prudence could not find the words to say it. Lord Ryland would not wish to marry her now.

"It was the fault of Lucknell and Clamarin, so do not tell me I can never, as I certainly can," Lord Ryland said in a gruff voice.

"You can?"

His fingers had cupped the necklace and his hand lay upon her chest. She felt the warmth of him, the vitality of him.

"Lady Prudence, I would carry on with the same intentions I brought with me this night. You can have no doubt as to what they were and continue to be. Would you do me the honor of becoming my wife?"

"After what you have discovered? Ought you not think it over? Would this not always be between us?" Prudence asked, hardly daring to hear his answer.

"I have never been more certain of a thing in my life," the lord said. "And I do not care to have even the air between us."

Lord Ryland took her in his arms. He was a beast of a man and his arms were strong. If she did not trust him, she would fear being crushed. But she did trust him.

His head lowered to hers.

Suddenly, he stepped back.

Why? Why did he pull away? Had he changed his mind? Had he realized he could not marry the cause of his father's murder?

"Do I frighten you, Lady Prudence?" he asked gently.

Prudence sighed in relief. He had not changed his mind. He'd only worried that she was still the frightened lamb, which she was decidedly not.

"I do not wish to frighten you," he said.

"Call me Pru, and I think you'd better try."

"Well, then," he said, pulling her closer. He kissed her, deeply, and she was not at all frightened by it.

She could feel her hair coming undone as he ran the fingers of one hand through it. He ran his other hand down the side of her body. She was not frightened of that either.

It was unlike anything she'd ever felt, and she most assuredly did not wish him to stop wherever his hands would like to go.

"Well!" a voice suddenly sounded behind her. Prudence untangled herself from Lord Ryland. It was her father, with Thomas trailing behind.

"He's gone and done it, hasn't he, my lord? He's asked Lady Prudence," Thomas said.

"I certainly hope so," the earl said.

"I have, Lord Copeland," Lord Ryland said. "I hope you approve the match."

"Oh, yes, yes, of course, it hardly needs to be said," the earl said, "but what was all the fuss on the ballroom floor? What's happened?"

As Lord Ryland told as much as he understood, the earl's surprise could not have been greater.

"Jóia never knew, she would have told me," the earl said. "When she was robbed upon setting foot on our shores, she told me a sealed box had been taken. It only contained a letter and she'd been instructed by Queen Maria Francisca that she was not to open it until she had married. She always wondered what it had said."

"I suspect the queen wished her to have the protection of a man before the diamond was known to be in her possession. Specifically, the protection of a man who had not married her for it," Lord Ryland said. "I believe the highwaymen who accosted her were likely Clamarin and Lucknell. They read the letter and have been trying to find the jewel ever since. They somehow came upon an anagram and thought the solution was Ryland, though it was in fact Landry."

"I gave the earl the exact same anagram," Thomas said. "Landry and Ryland, same letters, meant to be. It's called fate."

"That's enough now, boy," the earl cautioned his young page.

Prudence reached behind her neck, unclasped the locket, and took it in her hand. "It is engraved in Portuguese on the back. *Os nossos corações vivem*. Our hearts live on."

"I believe the hearts referenced are the Távoras who were executed for the alleged plot to kill the King of Portugal. I know, from following that family's history, that they were likely set up by the prime minister. At least, many I find credible believe so," Lord Ryland said.

"You followed the history of the family?" Prudence asked.

"Yes, my mother survived the attack that killed my father, as did the servants in attendance. They all recalled the highwaymen demanding the Lisbon Diamond. It was last known to be in the possessions of the Távoras. That was how I began my quest."

The earl appeared exceedingly grave. "Do you say then, Lord Ryland, that my wife was the cause of your father's murder?"

"I say no such thing, my lord. The diamond was rightfully hers. Thieves took my father."

"Sometimes," Prudence said, "I have almost felt the locket glowed in some fashion. There is a small pinprick of a hole on both the top and bottom and in direct sun I have sometimes noticed a prism of light from it. I thought it was the gold glinting, but then it would have had to be hollow and it *is* rather heavy…"

Lord Ryland moved to the desk and took out a sheet of paper from the drawer. He reached out his hand for the locket. Holding it up, he held a candle's flame close over the small opening at the top. A prism of rainbow colors fanned out from below and across the paper.

"There is no doubt," he said, "it is the diamond."

"I am astonished," the earl said.

"Count me double," Thomas piped in.

The earl turned to his page and said, "Young man, you talk as much as an old woman, but I warn you now—not a word on this matter. Not one word."

Thomas looked suitably warned and nodded.

"I will go and see if your men were able to catch up to the two rogues who have fled," the earl said.

Lord Ryland said, "I ought to go, my lord. They are my men, after all."

"Certainly not," the earl said. "You will stay here with Prudence. She is *my* jewel and I wish her well-protected."

With that, the earl turned on his heel and left, with his page trotting after him.

The door closed and Lord Ryland swept her in his arms again. "And now you are my own jewel."

Between kisses, Prudence said, "What should we do with it? My mother never knew what she had, but if she'd known the heartache that came with it, she would never have given it to me. She would have rid herself of it, I am sure of it."

"Is that what you wish to do?" Lord Ryland asked, kissing her lashes lightly. "You do not care to flounce about sporting the most magnificent diamond the world has yet known?"

"I want nothing to do with it," Prudence said, "and I certainly do not wish for you to have to look upon it round your wife's neck as a reminder of what it has wrought."

Lord Ryland bent down and nuzzled that recently mentioned location. "Oh yes, let me not forget my soon-to-be wife's neck."

Prudence was becoming very distracted, but she really wished to have a decision made. The faster she could rid herself of that diamond the better.

"Might we sell it, Lord Ryland?" she asked softly.

Lord Ryland kissed along the side of her neck. "Anything you like," he whispered. "My name is Ambrose."

"Ambrose. Oh, I know," Prudence said, "we'll sell it and use the money to fund your schools. My mother would like that."

"Very well," Lord Ryland said, working his way to her lips.

"I am glad it's settled."

"Do stop talking, Pru," Lord Ryland said, laughing.

He kissed her then, long and deep, and she did stop talking.

They eventually found themselves on the chair behind the desk, Prudence settled comfortably on his lap, though she could not explain exactly how she'd got there.

The lord began a trail of kisses beginning at her wrist and Prudence's thoughts were all very cloudy and wonderful.

Until something suddenly occurred to her. The vow she'd made to herself.

"Oh dear," she whispered. "I did promise myself that I'd be very forceful in making you understand that I am not to be bossed about."

"Understood," Lord Ryland said, continuing on with his journey up her arm.

"Now, I do not believe you have taken me seriously," Prudence said.

"I have taken you quite seriously," the lord said. "You'll see."

Prudence leaned back and gave way to kisses. She supposed she would see.

THE NEXT DAYS found Lady Featherstone's house a hive of activity. It was inevitable, as there had been so many people who'd witnessed at least part of what occurred at Lady Tredwell's masque.

Lord Ryland's men had rushed into the ballroom, Lady Prudence had been whisked away, the men had given chase to two gentlemen in dominos, and the end of it was Lady Prudence and Lord Ryland were engaged to marry.

The *ton* was never reluctant to create a story without enough facts to go on and so all sorts of scenarios were posed. That Lady Prudence had been on the verge of a kidnapping eventually won in the game of "I don't know much but I'll invent what I don't."

Naturally, there had been a flood of visitors wishing to hear more from Lady Featherstone.

Prudence and Lord Ryland had decided to disclose the existence of the diamond and that it was going for sale. They allowed the *ton* to believe that the mysterious men in dominos were intent on stealing it, but nothing further than that. They thought it wise to make public that it would be sold, so that never again would anybody darken their doors looking for it.

Lady Featherstone held court, regaling her subjects with what she knew, which was actually not all that much. It hardly mattered though, as she took great delight in nodding sagely and saying, "Now, *that* piece of the tale I am not at liberty to reveal."

As for Lord Ryland and his lady, he and Prudence made themselves scarce while these endless lines of people traipsed in. They took to going out in the lord's closed coach to tour the park, making circles round and round until the coachman was directed otherwise.

It was the sort of fine weather that would have suggested an open carriage, so no little comment was made on Lord Ryland's carriage circling round with curtains closed. It was even seen there when it rained, and matrons were scandalized to imagine what went on inside it.

Prudence was not scandalized at all, but rather, delighted. There was much she had not known, but was happily finding out behind those closed curtains.

Her lord was the same lion of a man he'd been upon their first meeting, but she was not the least bit overwhelmed or frightened by him now.

After all, why should she be? She had become the lion tamer.

After a special license had been obtained and they were married in St. George's Church, she discovered all that went on between a man and a woman, and what a discovery it was. She had never been a fool in those matters and had understood the facts. But the *facts* did not hint at the whole. The facts had never hinted at the marvel of it.

Lord Ryland took her to his house in Ramsgate—a rambling old house by the sea. They brought neither valet nor maid and only kept on the rather discreet lady who acted as both cook and housekeeper during the day and left for her sister's house at night.

This occasioned Ambrose to become expert with a lady's buttons and Prudence to become skilled at a gentleman's neckcloth.

Though, in the end, those items of clothing were far more often off than on.

If the housekeeper noted a trail of stockings and underclothes flung haphazardly on the stairs, she said nothing about it.

THOUGH LORD RYLAND'S men had been sent to every port, Mr. Clamarin and Lucknell were able to get away, making their way to America. They'd had the luck to book passage on a ship bound for Boston just hours before it set sail.

Lord Ryland might have followed them there, but there were other things to attend to now.

In the end, the lord would not have the satisfaction of seeing his father's murderers hang, but he knew who they were, what they'd done and why, and he knew they'd fled with next to nothing and would have a miserable time going forward.

Ambrose had a good idea of the difficulties and hard labor involved in establishing oneself in America without an abundance of funds and did not think Mr. Clamarin, in particular, would last long at the effort. He supposed they'd be dead of yellow fever or some other disease quick enough.

Most of all, Ambrose knew he'd won the real prize and the Lisbon Diamond be damned. The funds raised from the sale of the jewel would go to expanding his schools. It would go to the rehabilitation of young people who, if left to their own devices, would become the next Lucknell and Mr. Clamarin.

He thought his father would be satisfied with that conclusion. His mother certainly was, as she had all but despaired of grandchildren.

BOYHOOD FRIENDS CLAMARIN, Lucknell, and Paxton had stumbled over the information about the Lisbon Diamond and had chased it through time.

One night so many years before, a ship had just landed from Portugal and began to unload its passengers. The three friends did what they always did—waited and watched for a likely opportunity.

They'd spotted an elderly woman and a younger woman, the younger well-dressed and with an array of expensive trunks, who seemed to be under nobody's protection but for the coachman they'd just hired. They'd followed the recently landed party until they reached a lonely stretch of road and then they attacked.

They were only able to make off with two trunks as some derring-do fellow on horseback came along to the rescue, firing a pistol in the air. Nothing they'd taken was of much value. They'd had high hopes when they'd come across a wrapped box. Especially when they'd read on the box that it was not to be opened until after marriage. It was a present and likely jewelry.

They'd been disappointed to only find folded paper, until they'd read the letter. It was a handsome script and the paper was obviously fine quality. Lucknell had haphazardly opened it and read it. Then he'd passed it on to his associates.

The Lisbon Diamond is rightfully yours and you have had it all along. A jewel of remarkable worth, only exceeded by your own. Good luck. M.

A diamond of remarkable worth. But where was it? Still in that coach?

They'd tried to catch up to the carriage, taking separate roads in different directions, but it had slipped from their grasp.

Mr. Clamarin had thought up the idea of checking the ship's manifest. After a suitable bribe they discovered the name of the older woman. They got the name of the girl too, Jóia, though they did not think it a real one. She'd come as the old woman's daughter, but the ship's captain said they were more like maid and mistress and the supposed daughter's accent was far too fine.

A year passed and they could not find the old woman, though they always had their ear to the ground, listening for any news of the Lisbon Diamond. It was their Holy Grail and they even made several trips to Portugal on various fishing expeditions.

Finally, they did track her down. She was a retired housemaid for the palace in Lisbon and she now lived in a small fishing village on the Portuguese coast. They kidnapped her and starved her, but she was a mad old thing.

She seemed not to feel her hunger and thirst and tortured *them* instead. She knew where the diamond was and they would never get it. She'd heard from another servant in the palace that the lady had been safely married and now it was too well hidden and gone forever. The old crone amused herself by setting them to puzzles and riddles that went nowhere.

At last, when she was too weak to fight them longer, she wrote out six letters on a piece of paper—D, A, R, Y, N, L.

She expired shortly after.

They had worked and worked on those letters and finally came up with Ryland. They were certain they had it right!

Over time, and Paxton having accidently killed Ryland's father, they were less certain. Perhaps the mad old woman had lied to them right to the end. But then, they'd heard of a family in Kent named Landry. That's when it all fell into place. The wife had been from Portugal. Her name was Jóia. They had finally found the answer!

It was in Kent that Paxton finally crumbled over the guilt of the two murders—that of the old Lord Ryland, and then the old woman. He'd left then, and wrote the note discovered in the dry box at the Seven Dials, almost assuring they would be eventually caught. When it happened that he'd been the only one who was *not* exposed, it drove him further wild and he ended his days in a madhouse.

And so those circumstances, and the unfortunate appearance of Thomas in Lord's Ryland's house, had set Mr. Clamarin and Lucknell on the path that would eventually lead them to America.

Over the next three years, though, they did sometimes wonder if it would have been better to have been hanged in England.

When they'd landed in Boston, they decided their only

chance to build something was to go west and claim a plot of land. They'd got lots of advice from enthusiastic and friendly Americans on how to do the thing.

Though, nobody had mentioned the winters that were one long blizzard blinding a person and freezing toes off.

Or the summers broiling under the humid heat while attempting to talk recalcitrant crops into growing so they did not starve.

Or the bears, cougars, bobcats, lynx, packs of wolves, coyotes, mosquitoes, or black flies.

And especially nobody mentioned the quality of female who would agree to live in a place that was always trying to kill every human on the horizon.

He and Lucknell had managed to build a rather drafty log cabin with two bedrooms no bigger than closets and a shared…well, Mr. Clamarin did not know what to call it. It was not a drawing room. He supposed it was just the common room. At least that room had a fireplace.

It was there that Mr. Clamarin and Lucknell brought two women willing to wed them.

Mr. Clamarin did sometimes reminisce about the days when he'd been a gentleman from Yorkshire. Though, if he did it out loud it generally earned him a cast iron pot thrown at his head by his very hardy but less than sympathetic wife.

Of course, he reminded himself to be grateful—Lucknell's wife threw pots at his head when he'd not said anything at all.

Finally, in the year 1816, both Mr. Clamarin and Lucknell succumbed to cholera.

As they lay on their deathbeds and the wind howled outside, Lucknell was terrorized and desperately bargained with God. Mr. Clamarin did not bother, as there was no bargain to be had. He knew exactly where they were going.

They had spent the entirety of their adult lives chasing a mirage and leaving murder and mayhem in their wake. The time had come to pay the eternal piper.

LADY FEATHERSTONE TOOK to sending letters using the cipher she'd got at Lord Ryland's house, though none of her recipients had the formula to unlock the jumble of letters so their contents forever remained a mystery.

The lady would continue to befuddle the society members with her convoluted theories at Lord Ryland's weekly meetings. As always, if Lady Featherstone said one way, everybody else began to look the other way.

The annual mystery ball was another matter entirely. Lady Featherstone would go on to win more prizes there. Whether everybody routinely fed her the answers was quite beside the point as she never noticed it.

The rest of the *ton* was pleased to do it, as nobody was more enthusiastic than Lady Featherstone and they were all very fond of her.

She went forward with confidence as the crack investigator, her brooch and her walking stick her signature pieces and Tulip her second-in-command.

Prudence's children were delighted with Lady Featherstone, as she played interesting games with them, such as *Catch the Rogue*. She was intent on training the next generation of investigators to carry on her work.

Lord Ryland only hoped his children were not taught the habits of whatever maze of illogic and leaps of unreason wended through the lady's mind. Though, he did not say so. Like the rest of the *ton*, he was very fond of her.

LADY HEATHWAY WAS proved right in her prediction that Lady Gresham would produce a girl because the fates would not dare thwart her in such a matter.

That adorable grandniece did eventually reach toddlerhood and Lady Heathway was as good as her word—she would not countenance being called *Bwandbaba*.

Rather, little Grace called Lady Heathway *Aunt Menlopee*, which was thought quite superior.

MISS RIGHTSTONE WOULD haunt society's ballrooms for yet another two seasons, while the duchess and the viscountess worked to corral anybody, even Mr. Vance, to take her into supper.

Such was becoming the lady's reputation that gentlemen appeared struck blind when she waved to them, while ladies found an urgent need to cross the street. This did not affect Miss Rightstone in any particular manner, as she paid so little attention to anybody else's feelings or opinions.

She might have been surprised to know that the duchess and her mother were on the verge of despair.

THE EARL KEPT up his correspondence with Lady Barlow, their letters getting on more and more intimate terms. Finally, he proposed, and then spent a terrible week awaiting the lady's response. At last, she accepted and they were married the very next month, sometimes residing at Copeland Hall, sometimes at Barlow Hall, and sometimes with Lord Ryland and Prudence in Town.

They got on famously together as they both preferred a quiet way of going on, plenty of sweets on hand, and the companionship they found together.

In the mornings, Lord Copeland walked the garden and picked his lady a posy. Lady Copeland would march out to the drive with Nurse Maddington, always surging ahead of that lady and coming back victorious. After their various modes of exercise were complete, they would meet in the breakfast room for heavily sugared tea and bowls of equally sugared fruit.

Should any little ache or pain present itself, which was often as they both tended to pay attention to the smallest feeling, they delighted in being solicitous with each other.

When Lord Copeland's gout flared, Lady Copeland instantly ordered lemon tarts, as everybody knew lemon was efficacious for the condition. If Lady Barlow was suffering a general enervation, Lord Copeland immediately asked that hot chocolate be brought to her bedside, as that always had a good effect.

Nurse Maddington didn't believe there was much wrong with either of them. She thought Lord Copeland had a touch of arthritis, not gout, as she noticed he forgot his cane as often as he remembered it and the disease did not progress. Lady Copeland had all her life enjoyed her days abed and would take to it periodically, though there was no particular cause. The nurse considered it her job to simply keep the two of them moving as much as was possible.

When grandchildren came, and they did for both the lord and his lady, Lady Copeland stitched stuffed animals with discreet pockets, while Lord Copeland filled those pockets with paper-wrapped comfits.

If some little drama had distressed a young person, Lord Copeland lent a sympathetic ear and then cheered them up with fairy cakes. If the children had escaped their nanny and required a hiding place, a distinct blind eye was employed when they hid in some little corner.

Never were there two grandparents who indulged the young ones in their sphere to such a degree and it was well that they traveled between two sets of them. Had they focused all of their efforts on only one set, they surely would have turned them into the most spoiled little blighters in the world.

THOMAS HAD COME as an accessory of the earl and Lady Barlow found him very amusing. She also found him exceedingly clever and convinced the earl to send him to school.

He excelled at his classes and was an excellent mimic, soon taking on the accents and stylings of the well-to-do. That, along with Lady Barlow dressing him like a little gentleman, meant he could pass for one anywhere. Eventually, she urged him to become a teacher.

This, Thomas would not agree to. He'd set his sights on being a valet for a great muckety-muck, especially after understanding how little some of them actually did all day.

Eventually, Depsford met a lady of his own and they opened an inn together. This gave Thomas the opportunity he'd been waiting for. With pressure from all sides and letters flying across England, Lord Ryland was prevailed upon to take Thomas on.

It *had* taken pressure from all sides and a bombardment of letters, as Lord Ryland well knew he would be subjected to an endless amount of talking, most of it nonsense.

For all that, though, Thomas was just as clever as Depsford and generally handy to have around. In very Depsford-like fashion, he drove Mr. Parker to distraction at every opportunity.

LORD RYLAND MOVED his society's operations out of the house well before Prudence moved into it. She did insist that he go back to holding his mystery ball, as she could well manage hearing of a murder on one night of the year as long as all the other nights were crime-free. As well, Lady Featherstone would have been quite bereft if the tradition was given up.

Aside from that, though, the house and its lord were run by Prudence. Lord Ryland was often heard to say, "Nobody but Lady Ryland directs me," or "You'd best find out how Lady Ryland wants it."

As it happened, when Ambrose had claimed to Prudence that he was indulgent to those he well liked, truer words were never spoken. It was no great leap to imagine his heights of indulgence to those that he actually loved. Nothing was to be spared in pursuit of Lady Ryland's happiness.

When daughters came, they very predictably twisted their lion-like papa round their little fingers. It often fell to Prudence to come down on the side of discipline, as her lord would acquiesce to nearly anything, short of burning down the house.

She had become accustomed to listening for tiptoeing little feet, two naughty girls having escaped their governess and in pursuit of their father.

All wrongdoings were admitted to him, as he could be counted upon to tell them they must not be downhearted about it. This allowed them to feel their consciences clear for having confessed, with no particular consequences.

All wishes, wants, and requests that landed on the outrageous side also went to him, and Prudence had been often startled by the result.

Puppies and ponies arrived. Sweets were found hidden in all sorts of locations. Bedtimes were thrown over. Baths were skipped. There had even been one very long evening when the girls had suffered terrible stomachs.

It was eventually discovered that their father had absent-mindedly agreed that they might have cakes for breakfast. And then again at midday. And then again for their dinner. After a day filled with cake, and only cake, they'd paid an uncomfortable price.

Their long-suffering governess had looked gravely at Lord Ryland, but she knew as well as Prudence that he was not likely to change his ways.

When the girls had been caught out at something and the necessary conversation was had, it invariably ended with two children staring at their feet and mumbling, "Papa said we might."

As for Prudence's own viewpoint, she did insist on a modicum of rationality in her daughters. Her highest priority for her girls was to send them into the world with the courage that it had taken her some time to find for herself.

The lion might have been well and thoroughly tamed, but it was the lamb that had got a backbone.

As that remarkable season that saw Lady Prudence and Lord Ryland marry had drawn to a close, the duchess was not unaware that all of her friends had launched a young lady, while she had not.

She had suspected all along that this would be the case. She had a natural discernment and selectivity that few possessed. She felt deeply the ideals of the highest dignity and nobility. She would not take on just any girl.

Her patience was soon to be rewarded. A young lady of the highest caliber had been located. Her lines reached far back in time, all the way to the Plantagenets.

This girl would bring the duchess all the glory that was certainly her due. This girl would marry at the highest echelons of society. *This* girl was to be the crowning glory of *The Society of Sponsoring Ladies*.

If only Mr. Vance would understand that point.

The End

About the Author

By the time I was eleven, my Irish Nana and I had formed a book club of sorts. On a timetable only known to herself, Nana would grab her blackthorn walking stick and steam down to the local Woolworth's. There, she would buy the latest Barbara Cartland romance, hurry home to read it accompanied by viciously strong wine, (Wild Irish Rose, if you're wondering) and then pass the book on to me. Though I was not particularly interested in real boys yet, I was *very* interested in the gentlemen in those stories—daring, bold, and often enraging and unaccountable. After my Barbara Cartland phase, I went on to Georgette Heyer, Jane Austen and so many other gifted authors blessed with the ability to bring the Georgian and Regency eras to life.

I would like nothing more than to time travel back to the Regency (and time travel back to my twenties as long as we're going somewhere) to take my chances at a ball. Who would take the first? Who would escort me into supper? What sort of meaningful looks would be exchanged? I would hope, having made the trip, to encounter a gentleman who would give me a very hard time. He ought to be vexatious in the extreme, and *worth* every vexation, to make the journey worthwhile.

I most likely won't be able to work out the time travel gambit, so I will content myself with writing stories of adventure and romance in my beloved time period. There are lives to be created, marvelous gowns to wear, jewels to don, instant attractions that inevitably come with a difficulty, and hearts to break before putting them back together again. In traditional Regency fashion, my stories are clean—the action happens in a drawing room, rather than a bedroom.

As I muse over what will happen next to my H and h, and wish I were there with them, I will occasionally remind myself that it's also nice to have a microwave, Netflix, cheese popcorn, and steaming hot showers.

Come see me on Facebook! @KateArcherAuthor